Inconclusive evidence...

Ward said, "Then you have no reservations about blaming the accident on Major Crowell?"

"None at all."

"No problem with the conclusion that he just went berserk . . . then flew *Cobra One* a thousand miles across the Pacific before it crashed?"

"None. A thousand miles is inconsequential for the XR-Twenty-One-Hundred—approximately twenty minutes. And pilot panic isn't an unheard of phenomenon."

"All right . . . for the sake of discussion let's suppose we agree that Major Crowell was at fault. There has to be a rational explanation for his sudden failure. Shouldn't the investigation have been widened to try to determine that? Was he ill, on drugs, being cuckolded, badly in debt? There's no mention in the report of Crowell's outside associates . . . or his family. Why?"

Hadley leaned forward. "I. . ."

Sabin silenced the colonel with a raise of a hand. "The investigation was kept in bounds on my order. What real purpose would have been served otherwise? The question raised by the crash of *Cobra One*, as is true in most aircraft accidents, was a simple one: Was it the fault of the plane or the pilot? All evidence supports the conclusion that it was not the fault of the plane. With that determined, why carry the investigation endlessly forward? I must caution you that you are dealing here with a highly classified project, with an imminent vital mission to be performed. It is in the national interest to conclude the investigation and get on with that mission."

PRESENT DANGER

Also by William J. Buchanan

A Shining Season

PRESENT DANGER

William J. Buchanan

PaperJacks LTD.

TORONTO   NEW YORK

PaperJacks

PRESENT DANGER

PaperJacks LTD

330 STEELCASE RD. E., MARKHAM, ONT. L3R 2M1
210 FIFTH AVE., NEW YORK. N.Y. 10010

Macmillan Publishing Company edition published 1986

PaperJacks edition published June 1987

This is a work of fiction in its entirety. Any resemblance to actual people, places or events is purely coincidental.

ISBN 0-7701-0512-2

For Milli

ACKNOWLEDGMENT

The author wishes to acknowledge a debt of gratitude to former comrades-in-arms whose reminiscences were invaluable during the research and writing of this book.

AUTHOR'S NOTE

THE MIDOCEAN CRASH and recovery of an experimental aircraft, as well as the circumstances surrounding the "Kamchatka Signal," as described in PRESENT DANGER, are based on events with which the author was associated. Portions dealing with the "Rodale Report" are based on interviews with persons closely associated with that suppressed document. With those exceptions, and references to recognizable historical events and persons, the book does not intentionally resemble reality.

1

THE island first appeared on radar. A shimmering yellow triangular-shaped blip at the top of the scope, range 300 miles, dead ahead.

The copilot adjusted the set for a sharper image. "Kingman Reef?" he asked. He was new to this area of the Pacific.

The aircraft commander glanced at the scope. "Right on schedule." He eased the controls forward, putting the giant, four-engine, C-130 Hercules into an easy descent.

The weekly 1,400-mile supply flight from Honolulu to Christmas Island was a boring routine shunned by the regular Air Force. The chore had been palmed off on the Hawaii Air National Guard as an opportunity for the "weekend warriors" to maintain flying proficiency. To sugar-coat the assignment, the route was modified to include a menial operational mission. Each week the Air Guard performed a low-level, visual check of unmanned, remote-controlled weather transmitters installed on the Line Islands, a mid-Pacific archipelago strung out southeasterly for 500 miles, from Kingman Reef on the north, to Christmas Island on the south.

Since takeoff from Hickam Air Force Base that Tuesday, Au-

gust 26, 1980, the copilot had continually monitored heavy
radio traffic from an event taking place a thousand miles to the
west. "You oughta hear this jabber, Major. There're at least a
hundred planes crisscrossing that search area. What the hell's
down anyway, Air Force One?"

The AC laughed. "More important. Operations says it's the
XR-Twenty-One-Hundred. Disappeared on a test flight from
Johnston Island last night."

The copilot emitted a low whistle. "Jesus! No wonder the
whole damn Pacific Air Force is up." He thought a moment.
"What's it like—the XR I mean? Any straight dope on it?"

"Scuttlebutt mostly. Superhyped recon job, homebased in
New Mexico, out here for overwater testing. Supposed to be
light-years ahead of anything else in the arsenal."

"Wonder what went wrong?"

"*That*, old buddy, is why they're looking so hard for the
pieces."

The Hercules reached descent altitude and the AC leveled
the aircraft gently. Ten minutes later a barely visible land mass
appeared on the horizon. The AC said, "Checkpoint dead ahead."

The copilot entered the time on his log.

Kingman Reef is the smallest deep-ocean island in the world.
Barren, unpopulated, its three-foot-high coral shoals shelter a
deep, triangular-shaped lagoon nine miles long and five miles
wide. In all but the severest squalls the lagoon remains placid
despite the pitch of the seas beyond the shoals. This stark contrast of calm water amid agitated seas reflects an easily recognizable radar image that is a navigational boon to trans-Pacific
flights. The Air Guard used Kingman Reef as the checkpoint
for beginning its low-level overflight of the Line Island group.

A few minutes before noon, skimming the ocean at a thousand feet, the Hercules approached the northern tip of Kingman
Reef. The seas were calm, the lagoon an azure mirror reflecting
high-scattered clouds. A tropical sun blazed directly overhead.
The flight path traversed the lagoon slightly east of center. Suddenly, at a point above the southern shoal, the copilot yelled,
"Hey! For God's sake . . . look!"

Startled, the AC scanned his instruments furiously. "What?!"

"Major! Take her around. One-eighty. Come back over that
south sandbar at the same spot."

The AC shot the copilot a glowering look. Then, relieved that the over-excited lieutenant hadn't spotted a ruptured wing, or flames spewing from an engine, the AC put the Hercules into a starboard bank. Maintaining steady altitude he leveled five miles north of the reef and retraced the previous flight path. Just above the south shoal, with the sun bearing straight down on the lagoon, the copilot yelled again: "There! Just inside the reef . . ."

"I see it!" the AC said.

He put the Hercules into a tight pattern around the reef and keyed his microphone. "Honolulu Control . . . this is Guard Five . . . over."

The radio response was immediate. "Guard Five . . . Honolulu. Go ahead."

"Honolulu . . . Guard Five. We've spotted a downed aircraft underwater just inside the south shoal of Kingman Reef. Visibility is blurred, but it's sure a strange looking bird. Over."

There was a pause. "Guard Five . . . Honolulu. Can you make out any features? Over."

"Roger, Honolulu. Swept-wing, concave fuselage . . . looks like forward stabilizers . . . over."

"Guard Five . . . stand by."

There was a four-minute silence, then the radio crackled again. "Guard Five . . . Honolulu. You are to abort, repeat, *abort* your scheduled mission. You will remain on present station pending arrival of air-sea rescue units. You will then return to homebase for debriefing. Did you copy? Over."

"Honolulu . . . Guard Five. Roger. Please authenticate."

"Guard Five . . . Honolulu. Authentication: three-two—five-two—nine-four-eight-alpha. Over."

The copilot hastily checked the code against page 32, group 52, of the authentication tables for that day. He nodded to the pilot.

"Honolulu . . . Guard Five. Roger. Over and out."

The AC set the autopilot to maintain the circular pattern above Kingman Reef.

The copilot asked, "Do you think it's the XR?"

"I'd bet a year's pay on it," the AC replied.

"But . . . what's it doing here? A thousand miles from where the brass reported it down?"

"That, ole buddy, is the embarrassing riddle some poor bastard in the Air Force is going to have to solve." The AC looked down at the shadowy image in the lagoon. "One thing's for sure . . . whoever's in that bird down there isn't going to be any help with the answer."

2

THE rain came down in torrents, hitting the sill and splashing through the open window onto the bed.

Jonathan Ward said, "Shit!"

He kicked off the covers, got up and slammed the window shut. Outside the sky hung low, leaden, threatening. "Good old Maryland liquid sunshine," he groused.

He sat on the edge of the bed and looked at the clock. 6:31. Still twenty-nine minutes before the alarm. He debated crawling back under the covers for the extra half hour, but decided against it. For him it had always been get-up-when-you-wake-up or a headache for the rest of the day. He pushed in the alarm, flexed his neck and back, yawned.

Something beside the opposite pillow caught his eye. He reached over and picked it up. It was a sterling silver earring shaped in the image of a tiny devil with one hand cupped to his mouth, as if exhorting the wearer to yield to temptation. Susan's other earring, he remembered, was an angel, similarly posed with cupped hand. He looked at the rumpled bed with a wry smile. He was glad the devil won out last night.

Where was Susan? The bathroom door was open so he ruled that out. There were no sounds from the kitchen. Then he remembered. Tommy's seventh-grade class was taking its field trip to the Smithsonian today. Susan had risen early to go to her own apartment to get her son ready.

Ward stood and stretched his naked six-foot frame again, long and hard. Thirty-two years old, 170 pounds, he was a handsome man with tawny features: slightly wavy dark-brown hair neatly trimmed above close-set ears; wide-spaced agate eyes that regarded the world confidently from beneath arched brows; a firm, square jaw often clouded by a heavy beard that required twice-a-day shaving. His well-toned physique was testimony to a vigorous hour-long handball session each noon at the Andrews Air Force Base gymnasium.

He started for the bathroom, but as he passed his bureau he stopped. His eyes locked onto an envelope, ripped open at one end, casually lying atop the dresser among handkerchiefs, billfold, pen, coins, paraphernalia from his pockets. The letter had arrived the week before. He'd read it through once, uttered an oath and dropped it in the wastebasket. That night, for reasons he couldn't understand, he retrieved it and threw it atop the dresser where he could not help but see it each day, though he didn't touch it again. Now, with a heavy sigh, he pulled the folded, single sheet of paper from the envelope and slumped in a chair. The crimped handwriting, in pencil, was barely legible:

Mon 15th

Dear Jonathan,

I can understand your surprise at hearing from me. There were times when I would have written if I had known where you were. Congressman Gregory got me your address from the Air Force.

I am very ill. Dr. Travis, yes, he's still practicing, says I have a few months left, six at most.

There are things we should talk about, Jonathan. After all you are my only heir. There's not much. The house, my car, a few odds and ends. Not much money, but Dr. Travis is charging me only what insurance covers. There are some things of your father's that you should have.

I want you to come see me, Jonathan. Will you do that? I pray you will.

Mother

Emotions in conflict, he rested his head on the back of the chair and stared at the ceiling. *There are some things of your father's* . . . She still knew how to hurt. After a while his jaw firmed. He crumpled the letter and tossed it in the wastebasket again. Done, over, finished, out-of-mind . . .

The bedside phone rang, startling him.

Susan? His spirits rose. His mind filled with visions of last night and he felt himself becoming aroused. There was still time before he had to leave for the base.

He stepped over and picked up the phone. "I'm ready if you are."

"Ward?"

Ward cursed beneath his breath. "Fred . . . what the hell do you want this time of morning?"

"Ah . . . and top of the morning to you, too, Major," Lieutenant Colonel Frederick Bates replied. "I don't want anything. But somebody does. I just got a call from Personnel. You're to be at the flight line at sixteen-hundred. You're going thirty days temporary duty to Kirtland. Forget the office today. Pack and settle things for a month's absence."

"A month's absence! Fred, what in shit's name are you talking about?"

"All I know's what Personnel said. They got a hurry-up request yesterday for your command records. Then, this morning word came down from The Man himself. Priority One orders. General McCollum's personal pilot is flying you out. It's a by-name request from the Air Force Research and Test Center. You're to report to a Colonel MacWatt on arrival."

Ward's irritation turned to real anger. "Dammit, Fred, I can't spare thirty hours away from the Evergreen project, much less thirty days. Out of the question. There's got to be a screw-up."

"Look, Jonathan," Fred Bates said evenly, "this isn't some wives club tea party you're being asked to RSVP. It's an order. From the man in that big five-sided building over in Arlington who wears four stars on his shoulder. If you insist on doing your prima donna act, go see him. Otherwise, I suggest you be at the flight line at sixteen-hundred."

Silence.

"Jonathan?"

"What?" Ward said stonily.

"Look . . . I'll cover Evergreen for you. Don't sweat it. And for God's sake don't do *anything* to get your ass in a jam with McCollum. That wouldn't be smart at all. For once, just follow orders. OK?"

Ward stared at the phone in exasperation. Then, without a word, he slammed it down, his mood now as dark as the stormy sky outside his window.

The immediate object of his anger was Bates. Ward could guess what his boss's reaction had been to the call from Personnel. Did he protest? Hell no. Did he complain that they were asking for the most indispensable engineer in the laboratory, at the most critical juncture in a high priority project? Bates? No way. Hell, he was a likable guy, mostly. But likable guys make piss-poor division supervisors. Let a ranking officer demand Bates's balls and he'd whip out a knife and start cutting.

What was it all about anyway? Kirtland Air Force Base? *New Mexico,* "Oh, Christ!" A stinking wasteland. Jackrabbits. Rattlesnakes. Sand dunes. Desolation. What for? Why a by-name request for him? What in hell did the Research and Test Center want with a signal analyst? They were a flying outfit. He was a ground-pounder.

There had to be a snafu. He looked at the phone and wondered if he should call Personnel direct. Going over Bates's head didn't bother him for a second. But Bates said the order came down from the Chief of Staff himself. A call to Personnel would be futile. No one of lower rank would question an order from General McCollum. And there was no higher rank in the Air Force.

"Bastards!" he cried aloud.

He went back to the chair and tried to get his thoughts in order.

Bates was right about one thing, he admitted without remorse. I *am* a prima donna. A loner, a poor team player.

He was also a first-rate electronics engineer, in a critical specialty of the field. He'd lost count of the job offers he'd received from civilian contractors. The letter last month from Sylvania, coming on the heels of his latest article in *Scientific American,* had invited him to name his own starting salary. His reputation was that good.

He'd been tempted. It would mean stability. And a hell of a lot more money. But he'd turned it down. Just as he had all the others. And, despite his present blue funk, he knew why.

He had enlisted at seventeen, hitchhiking and walking all night from his small-town Kentucky home to Paducah to take the oath. Underage, he had forged his mother's signature to the consent papers, explaining to the recruiter that his father had died years before. The forgery was unnecessary. His mother would have signed readily. But he had not asked, had not wanted to give her the satisfaction.

Miles from his roots, he thought he had escaped the desperation of his life. Then, gradually, the furies that drove him returned. During basic training at Lackland Air Force Base, Texas, he was put on report twice. Minor infractions. Absolution earned by extra duties.

Six months later, assigned to the Lackland motor pool, he was ordered by his sergeant to work back-to-back weekend shifts.

"Screw you!" he told the sergeant, and went to town to get drunk.

The sergeant brought charges, recommending general discharge for inability to adapt.

The CO, a rough-hewn, over-age-in-grade captain who had served twelve years enlisted duty before winning a commission in Korea, cast an avuncular eye on the skinny, sad-faced youth who stood before his desk. "At ease, Airman."

The CO studied Ward's file, puzzled by the aptitude scores recorded there. "You got ninety-three in technical potential. What the hell you doing driving a truck?"

Ward shrugged. "Guess they needed a truck driver."

Precisely, the CO mused, silently bemoaning the mercurial whims of the military. Some nincompoop personnel clerk in headquarters had needed a warm body—any warm body—to fill a quota. Key punched. Private Ward's card drops out. Presto! Quota filled. End of problem—for the clerk.

"Sit down," the CO barked.

Ward did as ordered.

"How come you didn't finish high school?"

Ward looked at his shoes, not answering.

Talkative bastard, the CO thought. Was there something sal-vageable there? He closed the file. "Airman, I'm supposed to cashier your ass out of the service. Maybe I should." He waited.

Ward shrugged again.

The CO shook his head. He looked through a booklet on his desk. "You good in math?"

"I get by," Ward said.

"Uh huh. Son, there's a basic electronics class starting up at Keesler in"—he referred to the booklet—"two weeks. I can get you enrolled. It'll get you outa Texas and outa my hair. And I'll see that the charges are dropped. Agreed?"

With little choice, Ward agreed.

And found deliverance.

To Ward, the exacting science of electronics was a world apart. Fascinated, with a hitherto untapped innate ability, he sublimated his former destructive energies into a furious quest for understanding the functions of capacitors, resistors, mag-netic pulses, electron flow—inanimate, impersonal *things* to which he could dedicate passion without fear of betrayal.

Fourteen months after opening his first electronics manual, he graduated from basics with a high school equivalency di-ploma, an Air Force Training Command award for scholastic merit, and a recommendation from the school commandant that he be considered for advanced courses.

The commandant's recommendation was approved. For the next year Ward attended on-base classes in algebra, trigonom-etry, calculus. Thus prepped, he competed for and won an Air Force college scholarship. In 1971, following three years ac-celerated study and shortly after his twenty-third birthday, he graduated cum laude from the University of Kentucky with a B.S. in electronics and a commission as a second lieutenant.

The following year he received his Masters from the Air Force Institute of Technology in Ohio.

And that, Major Jonathan Ward mused, concluding his in-trospection that rainy morning in his Maryland apartment, was why he had turned down all the civilian job offers. The Air Force had taken him when no one else wanted him; had, after a shaky start, nurtured him, educated him, given him a purpose in life. With few loyalties to bind him, his loyalty to the Air Force was unequivocal.

But New Mexico!

He moaned. Thirty days away from Susan. A month deprived of that exquisite body. *That* was too much to ask of any man.

He considered options. If he couldn't convince the powers-that-be on this end that an error had been made, he'd simply have to convince those at the other end. Who was it Bates said he was to report to? A Colonel MacWatt. Well, he'd bucked heads with colonels before. He'd handle MacWatt when he got to Kirtland. In the meantime, he had the day at his disposal.

He went to the bed and picked up the suggestive earring. Then he dialed Susan's number. She answered on the second ring.

He said, "I've got something of yours."

"Oh?" Her voice was without emotion. "I thought that's where it might be."

"Would you fix a guy some breakfast?"

"Aren't you going to work?"

"Change of plan. Look . . . first a shower, then I'll tell you all about it over bacon and eggs. Deal?"

There was a brief silence. Then she said, "Sure. Come on up."

He cradled the phone and wondered about her hesitancy. He decided she'd had another spat with Tommy. Well, he knew just the thing to improve her disposition.

Her apartment was two flights up. When she opened the door he caught his breath. She was wearing a sheer green peignoir and matching robe that accentuated every sensuous curve of her body. Her long ebony hair fell straight down her back. She had cleansed her face of makeup. She was gorgeous.

"Coffee's on the table. I'll get your plate."

He sat down at the kitchen dinette and poured for both of them. "Did Tommy get off?"

"Yes."

She brought a plate of scrambled eggs, bacon and toast, put it before him and sat down. He skipped salt, shook pepper on the eggs and began to eat.

She watched him for a moment. "What's the big change of plan?"

He broke off a piece of toast. "Bates is sending me to New Mexico this afternoon. For thirty days, he says. What do you think of that?"

She sipped her coffee. "Part of the job I guess."

"Part of the job!" He laughed derisively. "Is that all the reaction I get?"

She took her cup to the sink and started washing the dishes. He watched her for a moment, puzzled. Then he wiped his mouth on a napkin, got out of his chair and went up behind her. He slipped his arms around her, opened her robe and cupped her breasts in his hands. "Hey there"—he kissed the nape of her neck—"why so glum?"

Without rinsing the soap from her hands she reached up and pushed his arms away. Then she tied her robe more securely about her.

It surprised him. And made him angry. "What the hell's eating you?"

She turned to face him. "We've got to talk."

He sat back down. "So . . . talk."

She leaned against the sink. "Last night . . . did you, well, feel anything?"

The question surprised him. "Feel anything? My God, it was great! I loved it. It's always . . ."

She shook her head firmly. "No, no. Not *it*. Did you feel anything . . . for me?"

His face was a perplexed mask.

She came to the table, sat down and put a hand on his. "Oh, Jon . . . I know you think we're good in bed. But in a relationship, there has to be . . . a growing together . . . a mutual giving. Sometimes, after we've made love, you get . . . well, distant. And I feel that I haven't been able to give you what you need . . . what . . ." She stood abruptly. "Oh Christ . . . I don't know how to explain it."

She went to the counter for a cigarette. She didn't return to the table. "There's something else," she said, exhaling smoke. "Les wants to come back."

"Les? That's a sudden turnabout isn't it?"

"Not really. He's been asking ever since the separation. That was my doing, you know. I was considering a reconciliation. For Tommy's sake, mostly. He needs a father now. Then . . . I met you . . . and we . . . well, it's been over three months. And I wondered what you'd say? About us, I mean."

There was silence. Broken only when she asked, insistently, "Jon . . . do you love me?"

"Love you?" He tipped the chair back on its rear legs, crossed his arms over his chest and gripped his shoulders tightly with both hands. "Well . . . if that's what you mean . . . sure . . ."

She laughed without mirth. "Oh, Jon . . . look at yourself."

"What?"

"What you're doing. You're trying to shield yourself. You're actually trying to pull yourself into a shell. Is it that bad?"

He was stung and she knew it.

She came to the table again and took one of his hands in hers. Her dark eyes welled with tears. "Oh, Jon . . . I love you. If that's all that mattered it would be so easy. But I need more now . . . Tommy needs more. Do you understand?"

He took a deep breath, then leaned forward and kissed her gently on the cheek. He stood. "I've got to do some thinking."

"Yes." She released his hand.

"I'm leaving this afternoon."

"Yes."

"I'll call . . . we'll talk."

She nodded.

"Maybe when I come back . . ."

"Yes . . . when you come back. Goodbye, Jon."

He looked down at her for a long moment then turned and left, his blue mood now returned in spades.

He went to his apartment to pack.

It was definitely not turning out to be his day.

3

THE man at the desk was asleep. Arm crooked for a pillow, he sat slumped forward atop a clutter of files and papers. His shirtsleeves were rolled two turns above the wrists. A burning fluorescent desk lamp illuminated his disheveled silver hair.

Near dawn the man stirred and looked toward the window. A thin shaft of daylight peeked from one edge of the heavy cerulean drapes. He sat up, yawned, tried to rub deep weariness from haggard eyes. After a few seconds he turned off the lamp, stood and went to the window. He was tall, with the solid, wide-shouldered build of a football player, which, indeed, he had been over three decades before at West Point. He opened the drapes, then arched his body and kneaded the muscles of his lower back with both hands.

The man was Major General Louis Burnside, Commander of the Air Force Research and Test Center (AFRTC), Kirtland Air Force Base, New Mexico. For a long moment this morning the general studied the view from his office window. Seventy miles to the west, towering huge on the horizon like a solitary sentinel heralding the new day, snowcapped Mount Taylor brilliantly reflected the first light. Slowly, the sun's rays receded down the frosted peak to the sere sprawling desert below. As always, the stark awesome beauty of the scene stirred Burnside deeply.

After a while he gathered up the scattered files from his desk and locked them in a field safe behind his chair. Then he crossed the spacious office to his private washroom. A drawn-faced stranger stared back from his mirror. The general took a couple of deep breaths, put a finger on his wrist and monitored his pulse. He frowned. He took a pill case from the medicine cabinet, shook out two red capsules and swallowed them with water. Then he removed his blue uniform tie and shirt, threw both into a hamper, and filled the basin with steaming hot water.

At 6:45 that morning Burnside's secretary, Ann Lucero, a half hour earlier than usual, bid a cheerful good morning to the security policeman stationed at the entrance to the commander's suite. "Good morning, Sergeant Jarrell."

The SP smiled. "Mornin', Miss Lucero."

Ann continued down the hallway to her office just outside the general's. With delicate care she arranged a fresh bouquet of white chrysanthemums she'd cut that morning in a vase on her desk, then sat down to scan *The Albuquerque Journal* before the workday began. Thirty-five years old, with fine Castilian features, Ann was strikingly pretty. On this morning she had dressed in a simple blue sheath that highlighted her shapely figure and short-cut auburn hair.

She spied a front-page story datelined *Santa Fe, Sep 24:* CARTER AND REAGAN NECK-AND-NECK IN NEW MEXICO.

She had just begun to read the story when she was distracted by the sound of running water. She closed the paper. Sergeant Jarrell should have told her that the general had already arrived. Or had he worked through the night again? That worried her. He hadn't looked at all well lately. She decided to order the coffee extra strong that morning.

In the washroom Burnside splashed on an expensive bay rum after-shave lotion, then reached into a wardrobe for a fresh shirt. While buttoning up he heard his secretary's stirrings. He pushed an intercom button beside the mirror. "Morning, Ann. Is coffee on the way?"

Ann's voice sounded through the intercom. "Good morning, sir. Yes, good and strong. Would you like breakfast sent in?"

"Donuts will be fine. And Ann . . . I want to see Colonel

MacWatt just as soon as he comes in. Better have Mister Coff-man sit in too."

"Yes, sir. General . . . you know that Mrs. Burnside's flight leaves this morning?"

A pang of remorse. He had forgotten. "Yes. What time?"

"Eleven-forty."

"All right. Thank you. Be sure to order plenty of donuts. You know MacWatt."

Colonel Robert MacWatt was a burly bear of a man. Six feet three inches tall, 260 pounds, he did not project the lithe image the PR posters proclaimed to be the typical sleek-groomed Air Force officer. He couldn't have cared less. As he entered General Burnside's office this morning, MacWatt was wearing a second-day shirt beneath his Class-A uniform blouse, barely pressed trousers, and shoes that looked as if they had never met the business end of a polish brush. It was generally conceded on base that if uniform socks weren't all black, MacWatt would surely have mismatched his.

General Burnside regarded his deputy with amused toler-ance. Years before, the general had embraced a wise command adage: *Some things you ignore with a fine dignity.* MacWatt's military bearing—or lack of it—was one of those things Burn-side ignored with a fine dignity. It was no secret in the Air Force that MacWatt's continuation on active duty after thirty years was due solely to Burnside's clout. For notwithstanding the colonel's seedy appearance, beneath his overlong thatch of graying hair there existed a first-rate mind. A mind that had saved Burnside's neck from the block too many times for the general to quibble over scuffed shoes.

MacWatt gave his best semblance of a salute. "Morning, General." His baritone voice had the gravelly timbre of a mid-western hog caller. He dropped his bulk heavily into an over-large brown leather chair.

In an opposite chair a stocky, moon-faced civilian blew his breath on the lenses of oversize horn-rimmed glasses and began to polish them with a handkerchief. MacWatt gave a brusque nod in the civilian's direction. "Gerald."

Forty-five-year-old Gerald Coffman returned the greeting with equal lack of enthusiasm. "Colonel."

Coffman was Burnside's technical advisor. In matters of pure technology his word in the command was second only to the general's. A fastidious dresser, Coffman was attired this morning in razor-pressed gray wool slacks, over-the-calf black silk stockings, highly shined wing-tipped shoes, a pale-blue shirt with a darker-hued knit tie knotted Windsor style, and a navy-blue blazer with a white linen handkerchief arranged deftly in the breast pocket. His sparse, chestnut hair was painstakingly brushed in a vain attempt to conceal a balding pate. His left eye was plagued by an erratic tic.

MacWatt did not like Coffman. Or his profession.

Ann Lucero entered with coffee in white china cups emblazoned with the Air Force seal, and a box of assorted donuts. Burnside took a plain donut and black coffee. Coffman took black coffee only. MacWatt took two jelly donuts and the cup of coffee that Ann had already sugared and creamed to the color of new leather.

Burnside instructed Ann to hold all calls. She moved a heavy ceramic ashtray to the table beside MacWatt's chair, left the room and stationed herself at her desk to guard the general against interruptions.

Burnside held up a half-inch-thick, bound document marked in bold red letters:

TOP SECRET
SENSITIVE INFORMATION
Copy *1* of 2 Copies

Burnside said, "You know what this is, Mac." A statement, not a question.

MacWatt shoved a pair of ill-fitting glasses over his ears, silently cursing, as he did each time, the Air Force's ridiculous one-size-fits-all policy for spectacles. Once again he vowed to go to a civilian optometrist. He peered at the document in Burnside's hand. "Yes, sir. Hadley's report on the XR-Twenty-One-Hundred crash." He removed the glasses quickly and took a large bite out of a donut.

Coffman cleared his throat. "General, if we are going to discuss Project Quickseal I suggest that General Sabin be present."

"Overruled," Burnside said bluntly.

MacWatt noticed the tic in Coffman's eye go wild.

Burnside turned back to MacWatt. "Have you read it?"

"Yes."

"So have I. Several times." Burnside's usually soft, Deep South drawl became flint hard. "What the hell was Hadley smoking when he came up with this pile of dung? And why, in God's name, did Sabin pick his own executive officer to conduct the investigation? Then approve such a half-assed job? Hell . . . that crash was only twenty-nine days ago. Yet, here's a final report on my desk for approval."

MacWatt was disturbed. Burnside's voice was on the raw edge of emotion. Under the general's command were twelve of the most highly sophisticated, top priority defense projects currently under research and development. Quickseal was one. Notably calm and self-possessed, even when confronted with the thorniest of command problems, it was unlike Burnside to become emotional. Few others had seen this disturbing late facet of the general's character. MacWatt regretted that Coffman was seeing it now.

MacWatt said, "It was General Sabin's prerogative to choose Colonel Hadley, or any other officer in the Quickseal test group, to make the investigation. He also had the authority of first approval before sending the report to you. That's all he's done. There's nothing out of line about the procedure."

Burnside was unimpressed. "Procedure be damned!" He opened the report and flipped through several pages. "Listen to this . . . here's a line from Hadley's findings: *Examination of the salvaged aircraft and its component parts revealed no structural, mechanical, or electronic failures that would have contributed to its loss.*'

"All right? Now, listen to this." He flipped forward to a page he had marked with a paper clip. "Here's one of the good colonel's conclusions: *'For reasons unknown and unknowable, Pilot Crowell lost control of his aircraft, panicked, declared emergency, and attempted to land on Kingman Reef. He misjudged the approach and crashed into the lagoon. Pilot Crowell was unable to extract himself from the cockpit and drowned.'*"

He closed the report and dropped it onto the desk as if he were ridding himself of carrion.

He rocked back in his large swivel chair. "Now, let's examine what we have here," he said, tallying each point by touching a finger. "First, the XR-Twenty-One-Hundred is the most advanced, most assiduously engineered aircraft in the world. Not even the Columbia got closer attention to detail.

"Next, every person in the Quickseal test group was hand-picked from at least five candidates. It's the singular, most professional test group in the Air Force.

"Next, the Quickseal pilot training program is second to none . . . as stringent as that for astronauts.

"And that brings us to Major Peter Crowell. He passed every physical and psychological stress test known to aerospace medicine. He was a decorated combat veteran. He flew every type of covert aircraft in the inventory. Why, he helped write the manual on the SR-Seventy-One. And now Sabin"—the general sat forward and slammed his open palm down on the report—"is telling me that a pilot that experienced, on a routine test flight, flew a thousand miles off course, lost control of an aircraft that can virtually fly itself, and crashed 'for reasons unknown and unknowable.' " He spat out the line from Hadley's report with contempt. "Damn it, Mac . . . what's going on over there in the Quickseal compound?"

During his tirade Burnside's face had grown wan. MacWatt took the cellophane from a Dutch Master panatella cigar. Deliberately stalling to give the general a chance to calm down, MacWatt bit the end off the cigar, moistened its entire length in his mouth, then lighted it with a throwaway lighter. Blowing smoke to the ceiling, he said evenly, "Nonetheless, there are significant points we can't ignore. Major Crowell did declare an emergency; the plane did go down; it was salvaged almost intact; and crash evaluation didn't find a single malfunction. It's puzzling. But those are the facts."

"Too damned puzzling," Burnside countered. "A perfect plane, a perfect pilot, no malfunction. Then what in God's name caused Crowell to lose control? Why was the plane virtually undamaged?" He tapped the Hadley report. "I'm certainly not buying this casual dismissal of the incident."

The general paused in thought. "Have you listened to the tape?"

"Tape?"

"Crowell's mayday transmission—it was recorded by Honolulu Control."

MacWatt shook his head. "No, sir. Just read the transcription." He waited for the general to clarify the question.

Burnside let it drop. "Tell me . . . what's my leeway in this?"

It was what all the preamble had been leading to, and MacWatt was glad the question was finally posed. He shifted his bulk in the chair. "The regulations give you several options, General. You can accept the report and forward it to the Chief of Staff as written; you can return it to General Sabin for reevaluation and revision; you can return it with an order that Hadley reopen the investigation; or"—MacWatt's voice took on pointed emphasis—"you can appoint an independent investigator, an officer outside Quickseal, one not so close to the incident, or the people involved."

The nuance in MacWatt's voice was unmistakable. Burnside smiled inwardly. *Why you crafty old reprobate.* It was clear now that MacWatt's opinion of the Hadley report was just as negative as the general's. The colonel had been playing devil's advocate.

Burnside mulled the options. Under no circumstances would he send a flawed report to the Air Force Chief of Staff. Gip McCollum would have his hide, and rightly so. Nor did he have any intention of returning it to Sabin. That left the final option. An independent investigator. Clearly the course MacWatt was tacitly proposing. Burnside made a mental bet that MacWatt had already picked his man.

Burnside said, "An independent investigator, you say. Accountable to whom?"

"To you."

"That would mean taking the investigation out of Sabin's hands."

"It's an authorized procedure."

Gerald Coffman inched forward in his chair. Following the rejection of his suggestion that General Sabin be present, the technical advisor had remained silent. But it was apparent that General Burnside was warming to the idea of a new investigator. Coffman said, "General, I feel we are in danger of making a grave error. May I speak freely?"

"Please do, Gerald."

"Thank you, sir." Coffman cleared his throat nervously.

"Gentlemen, I feel that you are perhaps failing to take into account the extremely sensitive nature of the Quickseal project. Outside of those in the test group, and the three of us in this room, not more than a dozen people know the true nature of the XR-Twenty-One-Hundred. As you know, the Pentagon quite successfully manipulated media reports of the crash. That subterfuge was expressly approved by the Oval Office.

"Now, I have read Colonel Hadley's report thoroughly. While I agree that it doesn't answer all the questions, I submit that it does have one overriding merit: It covers the facts as far as they are ascertainable without jeopardizing Quickseal." He paused for emphasis. "That merit alone, in my opinion, justifies the report. A new investigation"—he looked pointedly at Mac-Watt—"particularly one by an outsider, could seriously compromise the project. I submit that it is in the interest of national security that the Hadley report be approved as written."

Nervousness abated, he ended on a pontifical note. Now he sat back in his chair with the air of a person who was quite pleased with himself.

Burnside's response was quick. "Thank you, Gerald. But I'm afraid that the true nature of the XR-Twenty-One-Hundred has already been compromised. The President let that cat out of the bag, didn't he? And for the poorest of reasons—to boost his reelection campaign.

"No, there's an overriding factor here. And it strikes at the very heart of Quickseal. Now, something went wrong out there in the Pacific. Something failed. Man or machine? I don't know. And it's quite clear to me that neither Colonel Hadley nor General Sabin knows either. And the question is far too important to gloss over. Now, it's no criticism of you, Gerald, but I'm going to disapprove the Hadley report and order the investigation reopened. With an independent investigating officer responsible to me."

Despite the disclaimer, the rebuff registered banefully on Coffman's countenance.

MacWatt could hardly suppress his pleasure. He didn't know which satisfied him most, Burnside's decision or Coffman's visible pique. Of course, the little prick would get his jollies tonight, feverishly penning a full account of this meeting to his civilian cronies in Washington. Surely he would underscore Burnside's indiscreet slap at the President. What a plum that would make for the next gathering of the Pentagon Backstabbers Association.

Burnside said to MacWatt: "About this new investigator. I want someone sharp, with an analytical mind. Someone who's not afraid to follow a lead wherever it takes him." He gave his deputy a subtle look. "I suppose it's a bit premature to ask if you have anyone like that in mind?"

MacWatt stubbed out his cigar in the ceramic ashtray and feigned thought. "Matter of fact, I might know just the man."

Uh huh, Burnside thought, bemused. He had won his mental bet.

Coffman stood. "Well, if the decision is definite . . . Is there anything else, General?" He made no attempt to hide his displeasure.

"That's it, Gerald. Thanks for sitting in."

Coffman left.

Burnside looked at MacWatt knowingly. "All right, Mac, who's the man?"

"Major Jonathan Ward, engineering type from Andrews. He'll be here tonight."

"Ward?" Burnside mulled the name. "Do I know him?"

"There's no reason for you to remember. He was at Hanscom when you commanded . . ."

"Ah-h-h," Burnside interjected. "The Kamchatka signal. Right?"

"Right."

"Good . . . good. From what I recall of that incident he should be quite up to it."

Burnside lowered his voice. "Mac, I want Major Ward to work directly with you. He'll be acting on my authority. I'll take full responsibility. But I want you to be his focal point. Put him in private quarters . . . VIP would seem best. Make sure he has whatever he needs. Now—this is important—I don't want anything he discovers, interim or otherwise, put in writing to this office. He can pass information to you verbally and you can brief me as you see fit. He can keep his preliminary notes in a field safe in his quarters. See that he has one. But nothing is to come through headquarters until he's prepared to make his final report, orally, to me. Is that clear?"

Puzzled, MacWatt said dutifully, "If that's how you want it, that's how it will be."

"Fine . . . fine. I know I can count on you."

Pause.

"Mac, there's another matter, a personal favor. Eileen is leaving for L.A. this morning. I'm . . . uh . . . tied up. Would you take her to the airport?"

MacWatt bristled. "Damnit, Lou, there's nothing on your desk so important that you can't take an hour to see Eileen off. It would mean a lot to her. Don't put this off on me."

"Mac . . . I'm asking as an old friend."

MacWatt debated whether to argue, to flatly refuse. He could, and he knew he could get away with it. Instead, he said, "What time?"

"Eleven-forty. Trans International. I won't forget it."

"Sure, Lou . . . sure."

The burly colonel turned and left the office without another word.

4

EILEEN Burnside sat with her hands folded in her lap, eyes downcast, oblivious to the to-and-fro hustle in the busy north terminal of the Albuquerque International Airport.

Seated beside her on the heavy burnt-pine-and-leather couch, Robert MacWatt could almost feel the hurt she was trying to suppress. She was still so lovely: golden hair without a hint of gray; heart-shaped face as flawlessly smooth as a woman's half her age; tall trim figure, fetchingly adorned this morning in a pink wool pants suit. Yes, in the looks department the years had been kind to Eileen.

She said without looking up, "He didn't come home last night."

"He was working, Eileen, in his office, all night."

He had blurted it out too quickly, the overemphasis on truth in this instance underscoring that in other circumstances her suspicions would have been genuine. He realized the gaffe and it embarrassed him.

She raised her head. "Dearest Robert. Always the faithful retainer. Whatever would he do without you? Whatever would *I* do without you? I know about those women. I've known for years."

"Eileen . . . please. There's no need to tell me . . ."

She put a hand on his. "But I want to tell you. Don't you see, Robert. You're the only one I can talk to about such things. The only one who . . . understands."

He remained silent. He knew she was right.

She continued: "There was a time, early in our marriage, when I might have left him. But then I got pregnant, and Roberta came and there was a new purpose in my life. Then, over the years, I came to realize that Louis did truly love me . . . need me. He couldn't express it . . . in words. But I knew . . . despite the others."

She gave his hand a squeeze and released it. "Anyway . . . there haven't been any others for years. That's not the problem."

He waited.

"He's ill you know."

"Ill?"

"He thinks I don't know; sometimes he forgets that I was a nurse. He's seeing a civilian doctor. He's taking pills for angina."

Angina. So that's the reason for the peakedness, MacWatt thought, the overirritability. He realized that he had suspected something like this for some time, but had never brought his thoughts to bear on it.

Eileen said, "He should have retired years ago. He promised to. But he always found some reason to stay on. This summer he started talking about it again. He was really serious. We made plans to build a home in Newport Beach, near Roberta and little Louis. A *home*, Robert. Not just another house. We had such great fun designing it together and mentally furnishing the rooms and figuring out the landscaping and all.

"Then, last month that tragedy with poor Peter Crowell happened. And something about it is driving Louis relentlessly. He's obsessed with that crash. I tried to help, to get him away. He promised to make this trip with me. It would have been so good for him. Yesterday he told me he couldn't go. Before, whenever that happened, I simply stayed home too. But this time I decided I was going whether he did or not. I've never done that before. So . . ."—her voice lilted in mock triumph—"this is a first."

She emitted a half laugh. "*The general's lady.* Some women

thrive on such things. Oh, I played the part. You know that, Robert. But I'm tired. So very tired of it all. Endless parties, visiting dignitaries, honorary president of the wives club, the twenty-four-hour-a-day demand on Louis' time. I've endured it. For thirty years. For Louis. Now I want it over. I want us to live life on our own terms, to have whatever time we have left for ourselves. Is that so terribly selfish of me, Robert?''

"No," he said with honest feeling, "it's very wise."

She looked directly at him. "Oh, Robert. So often lately I find myself wishing that we could go back . . . to Itazuke. It all seemed so simple then."

Itazuke. The name resounded in MacWatt's memory. *Itazuke* . . . where it all began, that Christmas so many years ago . . .

The Korean War was six months old that December 1950. Three months earlier, First Lieutenant Robert MacWatt, 25, flying a lone reconnaissance mission over Wonsan, took a direct hit from a North Korean ack-ack battery. He maneuvered his flaming F-80 seaward and ejected, just as the plane exploded. He was plucked from the Sea of Japan by a Navy air-sea rescue helicopter and hospitalized aboard the carrier *Essex*. There doctors determined that the blast from the exploding jet had caused him irreversible audio nerve damage. Although not severe enough for a hearing aid, the injury reduced his hearing "below the threshold required of Air Force pilots." He was permanently grounded.

His flying career ended, Lieutenant MacWatt applied for immediate discharge. The request was denied "for the duration of the national emergency." Three weeks later, he was assigned as an aircraft control officer to the Air Defense Control Center (ADCC), Itazuke Air Base, Japan.

The war was not going well that first winter. Fighting with obsolete equipment that American forces had abandoned on countless Pacific islands at the end of World War II, United States troops were outmanned, outgunned, and often outmaneuvered. The ADCC was the combat eye for the Air Force during those hectic early days. Around the clock, USAF pilots based on Kyushu, the southernmost Japanese island, flew sorties against onrushing enemy forces in Korea. The task of directing them to their targets, then guiding them safely home, fell to the control officers who manned the farseeing radar scopes in the darkened, cavernous room that was the heart of the ADCC.

One midnight, two weeks before Christmas that first December of combat, a red light flashed on the intercom at Lieutenant MacWatt's console. The chief watch officer's voice came through the box. "Mac, we've got a mayday from an F-86, callsign Blue Knight Two . . . somewhere in I Sector. Take it."

MacWatt expanded the range on his radar scope to 150 miles. There were seven widely separated blips at various bearings, all, MacWatt knew from the operations log, F-86s returning from a night strike near Taegu. He tuned his radio to the emergency frequency and keyed his mike. "Blue Knight Two, this is Topkick. What's your condition?"

The radio crackled. "Topkick . . . Blue Knight Two"—despite the static MacWatt could discern a rich, southern accent— "I took a wing and fuselage hit. No instruments, no cockpit lights. Controls very unstable. It's dark as the devil's asshole up here, old buddy. Sure would appreciate it if you'd tell me where I am."

MacWatt smiled, but kept his voice even. "Roger, Blue Knight Two. Are you squawking IFF?"

"It's on. If you don't read me I reckon the transponder was hit."

There was no coded identification signal on MacWatt's scope. "Blue Knight Two . . . I'm not getting a squawk. I'm going to determine your position. On command begin flying a starboard box. Count fifteen, slowly, on each leg before changing course. Start *now*."

At the twelve o'clock position near the top of the scope, one of the tiny beads of light, indicating an aircraft high above the Korea Strait, began to move in a square pattern. The latest weather for the stormy strait reported swells to eight feet. No plane could survive a ditching in such seas, no pilot would survive if he ejected. MacWatt plotted the plane's position and checked his height finder. It read 18,000 feet. "Blue Knight Two, I've got you at angels eighteen, twenty miles east of Kyongju, seventy miles due north of this station. I'm going to bring you home. Can you maintain level flight?"

"Old buddy . . . if this baby's wings don't fall off I can fly her by the seat of my pants. You just point the way."

Gutsy bastard, MacWatt thought. "Roger, Blue Knight Two. Come slowly starboard . . . begin now." The blip veered right. "That's good. Keep that turn . . . slowly . . . a bit more . . . begin to ease out . . . *now*. No . . . you overshot. Ease back port . . . slowly . . . slowly . . . *now*. Good. You're heading one-eighty. Maintain and follow my instructions."

For the next fifteen minutes, talking without cessation to reassure the stricken pilot that he was not alone, MacWatt vectored him, keeping him on course and at proper altitude.

Suddenly Blue Knight Two's voice called out in broken vibrato. "Topkick . . . I've just developed . . . heavy vibrations. I must have . . . taken an engine . . . hit too."

Jesus! MacWatt thought. What next? He took a couple of deep breaths. It was imperative to keep his voice calm. "Roger Blue Knight Two . . . you should be seeing coastal lights now. I estimate you can eject over land in two minutes."

"Negative! Like I . . . told you . . . Topkick . . . I'm not punching out . . . of this baby . . . until she . . . coughs up her . . . last breath. We've been through too . . . Hey! Runway lights! Beginning descent . . . *now*."

"Blue Knight Two . . . you're cleared for emergency landing. Good luck."

"Sayonara, Topkick . . . See you in church."

MacWatt pushed back his chair and glued his eyes on the crash-alert light on the control board at the front of the ADCC. If that red light began to blink it was a signal that a crash had occurred at or near Itazuke strip. The sweep-second hand on the clock above the control board crept through one minute . . . two . . . three. MacWatt held his breath. At the end of five minutes he sat back and let out a long sigh of relief. The red light remained unlit. Blue Knight Two had made it.

Forty-five minutes later the watch officer called MacWatt to the booth. "You got a call."

MacWatt took the phone. A distinctive southern voice came through the receiver. "Lieutenant, they tell me you're the one who saved my ass from a midnight dunk in the briny. I intend to thank you proper. When's your next shift break?"

"Tomorrow night."

"Good. Officers Club. The biggest Kobe beefsteak in the house, and all drinks on me. See you at seven."

It was more like an order than an invitation. Besides, the treat wasn't necessary. MacWatt had only done his job. But he thought, why not? "Sure, who'll I look for?"

"Lou Burnside. I'll be at the bar."

An attraction of opposites, they hit it off from the start. First Lieutenant Louis Burnside, from Gulfport, Mississippi: tall, muscular, blond, handsome, West Point ('48), superbly self-confident, outgoing, unreservedly committed to the Air Force, flying, and the pursuit of beautiful women. Robert MacWatt, from Keyser, West Virginia: taller, passably good looking, dark-haired, heavyset with a beginning paunch, graduate of West Virginia University, shy, and, now grounded, indifferent to a military career. He never talked of his experiences with women.

Before dinner that first night Burnside ordered a brandy alexander, heavy on the nutmeg. MacWatt ordered Glenlivet on the rocks.

"Fancy tastes," Burnside chided. "I thought all you hillbillies drank corn liquor."

MacWatt downed a mighty gulp of Scotch. "Not when someone else's paying."

Burnside laughed. "Touché." He knew he was going to like this rough-hewn hulk of a man who had surely saved his life.

Late afternoon, Christmas Eve, the two lieutenants sat at the bar rolling dice for drinks. The Officers Club was resplendent with pungent pine wreaths, fresh holly, red and green ribbons, silver bells, and an enormous soft-lit Star of Bethlehem, all painstakingly erected by Japanese employees to assuage the uprooted Americans' homesickness during this, their special season of the year.

The trappings depressed MacWatt. He pushed the dice cup to Burnside. "Helluva time to be away from home."

"Hey," Burnside replied, "this is the Air Force. You *are* home."

"Your ass!"

Burnside rolled two deuces and cursed.

MacWatt drained his glass and ordered another Scotch. "Pay the man."

Burnside put more money on the bar. "Mac, I think I know

just the thing to cheer you up." He lowered his voice conspiratorially. "Get a load of that vision of loveliness across the room."

MacWatt followed Burnside's gaze. At the cashier's desk across the foyer a stunning Japanese girl in stylish western dress was clearing the register of the afternoon receipts in preparation for relinquishing the job to the night cashier. From time to time the pretty girl cast anthracite eyes toward the bar where the two lieutenants were sitting.

MacWatt snorted. "Michiko? No way, friend. That's field grade stuff . . . strictly colonels and above."

Burnside winked. "That's what *they* think. Look, she's got a friend. There's this secluded little inn in Fukuoka—hot tub, clove-oil rubdowns, fun in the futons. You can have Michiko or her friend, makes no difference to me. Be good for what ails you."

It was the favorite off-duty sport at Itazuke, but MacWatt shook his head. "I'll find my own girls."

Burnside shrugged. "OK. Be a stick-in-the-mud," he said good-naturedly. He finished his drink and stood. "I'll let you know what you missed."

"I bet."

Burnside crossed the foyer and said something to Michiko that made her glance toward MacWatt and laugh. Then Burnside tossed a smug salute toward the bar and left the club with the lovely Japanese girl on his arm.

The day after Christmas, Burnside was ordered to Pusan for two weeks' temporary duty. That evening MacWatt sat alone at the bar. Halfway through his first Glenlivet he noticed a WAF second lieutenant sipping a tall drink at a table in the rear of the darkened room. She had pulled the candle-lantern close and was apparently writing a letter. MacWatt motioned the bartender to him. "Tadashi, who's the WAF?"

"Nurse lady. First day from stateside. No Itazuke boysan yet. You hurry, roost in her nest first. Ha!" The all-knowing Japanese bartender grinned widely at his crude suggestion.

MacWatt glanced at the girl from the corner of his eye. She was blonde, pretty, and although her uniform paid her no compliments, her shapely legs suggested a comely figure.

MacWatt mulled the wisdom of Tadashi's advice. Certainly

as soon as the new arrival's presence on base was widely known she would never be alone in the club again. He drained his drink, ordered another, and tried to screw up his courage.

Fifteen minutes later the nurse finished writing, put the tablet into her purse and got up from the table. Lamenting another lost opportunity, MacWatt watched her leave the bar.

He thought about dinner but decided he wasn't hungry. He went to the cloakroom and rummaged among the all-too-similar blue topcoats. Finding his on a back rack he threw it on, shoving his arms hard through the sleeves. His hand struck something. He turned to see the new nurse, hat askew, go sprawling against the wall. "Oh my God!" he said.

He grabbed the startled girl by the shoulders and yanked her to her feet. Her head snapped back sharply, her hat toppled to the floor and she was propelled against MacWatt in a smothering embrace. Quickly he pushed her bolt upright, retrieved her hat and placed it roughly on her head.

Suddenly, the girl thrust both hands high into the air. "I surrender!" she cried.

Completely addled, MacWatt stammered, "I . . . uh . . . Bob MacWatt . . . you're . . . look . . . I . . ." Somehow he managed a muddled apology.

The girl adjusted her hat. Then, with a sympathetic smile, she extended her hand. "Eileen Cannon. Do you always come on so strong to girls, Bob MacWatt?"

Blushing scarlet, MacWatt took the proffered hand. "Is there *any* way I can . . . Say, have you had dinner? There's a fine Japanese restaurant, eighteenth-century setting and all, not far. It's the least I can do."

The invitation had come in a rush of words and, once they were spoken, he was appalled that he had been so bold as to make the suggestion.

To his surprise, she accepted.

The picturesque, rambling old restaurant, once a private estate, was nestled among ancient pines and meticulously pruned evergreen shrubs on a secluded acre. The century-old garden, lighted by colorful overhung oriental lanterns, was separated from the building by a miniature moat that was spanned by an arched wooden bridge. Eileen stopped on the bridge to admire the first Japanese garden she'd ever seen.

MacWatt said, "In the summer it's ablaze with flowers. And each night they release thousands of fireflies to flicker like tiny candles among the trees and shrubs."

"Oh-h-h . . . that I've got to see!"

"Yes," he agreed expectantly.

In the restaurant foyer they removed their shoes and donned coarse reed slippers. A kimono-clad hostess led them to a private dining room, where they sat on a tatami-matted floor with their feet resting on a ledge in a pit beneath the low mahogany table. On the sandy bottom of the pit, a bed of glowing charcoal kept them toasty warm. The sliding, paper-thin shoji panels that made up the walls of the room were overlayed with lacquer-preserved maple leaves of different hues, depicting the changing seasons of the year. In one corner, a narrow silkscreen painting of a cascading waterfall hung from ceiling to floor. In another corner, rooted in a cloisonné planter, was a full-bodied, dwarfed pine tree no more than twenty-five inches high from base to crown.

Eileen was enchanted. "It's all so lovely, so elegant, yet so . . . I suppose the word is *tasteful*. They seem to accomplish so much with so little."

"Yes, they're masters at it."

MacWatt was no less enchanted. But not with the surroundings. During the taxi ride from base Eileen's refreshing lack of guile had put him at ease, had assuaged his inherent timidity that caused him to be tongue-tied in the presence of most women—particularly one as beautiful as she. And she was beautiful, he thought, trying not to be obvious, but unable to keep his eyes off her. She was younger than he, twenty-two he guessed from her revelation that she had graduated from nursing school that fall. She had a smooth, symmetrical face, vivid blue eyes, and the full lips that he found so sensual in women. The anticipation of her first assignment, her first time on her own, filled her with an exuberance that made her glow.

At one point he asked, "Do I detect the Southwest in your voice?"

She raised her head in exaggerated pride. "Marble Falls, Texas, suh!" She relaxed. "And you? Midwest?"

"West Virginia. But flatten it out and it'd be as big as Texas."

They laughed at the parochial joke.

He wondered why she had entered the Air Force and finally found the nerve to ask.

"Well," she replied thoughtfully, "There's the war, of course. I could claim patriotic duty. But that's stretching the truth. I don't know . . . it's difficult to explain. I love my family dearly, and my home. All my friends are perfectly content with the expectation of living out their lives, and eventually dying, in Marble Falls. But I've always been different . . . a maverick I guess. I don't know why. But I always wanted to see what lay on the other side of the mountain . . . beyond the prairie. Does that make any sense to you? It sure doesn't to my poor parents."

"Yes," he said. "It makes sense."

Dinner was sukiyaki, ceremoniously prepared at the table by a pretty, kimono-clad girl who deftly braised razor-thin slices of beef, green onion tops, Chinese cabbage, giant dried mushroom, tofu, and pea pods in a simmering, pungent blend of soy sauce and saki, then served the savory result atop boiled rice in ornate lacquered bowls.

Eileen found the chopsticks difficult to handle.

"Would you prefer a fork?" MacWatt asked solicitously. "They keep them on hand."

"For butterfingered Americans? No!" the plucky girl replied.

He showed her how to wedge the bottom stick between her palm and third finger and use her forefinger and thumb to manipulate the top stick like a wedge. She began to master the technique. She flashed a dazzling smile. "Just wait 'til the folks in Marble Falls hear about *this*."

They decided to walk the two miles back to base. The night was cold, but clear, the stars cool emeralds in an inky sky. Knowledgeably, MacWatt explained the sights, sounds and smells of Japan.

The narrow unpaved road, absent of people, led between rows of tiny shops now shuttered for the night. In the middle of one block, a dim streetlight illuminated an unobstructed shop window. They stopped to admire a cluttered display of antiques and crafts. Prominent on a center shelf was a huge china platter etched with the fierce likenesses of two ancient figures bearing long staffs.

"Izanagi and Izanami," MacWatt explained. "The deities who

formed Japan from the primordial mud during the first great kamikaze."

"Kamikaze . . . I thought that was an airplane."

He laughed. "That's understandable. But it means Divine Wind. Izanagi and Izanami are still worshipped in some sects."

All at once Eileen stooped low and gave a cry. "Oh, how exquisite!" On a lower shelf, displayed in a small black velvet case, was a single jade stone mounted on a plain gold band.

MacWatt bent over and studied the ring in the weak light. "Looks like good quality. You can usually tell from the deep emeraude coloring. You've got to be careful about jade over here."

"Well, then, Robert . . . whenever I venture out shopping I'm just going to have to entice you along."

"It's a date," he said hastily, and silently prayed that she shopped often.

At the doorway of her quarters he apologized again for the fiasco in the cloakroom. She stood on tiptoe and kissed him on the cheek. "It was worth every bruise." She bade him good-night.

Next afternoon he called her and they dined that evening in the Officers Club. The following evening he hired a car and driver and showed her the sights of Fukuoka. Saturday night he took her to the river to watch fishermen on floodlighted barges entice huge cormorants into the water to swoop up carp and perch in their expandable throats, then disgorge the catch into the boats.

"How fascinating!" Eileen said, and clung to MacWatt's arm all the tighter.

She was the only woman with whom he had ever been completely at ease, and by the second weekend he admitted what he had known from the beginning. He was deeply in love. He wondered if Eileen felt the same? They never discussed it. But surely she must be aware of his feelings toward her. She had turned down other dates to be with him. That was a good sign.

Early Friday afternoon, at the end of his shift, he took a taxi to the little antique shop near the old restaurant. He carefully scrutinized the jade ring Eileen had admired, satisfied himself that it was, indeed, a fine stone, and bought it. On the ride home he practiced the speech he would make that evening when he presented it to her. He decided not to propose . . . not just yet. That would be too presumptuous. But perhaps in time.

In the club that evening Eileen toyed with her food, barely eating. Her face was strained.

"Eileen, what is it?" he asked.

She put down her fork. "Oh, this *damned* war!"

She grabbed up her napkin and dabbed at her eyes. "I'm sorry. I have no right to bring my problems to you."

"No . . . it's all right. I want to hear."

She took a deep breath. "This afternoon . . . a kid . . . not more than eighteen. He took a shell fragment in his brain. We got it out. But the surgeons say he'll never be more than a vegetable. So young. So . . . very . . . very . . . young." She shook her head forlornly. "Oh, Robert. What am I going to do? I'm a nurse. I'm supposed to be able to take these things. But . . ."

He put a hand on hers. "I know . . . I know."

He wondered if this were the proper time? He slipped his other hand into his pocket for the ring, felt the chill of indecision and decided to wait a while.

She smiled thinly. "Thank you, Robert, for listening. It helps. Now . . . let's finish our dinner. I promise to leave my work in the hospital from now on."

After dinner she ordered Cointreau. He chose Drambuie.

Despite her efforts to conceal it he could tell that she was still depressed. He downed his cordial in a gulp. Then, with settled determination, he reached into his pocket and clasped the black velvet ring box firmly in his hand. "Eileen, I . . ."

A voice called out, "Hey, Mac!"

Eileen looked up to see a handsome blond pilot, still in his flying suit, striding across the room toward their table.

Louis Burnside cast an appreciative eye on Eileen. "Quick, Mac, introduce us. Don't let me fall in love with a complete stranger."

MacWatt swore beneath his breath, made the introduction, and prayed that Burnside would leave.

Burnside lifted Eileen's hand and kissed it with a flourish. Then he pulled a chair to the table and began to relate anecdotes about his trip to Korea.

MacWatt suffered in silence.

Eileen, gloom dissipating, found the stories amusing.

"There's this Lieutenant Buckhannon," Burnside began another tale. "We met at an operations briefing in Pusan. He runs a gap-filler radar site on Unishima—that's a tiny island in the Strait. Well—he was telling me one night—it so happens that Unishima is smack in the midst of one of the best abalone beds in the Far East. Abalone are harvested by divers, you know, and when the divers would work the waters off the island, Buckhannon's men would desert their posts in droves. Damn near shut the place down."

"But why?" Eileen asked.

MacWatt frowned at Burnside and said, "Abalone divers are young women, Eileen. They work nude."

"Oh."

"Exactly!" Burnside exclaimed. "Poor Buckhannon. His first command, and things were going to hell in a hand basket. But, he rose to the occasion."

"What did he do?" Eileen asked, enthused now.

"Well, he called his NCOs together and they worked out a plan. During abalone season they rearranged schedules so that half the men—a skeleton crew—would operate the site. The other half went 'abalone diving.' Next day they'd swap places and the other half would get a shot at the action. It made a shambles of standard military procedure, but it worked. And Headquarters was none the wiser." Burnside gave an admiring chuckle. "Good old Buckhannon. He'll make general for sure, if he doesn't get court-martialed first."

Eileen laughed.

The lights dimmed and across the ballroom a Japanese band began to play note-perfect renditions of Glenn Miller classics.

Burnside smiled at Eileen. "Care to dance?"

She took his hand warmly.

As he watched the two of them embrace to the music, MacWatt realized that he had never asked Eileen to dance. It was just as well. He was two left feet on a dance floor.

The music stopped. Eileen was laughing gaily at something Burnside was saying. The band struck up again and they glided into another dance. And another. Seemingly oblivious to their sullen friend at the table, they danced the evening away.

In the BOQ that night Burnside complimented his pal. "I'm impressed, Mac. Is there, uh, anything on between you two?"

"On?" MacWatt was embarrassed. "Naw . . . nothing like that. We're just friends."

"Well, you might be missing the boat. A man could do much worse."

Yes, MacWatt agreed in silence, a man could.

For the next two weeks the three lieutenants were an inseparable trio: dinners at the club; movies on base; opening night at *Blithe Spirit*, by the NCO Club Little Theater group.

One Sunday Burnside treated them to dinner at the Bamboo Club, a Japanese establishment in Fukuoka that catered to American officers. While MacWatt swilled Scotch, Burnside and Eileen danced. Sometime during the evening Burnside summoned a roving photographer to the table. "All right, teammates, smile at the birdie." Just before the flash, he slipped his arm around Eileen. MacWatt managed a pathetic grin.

During the taxi ride back to the base Burnside announced, "Afraid you two'll have to get along without me for a while. I've got a dawn mission."

"Oh, Louis . . ." Eileen's voice revealed her concern.

"Nothing exciting," Burnside said. "I'm flying a Saber up to Nagoya for some special gear. I should be back Wednesday."

"Three days," Eileen said plaintively.

Three days! MacWatt thought. "Hey . . . good trip, hear? We'll miss you." His spirits soared.

The next afternoon MacWatt got to the club early. He sat in the foyer anxiously fondling the jade ring. He had carried it in his pocket constantly, cursing his earlier indecision, eager for another opportunity to be alone with Eileen.

She didn't show up for the cocktail hour.

As the dinner hour approached he reserved their usual table and sat watching the doorway.

The dinner hour passed.

At 8:15 he went to the lobby and phoned her quarters. No answer. Was she working late? He looked up the hospital number and dialed the nurse's station on Eileen's ward. A strange voice answered. He asked for Lieutenant Cannon. The strange voice responded, "Lieutenant Cannon didn't come to work today. She's on a three-day pass."

MacWatt felt an icy lump in his stomach. "Oh? Do you know where she went?"

"She signed out for Nagoya."

He sat at the bar, drink in hand, gazing forlornly at the jade ring. It had been a lost cause from the beginning, he knew that now. He'd only been fooling himself. Who was he, anyway, to think that he could have won the heart of such a beautiful woman? He hadn't eaten, but he didn't care. He wondered if he'd ever be hungry again. He shoved the ring back into his pocket and called to the bartender, "Tadashi . . . Glenlivet . . . the whole bottle."

The Japanese frowned and shook his head. "No. Against club rule. No whole bottle."

The hulking lieutenant stood to his full height and stared down at the hapless little bartender with fire in his eyes. Tadashi grabbed the bottle of Glenlivet and shoved it across the bar. "Club rule damned crazy. Ha!"

MacWatt laid a pile of bills on the bar, grabbed the bottle, and walked through the somber night to his quarters, alone.

First Lieutenant Louis Burnside and Second Lieutenant Eileen Cannon were married in uniform in the all-denominational chapel on Itazuke Air Base on January 30, 1951. Standing with the groom, Best Man Robert MacWatt suffered through the ceremony with stoical resolve. That afternoon he accompanied the newlyweds to the airstrip to catch the daily flight to Tokyo for a week-long honeymoon. Just before boarding, Eileen pulled him close and kissed him on the cheek. "Oh, Robert, dear . . . how can I ever thank you for introducing me to the loveliest man in the whole world?"

Next day, MacWatt applied for immediate reassignment to Wakkanai Radar Station, on the remote northernmost tip of Hokkaido, the "Japanese Siberia." Surprised to have a volunteer for duty dreaded by most officers, Headquarters approved the request. MacWatt departed Itazuke the day before his friends returned from Tokyo. In time, the sought-after isolation of Wakkanai helped ease the ache in his heart. He got through it. But he knew he'd never get over it.

In the years that followed, at Eileen's insistence, they kept in touch by letters. She chided him at first for "deserting us at Itazuke." But in time, her frequent, always upbeat correspondence became a welcome expectation in MacWatt's otherwise lonely life. Through her letters he kept abreast of Eileen's dexterous balancing of her roles as Air Force nurse and homemaker, and, though she never made a big thing of it, of Louis' skyrocketing career. Never one for professional jealousy, MacWatt was pleased that his friend, whom he'd early recognized as a comer, was realizing his potential.

In January 1954, Eileen wrote joyously that she was pregnant. "I must now resign from active duty. But, as I'm sure you can understand, that's fine with me. I much prefer the role of wife and mother to that of 'career woman.' " That summer the Burnsides' daughter was born. "We're naming her Roberta, after our dearest friend."

Following the Tonkin Resolution in 1964, Burnside, now a major, was assigned to Vietnam. The year-long separation was a fretful time for Eileen, and her letters to MacWatt became more frequent. He responded to each, bolstering her courage, reassuring her. In 1965, with 114 fighter-bomber missions to his credit (four more than he flew in Korea), Burnside returned home. Three months later, citing the need for experienced officers in the war, he volunteered to return. He was assigned to Bangkok as advisor to the Thailand Air Force. From Bangkok he wrote his first and only letter to MacWatt. It was a surprisingly candid revelation of Burnside's growing disenchantment with the American presence in Southeast Asia. MacWatt knew that Burnside was venting frustration to the only other officer he would trust with such career-threatening insight. MacWatt felt honored.

Then, Burnside's letter concluded: "But there are compensations. Remember Michiko, the passion-pot at the Itazuke O' Club? Well, these doe-eyed Thai beauties know tricks that put her to shame!"

With a throaty curse, MacWatt crumpled the letter. This, too, was information that Burnside felt safe in writing to his old buddy. MacWatt despised being privy to it. He prayed that Eileen would never learn of this perfidious side of the man she considered "the loveliest in the world."

By 1972, Lieutenant Colonel Robert MacWatt was recognized as the Air Force's foremost authority on ground radar operations. He was also recognized as having reached the end of his career. There would be no further assignments, no further promotions. His studied unmilitary bearing, his sometimes callous disregard for rank and protocol, had roiled too many senior officers to whom such perquisites were inviolable. MacWatt anticipated the end of his career without regret. He despised the cliques and cabals of Washington, the political bullshit that was part and parcel of higher rank. Then, in the spring of that year, he received orders to report for ten days special duty to the Commander, Air Forces Iceland—Colonel Louis Burnside.

In the twenty-two years since Itazuke their paths had crossed only twice. In 1955, MacWatt caught a cargo flight to Norton Air Force Base, California to attend Roberta Burnside's christening. Then, in 1964, just before Louis left for Vietnam, the Burnsides visited MacWatt at Keesler Air Force Base, Mississippi. Though he had dreaded each visit beforehand, MacWatt looked back on them afterwards as happy occasions.

The reunion at Keflavik, Iceland, was no less heartwarming. MacWatt had a made reservation at the BOQ, but Eileen wouldn't hear of it. "You're staying with us and that's that."

That evening in the AFI Commander's quarters, while Burnside mixed before-dinner cocktails, MacWatt adjusted his ample girth in a chair and noted wistfully how much kinder the years had been to his friends. Lou's hair was whiter, there was a more rugged maturity to his still-handsome face, but surely he could still fit into the uniform he wore as a plebe at West Point. Eileen was, well, still so breathtakingly beautiful—tall, trim, endearing. Roberta, now eighteen, and as willowy curvaceous and radiantly pretty as Eileen, had inherited the best from both parents. And it was she now who, with that magically lyrical voice that MacWatt had found so enchanting in her mother so many years before, entertained him with stories of the Land of Fire and Ice. "It's such an off-putting name, *Iceland*. But it's not that at all. The original settlers named it that, you know, to deceive the marauding Vikings. But it's not icebound. Oh, there're glaciers, but, Uncle Robert, you should see the deep meadows, the lush green sheep ranches, the beaches . . . well, they're mostly pebbles . . . but they're so picturesque."

Eileen said, "Perhaps you should drive Uncle Robert out to visit the whale processing plant."

Roberta gave her mother a dirty look and made a face. "Yuk!" They all laughed.

"I get the picture," MacWatt said.

"But there is Tern Day," Roberta added quickly. "Any time now."

"Tern Day?"

"They come in from the sea . . . millions of them. They lay their eggs on the beaches and the farms and the rocklands. Everyone—children, adults—goes out with baskets to gather them. It's like one enormous Easter egg hunt. Mom uses them to cook with. Would you go with me, Uncle Robert?"

MacWatt was sincerely touched. "Honey, that's the most exciting invitation I've had in years. But remember, I'm here for only a few days. I think I'd better concentrate on whatever it is your father called me up here to do."

From the corner of his eye he saw his hosts give each other a furtive glance. Burnside said, "Yes, ah . . . well, we can go into that tomorrow. But tonight, no shoptalk." He raised his glass. "To good friends, forever."

In high spirits, they raised their glasses in a mutual toast.

The office was spacious and well-appointed, as befitted the senior Air Force officer on a NATO base. Burnside stood beside a wall map of the North Atlantic. MacWatt listened.

"This corridor"—Burnside used a pointer—"is one of the most crucial to the defense of North America. Each night the Russians send their Bear bombers down the Norwegian Sea past the Faroes, or through the Denmark Strait, enroute to the U.S. and Canadian coasts. They're probing, of course, testing our ability to intercept them." He laid the pointer down and sat at his desk. "That's why I sent for you, Mac."

"Oh?" MacWatt said, skeptical.

"We've got four primary radar sites operating twenty-four hours a day. I need to know if they're at peak efficiency, if everything's going as well as it should. Sure, I get rosy reports from my staff. But they don't have your background. You're the best in the business. I'd like for you to examine the operation, let me know if we're doing things right. Will you do that for me?"

MacWatt said bluntly, "No, I won't."

Burnside was taken aback. "What?!"

"I said I wouldn't do it. Look, Lou, where in the hell do you think I'm coming from? I've chaired the radar evaluation board for the Joint Chiefs for three years. There's not a red alert intercept made anywhere in the world that I don't know about within ten minutes. I know your record . . . I've taken a particular interest in it. Since you took command up here the intercept rate has been a hundred percent; your radar down times are eleven percent lower than any comparable station on the Dew Line. Now, how about dropping the bullshit and telling me the real reason you sent for me?"

For a moment Burnside's face was stern, then it erupted into a grin, then he let out a hearty laugh. "All right, keep your shirt on. I *was* testing you. I wanted to see for myself if you're really the crusty outspoken bastard everyone says you've become. I can see that you haven't been slandered." He swiveled back in his chair. "OK. No more bullshit. Mac, the word I get from down your way is that some of the moguls are trying to nudge you out to pasture."

MacWatt shrugged. "Might be best."

"Now who's bullshitting? You know as well as I do that the Air Force is damned short of officers who aren't afraid to speak their minds. We need men like that." He cast a wry glance at MacWatt's midsection. "Even if they do have to buy their uniforms from Omar the tentmaker."

"Hummph," MacWatt snorted, unoffended, but wondering where this conversation was leading.

"Mac, the new brigadier list will be out in two weeks. My name will be on it."

For the first time, MacWatt brightened. *"Brigadier General Louis Burnside."* He spoke the words slowly, savoring them. "By God, Lou, that is good news. Congratulations. I'm proud of you. I mean that sincerely."

"I know you do. And I appreciate it. But I want more than your congratulations. I want you."

MacWatt was puzzled. "I don't understand."

"I've been given the word, unofficially of course, about my new assignment. Hanscom, Massachusetts. I'm going to head up the EDC."

"The Electronics Development Command. Quite a plum for a new brigadier."

"Yes. But you know what the score is there. Half the complement is civilian. High-ranking civil service types, scientists and engineers. Not the easiest folks in the world to work with. That's where you come in. I want you to be my deputy, to ride herd for me, to see to it that things get done as they should. I've already spoken to the Chief of Staff. All it takes is your OK." He looked at MacWatt expectantly.

"Deputy Commander of EDC," MacWatt said thoughtfully. "That's a full-bull billet, Lou. I'm just a lieutenant colonel."

"I can fix that too."

"I was honestly looking forward to retirement. It isn't that I'm intimidated by those Pentagon assholes."

"I believe that. But it's just for two more years. You can do that standing on your head. And it'll mean a boost in your retirement check. How about it?"

MacWatt shifted uneasily in his chair. "I just don't know, Lou. I'm honored . . . but, well, I'll have to think on it."

"Sure. You're at my disposal for ten days anyway. But I'll have to know before you leave."

"Fair enough."

On following days, whenever the opportunity presented itself, Eileen added her pitch. "Please say yes, Robert. Louis truly does need you. And it would be just like old times, the three of us together again."

He wondered how "the three of us together again" would work, but said nothing.

At the end of a week, still undecided, MacWatt hosted his friends for dinner at the Keflavik Base Officers Club. In the middle of the meal Burnside was paged to the phone. He returned to the table in a dark mood. "Eileen, I've asked Lieutenant Haywood to see you home. Mac, you come with me."

They drove to base operations. On a hardwood bench in the passenger terminal, a lone airman, dressed in Class-A blues bearing two stripes, sat with one arm draped over a packed flight bag. The airman rose when Burnside and MacWatt entered. Burnside went directly to the man. "All right, Perkins, tell me again, exactly what happened?"

Airman Perkins repeated the story he had related on the

phone. That morning he had received a telegram from his wife in Lubbock, Texas, saying that one of their children was seriously ill. The Red Cross in Keflavik confirmed the wire. Perkins booked emergency-leave passage on the regularly scheduled Air Force passenger flight to the states that evening. Ten minutes before boarding time he was called to the passenger desk where the loadmaster informed him that he had been bumped by a major returning home on routine leave. Perkins asked for the name of the transportation officer in charge of the passenger manifest so he could appeal the decision. The loadmaster replied, "His name's Major Rawlings. Won't do you no good though. He's the one who bumped you."

Hurt and enraged, Airman Perkins defied the chain-of-command and called the highest ranking Air Force officer on base, Colonel Burnside.

Burnside shook his head angrily and looked at his watch. The passenger flight had been airborne for thirty-seven minutes. "Perkins, you wait right here."

Three minutes later Burnside, with MacWatt in tow, stepped off the elevator into the control tower situated high above the operations building. Burnside glanced at the flight board for the call sign of the passenger flight that night. Without fanfare he said to the startled chief controller, "Get Air Force Six-Eight on the horn. Tell him to return to this base immediately."

Sensing it was not the time for questions, the chief controller complied.

Moments later an incredulous voice came through the radio: "Keflavik, this is Air Force Six-Eight . . . say again. Over."

The chief controller repeated the order, adding that it came from the AFI commander.

"Keflavik . . . Air Force Six-Eight. This is not an AFI aircraft. I have a schedule to keep. Unless you can give me a priority reason I cannot comply. Over."

Burnside grabbed the microphone. "Air Force Six-Eight, this is Colonel Louis Burnside, AFI commander. What is your aircraft commander's name? Over."

Pause. "Captain O'Dell, sir . . . over."

"Captain O'Dell, I have five F-One-O-Four interceptors sitting on the runway in readiness. Unless you turn that bird around within the next thirty seconds I'm going to send them up to help you make that decision. Is that priority enough? Over."

A longer pause. "Yes, sir. Returning to base. Over."

Fifty minutes later Colonel Burnside boarded Air Force Six-Eight and personally escorted Major Rawlings off the aircraft. The hapless major was ordered to report to Burnside first thing next morning. Then Burnside escorted Airman Perkins onto the aircraft and sent it on its way again.

Though no one involved with the incident that night realized it at the time, they had witnessed the birth of a legend. In coming years, Louis Burnside would be regarded affectionately by enlisted men throughout the Air Force as "the GI's general."

As Air Force Six-Eight lifted off the runway for the second time that night, Robert MacWatt turned to Louis Burnside. "Lou, I'd be proud to be your deputy."

When they told Eileen, she squealed with delight. Burnside opened champagne. When they raised their wine glasses MacWatt toasted, "To the three of us, together again . . . just like old times."

The "two more years" Burnside predicted evolved into four. At EDC, Brigadier General Burnside made the decisions and set the goals. Colonel MacWatt saw to it that they were adhered to, to the letter. If he sensed that a decision was wrong he argued. He won some, lost some. But the ones he won saved Burnside from serious error, and the general recognized it. The burly colonel had become his right arm. No other command deputy in the Air Force enjoyed more authority.

Then, in 1976, at the peak of his power, but feeling that his commitment to Burnside had been fulfilled, MacWatt once again applied for retirement.

When the request hit Burnside's desk the general summoned his deputy. "Mac, there's something I want you to see." He handed MacWatt a paper. It was a list of officers the President had approved for advancement to the rank of Major General. The name heading the list: Brigadier General Louis Burnside.

"A second star," MacWatt said. "About time."

"They're giving me the Air Force Research and Test Center."

"Kirtland," MacWatt acknowledged.

"It's going to be a tough assignment."

MacWatt laid the list of names back on Burnside's desk. "You can handle it."

"I can . . . if you come along."

"Oh, bullshit, Lou . . ."

"No, Mac. No bullshit. You know as well as I that I couldn't have done the job here, couldn't have accomplished half the projects if it hadn't been for you. But this is peanuts compared to AFRTC. That's the highest-priority R and D outfit in the Air Force. New planes, new weapons systems, new concepts. No, it's not bullshit, Mac. I *need* you. Come with me to Kirtland. Two more years. That'll make a full thirty for both of us. We'll go out to pasture together. What do you say?"

And so MacWatt relented.

In the next two years the command team of Burnside and MacWatt revitalized the Air Force Test and Research Center at Kirtland Air Force Base, New Mexico. Staffs were restructured, projects were revised, lead times between concept and proto-type were shortened. By 1978 AFRTC was rated the most efficient R&D organization in the Department of Defense. MacWatt was pleased. But he looked forward to summer when he and Burnside would relinquish the reins of command to others.

In May, Burnside confided anew in his deputy. "Mac, how much do you know about the Stealth project?"

MacWatt lighted a Dutch Master panatella. "What I've read in the top secret summaries. Radar evasion aircraft. Pretty far-fetched from what I gather."

"Not so much as you might think. Did you know there's a prototype ready for testing?"

"No, I didn't."

"Not the primary, an offshoot. The XR-Twenty-One-Hundred. The Chief of Staff wants AFRTC to honcho it."

MacWatt blew smoke. "I thought that was an Edwards project."

"Correct, for the primary. But the XR-Twenty-One-Hundred is a reconnaissance plane, with an advanced state-of-the-art navigational system. Years ahead of anything flying today. General McCollum wants the first operational model on the line by the fall of 1980. That means only two years to wring out the bugs. The project will move here under the codename *Quick-*

seal. McCollum has handpicked a brigadier to head it up—Bart Sabin."

MacWatt snorted. "Golden Boy himself. Someone's in for headaches."

"Ah . . . yes. Well, McCollum has asked me to stick on active duty for a couple of years to supervise Sabin, to keep Quickseal on track. Mac, I think we can bring it off."

MacWatt shot Burnside a flinty look. "Did you say . . . *we?*"

"Yes . . . you and I. It'll be our capstone. The most important project we've ever ramrodded . . ."

MacWatt shook his head defiantly. "Uh uh. No way. If you want to prolong your agony that's up to you. But count me out."

"I've already told the Chief of Staff you'll stay."

"You what?" MacWatt sat bolt upright in his chair. "What the hell gave you the right to do that?"

Burnside's face creased into a wry smile. "Because I know you, Mac. You could never pass up the opportunity to lock horns with a stuffed shirt like Bartholomew Sabin."

MacWatt sat back, his brow knitted in thought.

Once again, he agreed to stay.

By the summer of 1979 the XR-2100 was flying covert test missions over New Mexico. In the summer of 1980 the project temporarily moved to the Pacific for final overwater radar detection tests. It had been an exacting two years, with frequent brainstorm sessions between Burnside, MacWatt, Sabin, Technical Advisor Gerald Coffman, and Chief Test Pilot Peter Crowell. But the ambitious milestones had been met, the XR-2100 would become operational on schedule. It was, as Burnside had wanted, the capstone of his long and distinguished career.

Then, in the early morning hours of August 26, 1980, the XR-2100 crashed at Kingman Reef, a thousand miles off-course, killing the most competent test pilot in the Air Force. And Major General Louis Burnside's world collapsed . . .

A loudspeaker blared, interrupting MacWatt's reverie.

Eileen stood. "They just announced my flight."

MacWatt pushed himself up from the bench. Eileen rose on tiptoes and kissed him on the cheek. "Thank you, Robert, for bringing me. For . . . everything."

He said, "Give my love to Roberta and little Louis."

He watched until she disappeared up the ramp into the loading jet. Then he turned and walked through the sprawling Albuquerque Terminal toward the parking lot, his mind still clinging to the past. It had all been for her. He knew that now. Oh, he'd been loyal to Lou. And he was proud of their team. But it wasn't loyalty or pride that had caused him to lose all those arguments about retiring, to allow himself to be persuaded to remain on active duty. No. He hadn't done it for Lou, or for ambition, or for the Air Force, or for any sense of serving a vital national interest.

He'd done it to remain close to Eileen.

5

MAJOR Jonathan Ward listened dully as Colonel MacWatt briefed him about the reasons for Ward's thirty-day assignment to AFRTC. Where, Ward wondered, had he seen this disheveled blimp of a man, this crude caricature of an officer, before?

Ward shifted in his chair impatiently, willfully tuning out the colonel's irritating gravelly voice. It had been an exasperating day from the beginning. First, the early morning call from Bates alerting him to this ridiculous assignment; then, that unsettling, and unsettled, episode with Susan; then a bumpy, overlong flight from Andrews. And now this: a boring recitation about some damned aircraft crash, a botched investigation, a disgruntled general who wanted the whole thing reinvestigated, and, most preposterous, the notion that Ward would willingly drop work on a truly important project at Andrews to pull the AFRTC fat out of the fire.

Ward noticed that the colonel had quit talking and was looking at him expectantly. *Did he ask me something?* Ward remained silent. After a moment the colonel smiled, reached into his desk and withdrew a bottle and two glasses. "It's been a long day. Would you join me in a drink?"

"No." Ward was in no mood for conviviality.

MacWatt poured three fingers of Glenlivet and downed half of it in a swallow. Then he looked back at Ward. "Well?"

So he did ask me something, Ward thought. It could only have been one thing. "Colonel," Ward said, "I'm sure the matter is top priority here at AFRTC. But you've chosen the wrong man. First, I'm not rated. I know next to nothing about flying and care less. Second, I'm involved in a high priority project myself, one just as vital as you claim Quickseal to be. Last, if I understand you correctly, there was nothing found wrong with the aircraft. It seems to me that you need the OSI, not an engineer. I see no reason why I should become involved."

Audacious bastard, MacWatt thought. Still, that characteristic might serve the disgruntled major well in the task ahead. MacWatt downed the remainder of the Scotch and set the glass aside. "Well now, let's examine your objections and see if they have merit."

He rocked back in his chair and laced his fingers across his ample stomach. "First, about being nonrated. The pilots have had their go at the investigation. Obviously they didn't do an adequate job or you wouldn't be here, right? But more to the point, the XR-Twenty-One-Hundred is not just a flying machine. It's a flying computer. *Electronics*, Major. A field in which you're eminently qualified.

"Second, Evergreen *is* a high priority program, agreed . . ."

Ward was surprised. He hadn't mentioned Evergreen by name.

"But," MacWatt continued, "it's in the initial research stage, with a four-year lead time and no guarantee of success. Quickseal is in the applied science stage, with an operational date this year. The failure of the XR-Twenty-One-Hundred . . . finding the cause of it . . . is of the greatest urgency.

"Last, as to the OSI. We're not talking about a 'whodunit,' such as the Office of Special Investigations handles. This investigation will require sorting through reams of technical chaff to uncover a few meaningful grains of truth. Not exactly what the OSI types are noted for.

"Now, as for your inability to see any reason why you should become involved: Let me assure you that your selection was deliberate, not random. And there're two very good reasons why you should accept the assignment."

"Oh?"

MacWatt sat forward in his chair and splayed both of his hamlike hands flat on his desk. He looked Ward straight in the eye. "If you don't do it," he said, his voice ominous now, "and do it right, *I'll have your ass cashiered out of uniform so fast you won't have time to salute the flag on your way out the gate.*"

It was as if Ward had been slapped. Stunned, face flushed, he sat stiffly upright. No one spoke to him like that! His first instinct was to respond in kind, to tell this gruff son-of-a-bitch where to get off. But something restrained him. Intuitively, he knew that he wasn't dealing with a Bates now. There had been steel and icy resolve in that cavernous voice. The old bastard would do it, *could* do it. Ward had heard of rogue colonels, men who for some reason or another had been passed over for star rank, but who nonetheless wielded power and influence far beyond others of their grade. He had not the slightest doubt that he was in the presence of such a man now.

MacWatt smiled and sat back. "Are you sure you won't join me in a drink?"

"Ah . . . I, uh, think I will."

"Good, good."

MacWatt poured a healthy shot. "Water?"

Ward nodded.

MacWatt added water from his desk pitcher and handed the glass to Ward.

Ward took a hefty drink, coughed, then breathed deeply as the fiery liquor helped him regain his composure. "It appears . . . that I have no choice."

"Well stated." MacWatt raised his glass. "Cheers."

Ward drank the remainder of his drink more slowly. "You said there were two reasons."

"Yes. Fact is, you owe one to General Burnside."

"Owe one?" Ward was puzzled. "I don't understand."

"You remember the Kamchatka signal?"

Remember? Lindbergh and the Atlantic. McAuliffe ("Nuts!") and Bastogne. In some people's lives events occur that forever thereafter are an indelible part of their legend. For Jonathan Ward, such an event was the Kamchatka signal.

On the night of October 14, 1975, a United States Air Force C-135 ferret aircraft on a mission over the Sea of Okhotsk recorded an electronic signal with no known counterpart. After failing to identify it, the Air Force signal laboratory in Tokyo rushed it by secret courier to the primary signal laboratory at Hanscom Air Force Base, Massachusetts. After three weeks of intensive analysis the Hanscom laboratory reported alarming findings. The signal revealed the existence of a new Soviet radar missile guidance system of sophisticated design operating on the Soviet peninsula of Kamchatka. Though there was no evidence of an actual missile firing, the radar had been "locked on" to the American ferret plane at the time it was recorded. It was only a matter of time, Hanscom laboratory concluded, before the new missile system would be operational throughout the Soviet Union and its territories.

On receipt of the Hanscom report, the Secretary of Defense ordered an immediate tri-service effort to gather information about the new system. Air Force covert aircraft were ordered to "probe" Kamchatka to provoke the system into operation for ferret aircraft and Navy surveillance ships to record. Covert agents were assigned to infiltrate the remote peninsula and photograph the missile site. Efforts to gather data on this threatening new Soviet missile system were assigned DOD Priority 1A.

Five months later, Jonathan Ward, then a captain, was newly assigned to the Hanscom signal analysis laboratory. As a part of Ward's indoctrination, the laboratory supervisor, Colonel Clinton, handed him a cassette recording of the Kamchatka signal. "Study it well," the colonel ordered. "We'll be getting a lot more like it soon."

In the soundproof booth assigned to him, Ward tested the Kamchatka signal for all essential parameters—beam width, amplitude, modulation, pulse frequency, signal strength. He was impressed. It was, indeed, a complex puzzle, and Ward's esteem for the engineers who broke the code soared. But how had they done it? Each day throughout that first week of training, and afterward during lulls in his routine duties, he studied the Kamchatka signal again and again. And as he did, he began to have doubts. The signal *could* fit those of a radar controlled guidance system. But there were too many spurious harmonics—random noises—for the radar's lock-on feature to be accurate. More disturbing, the amplitude of the signal indicated a transmitter of unbelievable power.

Ward mentioned these discrepancies to Colonel Clinton.

Clinton was a small, intense man with grandiose ambitions and a patronizing air toward those of lower rank. "We considered all that, Ward," he huffed. "The harmonics simply mean the Russians haven't worked all the bugs out. As for the high signal strength"—he gave a wry wink—"our boys were obviously a wee bit closer to the site than they care to admit. That happens, you know. Think it through and you'll see that there're no other viable explanations."

In a pig's ass, Ward thought.

That afternoon Ward went to the tape library, checked out the entire nine-hour intercept tape for the 10/14/75 Sea of Okhotsk mission and took it to his booth. The Kamchatka signal was recorded at 1202:33Z. He carefully analyzed every signal recorded thirty minutes prior to and thirty minutes following that time. There was no indication of a recorder malfunction. That left the colonel's supposition to ponder. Could it be that the ferret aircraft was, indeed, almost directly over the missile site at the time of the recording, instead of fifty-five miles away as the flight plan indicated? There might be a way to check. It was a long shot, but sometimes flight crews remarked about errant flight changes. And all cockpit conversations were recorded.

He obtained the cockpit voice recording from the library and monitored it for a half hour on either side of 1202:33Z. It was a hodgepodge of pilot/copilot chitchat, with occasional comments about flight progress. No mention of being off course, intentional or otherwise. Ward sighed with resignation. His doubts were ill-founded.

He rewound the tape and prepared it for return to the library. But something was pricking at his mind. It was an offhand remark made by one of the crew halfway through the recording. Of no consequence, surely. Without knowing why, he replaced the tape on the playback unit and advanced it until he found the disconcerting remark again. It was the copilot's voice: "There goes number two again."

Number two?

Ward punched the rewind button and listened again. At the sound of the copilot's voice Ward read the time from the tape . . . 1202:33Z.

"Jesus!" Ward was excited now.

He picked up the phone and dialed flight maintenance. A gruff voice answered. "Maintenance . . . Sergeant Terrell."

"Sergeant, this is Captain Ward. Do you happen to have a one-thirty-five engine on the blocks?"

"Two of 'em. Why?"

"I'll be right there."

He stopped by supply, grabbed a suitcase-size Akai reel-to-reel recorder off the shelf and checked to make sure it had a blank tape. Then he ran to his car. He was at the flight line in ten minutes.

Master Sergeant Terrell spat an amber stream of tobacco juice into a bucket on the hangar floor. "Damn, Captain . . . I don't know. We're trying to smooth 'em out, not foul 'em. Are you sure this is important?"

"It is, Sergeant. Believe me."

"All right, sir . . . if you say so."

The hangar was the size of a football field. Near the large track-riding front doors a C-135 jet engine was mounted on a test frame. Ward made some mental calculations. The Kamchatka signal was recorded in the Very High Frequency range. The VHF antenna on the ferret aircraft was located on the underside of the fuselage, just forward of the tail section—about forty-five feet from number two engine. Ward stepped off fifteen paces to the rear and to one side of the test frame. He set up the Akai recorder, switched it on and waved to Sergeant Terrell.

At the test control panel Terrell slipped a pair of noise mufflers over his ears. Ward did the same. Then Terrell manipulated some controls. The huge engine began to whine, then increased in pitch and revolutions until it was running at cruising speed.

Terrell looked at Ward. Ward nodded. With the flip of a switch Terrell shut off the fuel supply to the engine, then instantly returned it to proper feed. There was a sharp retort, like the crack of a high caliber rifle, before the engine settled again into a steady hum. For the next fifteen minutes, while Ward recorded the entire procedure, Terrell performed a series of operations designed to cause the jet engine to malfunction.

Colonel Clinton stared dumbfounded at the evidence on his desk. At his side, Ward arranged the display in sequence—a graph of the Kamchatka signal superimposed over a graph of the recordings he'd made at maintenance. "You can see they're identical. The malfunction created an electromagnetic pulse. Almost every parameter checks."

Tiny beads of perspiration formed on Clinton's brow. Ward's evidence was indisputable. The famed Kamchatka signal was no signal at all. *Those stupid fucking idiots had recorded their own engine noise!*

The dire implications did not escape Clinton. He was the one who had approved the analysis. It was he who sent the urgent intelligence report to the Chief of Staff. *A new Soviet missile system.* Oh, Christ! At this very moment in Europe and the Far East special covert missions were being flown, agents in the field were risking their lives, all in search of a phantom. He moaned to himself. It could ruin him, all that he had worked for, at a moment when the silver star of a brigadier was almost in his grasp.

Colonel Clinton took a deep breath then stood grandly and grasped Ward's hand. "Excellent work, Captain. Absolutely brilliant. Now, this has to be hush-hush, you understand. I must take certain steps . . . things must be done. Bring me all your recordings, all your readouts. I'll take personal charge from this point. But this will go in your record, you can count on that."

Two weeks later Ward received reassignment orders to Keesler Air Force Base, Mississippi. "It's a step up," Colonel Clinton assured him. "Instructor at the signal analysis school. I had to pull some strings, but you deserve it."

MacWatt's deep voice brought Ward back to the present. "Do you know why your assignment to Keesler was canceled?"

Ward shook his head. "There were rumors. I never got a straight story."

So MacWatt told him.

One morning, two weeks before General Burnside and MacWatt were to depart for Burnside's new command in New Mexico, the general called MacWatt to his office. "Mac, why is the signal lab transferring an officer who's been here only a couple of months?" He handed his deputy a copy of a reassignment order that had just reached his desk.

MacWatt looked at the name on the order: Captain Jonathan Ward. "I don't know, but I'll find out."

The personnel officer was defensive over the phone. "It was

Colonel Clinton's doing, sir. He was insistent. I didn't question it. Is there something wrong?"

"I'll let you know," MacWatt said, and hung up.

Colonel Clinton shifted uneasily in the chair. He could read the doubt in the deputy commander's eyes—those damned dissecting eyes. *He knows I'm dissembling.* Clinton took a handkerchief from his pocket and wiped his palms. "All right . . . I should have brought it up sooner, I guess. Anyway, here's the whole story."

And he told MacWatt about the Kamchatka signal.

It was an incredible story, but that wasn't what concerned MacWatt. "You've been sitting on this for over two weeks?"

Clinton licked his lips. "Look . . . I, uh . . . was going to take care of it. I was just trying to find a . . . well, some reasonable way to do it. It's a sensitive issue. Hell, Mac, you know what I mean?"

"Yes, I know what you mean." MacWatt thought for a minute. "Clint, I want that signal data brought to me within the hour, every last item. Bring it yourself. Understand?"

For the first time since he'd entered MacWatt's office Clinton felt a surge of hope. "Yes . . . I'll do it personally. No problem."

No problem my ass. "How many years you got toward retirement, Clint?"

Suddenly, the room turned chilly. "Twenty-six. Why?"

"It's a good time of year for it. Why don't you bring your retirement request with the other stuff?"

Clinton half rose from the chair. "Now wait just a goddamned minute, Mac . . ."

"Either that," MacWatt cut in sharply, "or be prepared to explain to a board of inquiry your reasons for covering up vital information at the risk of other people's lives."

That afternoon the Kamchatka signal was exposed for what it was, Captain Ward's reassignment orders were canceled, and Colonel Clinton applied for early retirement. One month later, after Burnside and MacWatt had left Hanscom, Ward was promoted to major and made deputy supervisor of the signal laboratory.

"So," MacWatt concluded his story to Ward, "if General Burnside hadn't questioned that order, you would have been shunted into a thankless billet. And you wouldn't have made major a year ahead of your contemporaries—at Burnside's specific recommendation, I might add."

Now Ward realized where he had seen MacWatt before. At Hanscom, surely, perhaps only a fleeting glimpse in those final weeks before he left for New Mexico. And, Ward thought with new insight, I suppose I do owe one to the general.

"All right," Ward said. "Where do I start?"

MacWatt pointed to a combination-locked aluminum suitcase sitting on the floor across the room. "It's all there, what we know so far. Hadley's report, supporting documents, Quickseal mission data, crash evaluation, statements from people involved, personnel files." He handed Ward a piece of paper. "This is the combination to the suitcase and some phone numbers you'll need. You'll be in VIP quarters. There'll be a guard on the door around the clock. No one gets in without your say-so. There's a field safe there, open. Do you know how to set a combination?"

"Yes."

"Pick one, memorize it, don't write it down. You'll be the only one with access to the safe. Keep everything about the investigation in it. Remember—no written reports. You can brief me anytime, day or night. You can reach me during duty hours through Miss Lucero. After hours I'll be in my quarters or available by air-page through the staff duty officer. OK so far?"

Ward nodded. "So far."

"All right. Once you're familiar with the documented material you'll want to interview the principals. With exception of those of us in headquarters, they're all in the Quickseal compound. Your top secret Quickseal badge is on file at the compound gate. If you have problems with anyone, remember that you're acting on the authority of General Burnside."

MacWatt reached into his desk drawer and withdrew a set of keys. "I've had a staff car assigned to you. Slot five, outside. A guard is waiting there to accompany you to your quarters. Do you want a driver assigned?"

"That won't be necessary."

"Good." He tossed the keys to Ward. "Any questions?"

Ward motioned toward the suitcase. "You say the personnel files are in there?"

"Yes."

"Yours?"

MacWatt smiled. "Right on top."

"No more questions." Ward saluted and left.

MacWatt poured another finger of Glenlivet. For a long moment he held it in his hands, not drinking, pondering the meeting that had just ended. He wondered if he had chosen the right man?

"I damn well better have," he said aloud, and downed the Scotch in a gulp.

6

THE cab crept bumper-to-bumper with snarled traffic along 10th Street, finally coming to a dead stop directly across from Ford's Theater. Gerald Coffman surveyed the roadblock ahead. "I'll get out here." The meter read $5.80. He grabbed his briefcase and umbrella (you could never tell about D.C. weather) and handed the driver six dollars. "Keep the change."

Disregarding the cabbie's nasty look, Coffman walked hurriedly south toward E Street. As always during his frequent trips to the capital, he felt a sense of exhilaration. He had started his career here, in Naval Ordnance, after graduating from M.I.T. in 1960. Hardworking, a brilliant technician, he soon caught the eye of the right people, and in 1962 he moved to the Pentagon as one of the original "Whiz Kids" on the staff of the Secretary of Defense. It was the golden era for ambitious young scientists in government. Brave New World—New Frontier—Camelot. Despite a reputation for stodginess in personal relationships, Coffman's professionalism won the respect of colleagues and superiors alike. Over the next decade he parlayed his talents through a series of key promotions to become, in 1975, the assistant to the Deputy Secretary of Defense for Science and Technology. Two years later, in a surprising decision, the scientific advisory board selected him for the job of technical advisor to the commander, Air Force Research and Test Center, Kirtland Air Force Base, New Mexico.

Bewildered and hurt by what he considered to be an undeserved demotion to a billet far removed from the seat of power, Coffman appealed to his superior.

"Gerald," the Deputy Secretary asked, "who do you know on the Senate Armed Forces Committee?"

It was an unexpected question. "Why . . . no one."

"Well, someone knows you. The assignment to Kirtland is a by-name request. It was personally delivered to the advisory board by the committee's chief counsel. That's not an everyday occurrence, Gerald. And whatever the reason, we have no recourse but to comply. That committee is our bread and butter."

So, convinced of the expediency—if not the justification—for the selection, and assured of compensatory rewards to come in his future, Coffman made the move to New Mexico.

At the corner of 10th and E he turned west on E Street, almost colliding with two oncoming Army officers. He moved aside with an uttered apology. The two officers merely glared at him and continued on their way. Coffman hurried on, thinking now about the military officers he had worked with over the past two decades. Mediocrities, most of them. Tangible reminders of the wisdom of the Founding Fathers in firmly subordinating the armed forces to civilian control. He could count the exceptions on the fingers of one hand. Burnside was one. Brilliant, but contrary. MacWatt? He was an ass. Why did a man as astute as Burnside keep such a buffoon on his staff? But there was no denying MacWatt's influence. Indeed, it was most assuredly the meddlesome colonel who had poisoned Burnside's mind against the XR-2100 crash report.

Just west of 12th Street, Coffman stopped before a sign that proclaimed: "Sea Catch Restaurant." A Washington landmark, the eatery was favored by discriminating seafood lovers. On a grill just inside a large picture window a black chef was preparing a house specialty, Norfolk Stew, succulent bits of assorted shellfish sautéed in pure butter. Coffman paled. His stomach was still queasy from a bumpy flight. He disliked flying in any weather and found it difficult to think of food for a full day afterward.

The restaurant's decor was nautical. Coffman waited until his eyes adjusted to the dimmer light, then looked around expectantly. He spotted the man he was seeking in a secluded booth in the rear corner of the room. The man was preoccupied with eating. Coffman was relieved. The man had waited. But, Coffman reflected, what choice did he have? It was an absurd question and Coffman banished it from his mind at once. This particular man had a wide array of choices—and he knew how to use every one of them to whatever advantage he desired.

Coffman threaded his way between the tables to the booth. "Senator."

Senator Nathan Beaumont looked up. "Ah . . . Gerald. Sit, my boy. Would you care to join me in a late lunch?"

Coffman's stomach churned. "Senator, I'm sorry. We were held up over Chicago." He suppressed an urge to belch.

"Come, come, Gerald. You mustn't be so sensitive. I wasn't being critical."

Coffman relaxed a bit. "Perhaps . . . a bottle of Perrier." The belch came involuntarily.

"Dyspepsia? Ah, yes . . . I recall. You dislike flying. That must be a terrible burden for one so deeply involved with the Air Force." The senator signaled the waiter and ordered Perrier water for Coffman.

Of medium height and build, possessing a flowing white mane and the leathery features of one who enjoyed the outdoors, Senator Nathan L. Beaumont was distinguished in both bearing and reputation. Internationally regarded as one of the rare first-rate products of the American political system, he enjoyed a spirited national following as well. In 1964, with a groundswell of public support, he entered the race for his party's nomination for the presidency. At the last minute, on the convention floor, he withdrew in support of Goldwater. He was currently the ranking minority member on the Senate Armed Forces Committee and the Foreign Relations Committee. It was an open secret in Washington that if the upcoming presidential election went as expected, Senator Beaumont could have his pick as chairman of either committee.

The senator dashed Tabasco on his food. "Norfolk Stew, Gerald. A feast for the gods, the very finest of sea fare. The only comparable freshwater delicacy is catfish. Properly prepared, of course, which so few nowadays know how to do. Have you ever hogged catfish, Gerald?"

"Hogged, sir?"

Beaumont chuckled. "It means catch them with your bare hands," he explained between bites. "Great sport. Wade right into their muddy domain and grapple them up with your fingers. My boys and I do it often on my farm on the Tallahatchie. Must watch out for the fins, mind you. The only acceptable way to prepare catfish is deep fried. We skin them out with great care, cut the meat into fist-size chunks, roll them in well-seasoned cornmeal—white corn, mind you—and drop them for exactly four-and-a-half minutes in a caldron of grease that is boiling so hard you can strike a match in it. Fresh lard is best, by far."

Gerald took a hasty drink of Perrier.

"Mighty good eating," the senator said. "Darkies love it."

Coffman was amused. Never before had he heard the term "darkie" actually used in conversation. He realized now that Senator Beaumont's reference to "my boys" was not to his sons.

Coffman sipped his sparkling water and silently contemplated the wisdom of the senator's choice of meeting places. The restaurant was centrally located, with few out-of-towners. The diners were mostly Washington clientele—civil employees unimpressed by the sight of government bigwigs. A meeting here, even with someone as recognizable as Senator Beaumont, was essentially private.

The senator asked, "And what reason did you give for the trip this time, Gerald?"

"Comptrollers meeting—fiscal year budget projections."

"Excellent. There's always a budget meeting in progress somewhere in the Pentagon, isn't there?"

The senator pushed his plate aside and withdrew a briar pipe from his brown tweed jacket. He filled it with aromatic tobacco from a leather pouch, tamped it gently, and lit it with a gold Dunhill lighter. He drew until the tobacco was burning well, blowing the smoke away from Coffman. "Now, Gerald, tell me about this new boy that General Burnside has brought in on us."

Coffman kept his voice low. "His name is Ward—Major

Jonathan Ward, from Andrews. He was at Hanscom when Burnside commanded there. His primary duty is developing the remote telemetering mode for the Evergreen project . . ."

"The permanent moon station," Beaumont commented.

"Yes. Ward's temporary orders—directly from the Chief of Staff—assign him to Kirtland for thirty days. Burnside wants him to reinvestigate the crash from the beginning."

"All because of Hadley's screw-up."

Coffman disagreed. "We can't lay all the blame on Colonel Hadley. He followed orders. It's that damned court jester MacWatt. He's got Burnside in his pocket."

Beaumont took the pipe from his mouth. "I'm not sure I buy that, Gerald. I've known Lou Burnside for many years. He's his own man. MacWatt influences him, surely. But I doubt if it's beyond a point where Burnside is unwilling to go . . . Have you seen anyone about that tic, Gerald?"

"Sir. Oh"—Coffman removed his glasses and rubbed his left eye—"uh . . . no . . ."

"I can recommend a good neurologist."

"Neuro . . . oh, I don't know. Maybe. Thank you, sir." He slipped his glasses back on.

"Anytime. Now, tell me . . . just what did go wrong with that plane?"

Coffman looked perplexed. "I simply don't know. No one else does either. And I don't think Ward will fare any better. For one thing, he's a malcontent, unhappy with the assignment. He'll probably rush things through, just to get it over."

"You know this firsthand?"

"No. But I know the Chief of Staff's pilot. Ward bitched about being pulled off Evergreen during the entire flight from Andrews."

"I see."

"On the other hand, Ward has a reputation for tenacity. And that bothers me. If he decides to put his heart into it he could become a threat." Coffman swallowed hard to suppress a rising bile. "Senator, I'm . . . I just hope things don't get out of hand."

"Come, come, Gerald. Aren't you overreacting? Just what can this Major Ward accomplish anyway? He'll be going over the same material, talking to the same people. Conceivably, he could reach the same conclusions." He paused. "Except . . ."

"Except what, sir?" Coffman asked anxiously.

"Have you ever flown a plane, Gerald? No . . . of course not. I was a pilot during the second war, you know. Eighth Air Force. B-Seventeens."

"Yes . . . a distinguished record, sir."

"Thank you. Anyway, when a plane goes out of control rarely does a pilot panic. There're no screams from the cockpit, no throttled cries. There's just no time for that. Instinctively, a pilot will fight for control right down to the final moment. And that, Gerald, is where Colonel Hadley screwed up: reporting that a man like Major Peter Crowell panicked and lost control. An unwise conjecture that says more about Hadley, I fear, than it does about Crowell. If I were a betting man I'd lay odds that right there is where Burnside parted company with Hadley's findings. Not from any influence from MacWatt."

Beaumont puffed on his pipe for a couple of minutes in silence. "Ah, well, Gerald. It's of little consequence really. Our work is nearly complete. The reinvestigation might make the task a bit more difficult, but by no means insurmountable. No, we will persevere."

Coffman said, "Senator, what if Ward decides to talk to people outside Quickseal?"

"Whom, in particular?"

"Crowell's wife."

"Ah . . . you're thinking about the professor?"

"Yes."

The senator thought about it. "That could make the gravy a bit lumpy, couldn't it?"

Coffman moaned. "Why . . . with all the women a man like Crowell could have had, did he have to marry Professor Moslin's daughter?"

Senator Beaumont chuckled. "Yes, that was an ironic twist of fate. But I see little to worry about. Major Crowell was a dedicated career officer, therefore discreet. I daresay his wife knows little about his military duties. As for our good friend, Professor Moslin, I can't envision him as a threat. Not at all. Delta Group has been under tight rein since Vietnam. We know every move the professor makes, particularly since his son-in-law's unfortunate death. We'll keep it that way until our task is finished, I assure you."

Coffman wished he could be as confident. "Are there any instructions, sir?"

The senator pulled an ashtray to him and knocked the spent tobacco from his pipe. "Yes. You must try, discreetly, mind you, to contain Major Ward—to keep the scope of his investigation within the confines of Quickseal, the same grounds covered by Hadley. Try not to be obvious, but keep abreast of where he goes, to whom he talks. Can you do that?"

Coffman hesitated. "General Burnside is playing things close to his chest—but, yes. We have ways to do it."

"Good . . . excellent. Keep me informed, night or day—you know how. If things look as if they might be getting out of hand I'll take steps from here."

The senator sat back in the booth. "Ah, Gerald, it's a sad state of affairs we face today. You're a bit young to remember us during my war—a proud nation, full of hope and vigor. Powerful and respected. *Ike*—there was a man. And Foster Dulles. Foster and I used to spend an occasional weekend together at my Maryland retreat, near Camp David. He was a gourmet cook—did you know that? We would dine sumptuously, discuss world affairs, the state of the nation, challenges looming on the horizon."

The senator's countenance hardened. "Oh, how I wish Ike and Foster were here today to handle this Iranian thing. Imagine it, Gerald. Americans—men and women—held hostage by a ragtag band of brigands. They would never have dared such impertinence in Ike's time. Never!"

He paused to let his agitation subside. "But the mood of the country is changing, Gerald. The people are fed up. You'll see that on election day, mark my word. And you must be prepared. You, and other young people who believe like you. Prepared to use your positions, your authority, however necessary, to revitalize this once-great country."

Early in his career Gerald Coffman had learned the value of listening, of remaining ever alert to detect weakness in others that might be used to advantage. He detected no weakness in Senator Nathan Beaumont.

The senator looked at his watch. "Now, I must get back to the hill. You will show up at that budget meeting, won't you? To keep up appearances."

"Yes. Tomorrow morning. I have a midafternoon flight back to Albuquerque."

"Fine. Now remember, Gerald, keep me informed. It's imperative that I know at once if Major Ward begins to stray. In the meantime, I'll see to it that our friend overseas gets a full report of our meeting."

Coffman leaned forward on the table expectantly. "I'd like so very much to meet him. Does he ever get back to this country?"

The senator shook his hoary mane sadly. "Not since he was disgraced by that pompous jackass from the Pedernales. But all that will be vindicated. Soon."

The senator rose and Coffman did too.

"*Very soon*," the senator averred. He shook hands with Coffman and left.

7

Jonathan Ward dropped the memorandum onto the desk
and tried to rub the fatigue from his eyes. The desk was strewn
with papers, file folders, aeronautical charts, pamphlets, memoranda for record, and copy #1 of Colonel Hadley's top secret
Report of Investigation—contents of the aluminum suitcase Ward
had gotten from Colonel MacWatt the night before. He'd been
at the desk since dawn and had finished a first reading of the
report and supportive documents by noon. Influenced by
MacWatt's briefing, he expected to find chaos. Instead, he found
a cogent, well-written report, each section methodically cross-
referenced to pertinent attachments and independent supporting material. Colonel Hadley knew his business—which was
more than Ward could say about the task confronting him.

At one o'clock Colonel MacWatt brought General Burnside
to the VIP quarters to meet his new investigating officer. The

courtly general inquired of Ward's comfort, assured himself that the major had the necessary tools (car, safe, recorder and playback unit, USAF credit card, petty cash) at his disposal, and impressed upon him that he was acting with the general's full authority. For a brief moment Ward had been tempted again to question the propriety of his assignment, but he glanced at the hulking colonel and thought better of it.

After the two senior officers left, Ward returned to the desk and spent the afternoon reading the material a second time. Slowly, a fascinating picture of what had happened on that fateful night in the Pacific began to emerge. By sundown he had chosen several documents to read again that night.

He pushed back his chair, stood and stretched long and hard, then went to the kitchen. The refrigerator had been well stocked, on MacWatt's order, before Ward arrived. He took out a can of Coors, pulled the tab and downed half the ice-cold beer in two swallows. The quarters, like the arid desert outside, were bone-dry. His skin itched, his hair had turned to straw. How, he wondered, could anyone ever adapt to this damned climate?

For a moment he considered going to the Officers Club for dinner. He looked back at the pile of papers on the desk and decided against it. Instead, he took packages of Swiss cheese, Danish ham, lettuce, a tomato and a jar of horseradish from the refrigerator and made a hefty sandwich on rye. He carried it and the beer back to the desk. Except for the infernal dryness, he mused, he couldn't complain about the quarters. In addition to the fully laden kitchen there was a good-size bedroom with adjoining bath; a separate living room with overstuffed chairs, couch, and color TV, an alcove for dining, even a well-stocked bar—all complimented by pale-blue textured walls and a deep-pile azure rug. It was a far cry from quarters he had stayed in on other bases. "Flag-rank digs," he uttered aloud.

He sat down at the desk, took a bite from the sandwich and fingered the stack of papers to be restudied. He picked up the first memorandum again:

MEMORANDUM FOR RECORD
Subject: Last Flight of COBRA ONE
1. At 2109 local time, 25Aug80, experimental aircraft XR-2100, callsign COBRA ONE, piloted by Major Peter Crowell, took off

from Johnston Island on its final scheduled test flight. The flight was designed to test the aircraft's computerized control system—STARGAZE—as well as the aircraft's ability to avoid radar detection. The aircraft was under STARGAZE control, with minimum control from the pilot. The mission required COBRA ONE to fly approaches against four C-135 Aircraft Warning and Control System (AWACS) aircraft stationed at different positions southwest of Johnston Island. Similar test flights on the five immediately preceding nights were successful.

2. COBRA ONE penetrated AWACS #1, #2, and #3 positions without detection. At 8000-yards-range Pilot Crowell activated his radar transponder, feeding a coded signal to the AWACS to verify the penetrations.

3. AT 2245 AWACS #4 radioed that COBRA ONE was overdue. General Sabin, Quickseal Commander, ordered the Command Post to attempt radio contact with COBRA ONE. The attempts were unsuccessful.

4. At 2330 the Quickseal Command Post received the following radio message: "MAYDAY . . . COBRA ONE . . . STARGAZE MALFUNCTION . . . OUT OF CONTROL . . . MAYDAY . . . MAY . . ." The message faded and was not repeated. The message was also received, and recorded, by Honolulu Control at Oahu. A tape of the mayday message is enclosed.

5. At 2340 an air-sea search and rescue operation got underway in the designated Quickseal test areas (AWACS areas). This operation continued throughout the night and most of the following day.

6. At 1214, 26Aug80, CINCPACAF reported that a Hawaii Air National Guard aircraft had sighted a downed aircraft underwater at Kingman Reef. Description of the downed aircraft fit COBRA ONE. Subsequent Navy salvage operations verified the identity.

7. Distance from COBRA ONE's last authenticated test position (AWACS #3 position) to Kingman Reef is 1,004 miles.

ELWOOD HADLEY
Lt Col, USAF
Quickseal Executive Officer

Pretty damned cozy, Ward thought. The Quickseal executive officer and investigating officer one and the same. Still, Hadley's memorandum was pertinent.

The next memorandum was from the officer in charge of the salvage operation:

MEMORANDUM FOR RECORD
Subject: Salvage Operations, Kingman Reef
1. On 26Aug80 LST *Grant County*, under my command, was conducting routine harbor dredging at Palmyra Island. At 1220 CINCPACFLT signaled *Grant County* to cease operations and steam to Kingman Reef. Priority One Mission: salvage operation, USAF aircraft. *Grant County* arrived at Kingman Reef at 1535 and dropped anchor 3,500 yards off the south shoal. USN Destroyers *Ladd* and *Adams* were already on station to provide salvage support. Sixteen Navy and Air Force aircraft were flying canopy above the reef.
2. At 1609, divers located the downed aircraft resting on its belly two fathoms below the surface on the lagoon side of the south shoal. Except for sheared-off gears the aircraft was intact. Pilot's body was strapped in the cockpit. Seat ejection mechanism was found in locked position indicating that the pilot did not attempt to eject. At 1704 pilot's body was removed to *Grant County* and placed in custody of the chief medical corpsman.
3. At 1715 CINCPACFLT signaled that Soviet covert operations ship *Kiev*, recently observed monitoring USAF operations at Johnston Island, was steaming flank speed toward Kingman Reef, ETA 1200 next day. CINCPACFLT ordered that if salvage operations were not completed by that time, *Adams* and *Ladd* were to intercept and keep *Kiev* at bay until salvage operations were completed. CINCPACFLT directed that not a single "nut or bolt" of the downed aircraft was to be left for the Soviets to recover.
4. At 1800 *Grant County* maneuvered shoreward, beaching at La Paloma Channel. Forward winch cables were attached to the submerged aircraft. Aircraft was slowly dragged from the water upon the south shoal. Floodlights were arranged on the shoal. Throughout the night crewmen disassembled the aircraft's stabilizers and wings. At 0610 next morning (27Aug80) the fuselage was winched across the shallow channel, through the forward ramp into the deck-well and secured. Stabilizers and wings were hoisted aboard by boom.
5. At dawn crewmen and divers began a systematic search of

the reef, lagoon, and seaward waters. At 0930 divers found the main gear, in two sections, submerged at three fathoms, fifty yards seaward of the northern tip of the eastern shoal. The nose gear was not found and is presumed to be submerged beyond recovery in the deepest part of the lagoon. No other parts of the aircraft were found.

6. At 1040 *Grant County*, accompanied by *Ladd*, departed Kingman Reef — mission accomplished. *Adams* remained on station to keep *Kiev* under surveillance. At 1240 *Adams* signaled that *Kiev* had landed a reconnaissance party on the reef. At 1835 *Adams* signaled that *Kiev* had departed "empty handed."

7. At 1604 USAF Hospital Helicopter 153 intercepted *Grant County* at sea and removed pilot's body for expeditious delivery to Hickam Air Force Base.

8. *Observations and comments:*

    a. All locations mentioned in this MFR are plotted on the enclosed navigational chart.

    b. It is my opinion that the pilot attempted an emergency landing on the extended east shoal of Kingman Reef, missed, and crashed into the lagoon.

WILLARD S. PAAR
LT, USN

It was a most interesting report. Ward unfolded the large-scale chart of Kingman Reef attached to the memorandum and studied again the locations Lieutenant Paar had plotted. It was evident, even to a nonflyer, that a pilot attempting an emergency landing on the reef had no option but to shoot for the east shoal. Even then, a survivable landing would be miraculous. Still, from the location where the main gear was found, Ward couldn't argue with Paar's conclusion that that was exactly what Crowell was attempting. Further, if a plane coming low in that direction missed the shoal and hit the lagoon, it would assuredly come to rest in approximately the location where *Cobra One* was found.

But why Kingman Reef—a thousand miles east of Crowell's last reported location, when his homebase, Johnston Island, was 500 miles closer?

Perplexing.

Ward pushed the empty sandwich plate out of the way, finished his beer, and picked up the next memorandum. It was from the chief medical corpsman aboard *Grant County:*

MEMORANDUM FOR RECORD
Subject: DOA (Crowell, Peter, Major USAF)
1. Date body received: 26Aug80
2. Description of body: White male, ht. 6', wt. 170, hair brown, eyes brown. No visible scars or extraordinary identifying features noted. No external injuries noted. Partial discoloration (purple) of lips, extremities, tongue, caused by water exposure.
3. Personal effects: Flight suit (USAF space type), stenciled CROWELL, P. MAJ; flight helmet (USAF space type), stenciled Crowell, P. MAJ (visor locked open); shorts, jockey, size 34; flight glove, left, size M (second glove recovered from cockpit); chronometer, wrist, USAF; ring, wedding band, gold, inscribed "Love is eternal, Janet."
4. Estimated time of death: Between 0100 and 0500 26Aug80. Estimated cause of death: Drowning secondary to aircraft accident at sea.
6. Polaroid photo and fingerprints set attached.

ALLEN ROGERS
SFC, USN

Ward picked up a folder marked PERSONNEL FILE-201. Inside was a glossy black-and-white photograph of a dark-haired young officer in uniform smiling into the camera. A name tag on the officer's jacket read: PETER J. CROWELL. Ward studied the pleasant, boyish face for a few moments. Then he picked up the Polaroid photo attached to Rogers' memorandum. It was taken from overhead (Ward could envision Seaman Rogers focusing down from a top bunk). The photo showed an obviously dead man lying nude on his back on a table. Ward compared the Polaroid to the glossy print in the personnel file. The contrast between the features—between life and death—was startling. But there could be no doubt. Both photographs were of the same man.

Attached to Crowell's file was a list of things Ward had jotted down earlier about Peter Crowell:

—Aeronautical engineer
—Advanced test pilot, covert rated

—Distinguished combat record, Vietnam

—Distinguished flying cross

—Outstanding efficiency reports, reportedly a loner but respected professionally

—Son of Lutheran minister, parents deceased

—Married, no children

The type of man, Ward mused, that every Air Force recruiter dreamed about signing up.

He put down the list and swiveled toward an oceanic map he had pinned to the wall. The map legend read: GLOBAL NAVIGATION AND PLANNING CHART—GNC 7—SCALE 1:5,000,000. The scale was in inches. He stood and placed his finger on the map at Oahu and traced a path southwest across the 750 miles of ocean to Johnston Island. From Johnston he ran his finger east to Kingman Reef—1,000 miles. Then back to Oahu. A near perfect triangle. He stared at the map and pondered the reports he had read. *What a bucket of worms.*

Deliberately, he traced the southern leg of the imaginary triangle again. Somewhere along that ill-fated thousand miles between Johnston Island, where *Cobra One* should have been, and Kingman Reef, where the plane was found, something extraordinary had occurred . . . some aberration that they had all overlooked. He glanced at the photo of Crowell again. Perfect pilot, perfect plane . . .

It had a familiar ring. MacWatt . . . at the briefing. Jesus, Ward thought, now I'm beginning to think like the old bastard!

He returned to the chair, his mind a kaleidoscope of the bits and pieces he knew, desperate for the pieces that were missing. He thought of Hadley's conclusion: ". . . for reasons unknown and unknowable . . ."

"Bullshit!"

It was there. Sure as hell, somewhere in the ponderous assortment of files, memoranda, charts, maps, tapes, photographs, was the key. What key? *What the hell am I looking for?*

For some reason, at that moment he recalled an event from his past.

His father had died when he was ten, leaving him the only child of a querulous mother who, having missed no opportunity to find fault with her forbearing husband, now turned her spite on her son. Unable to find solace in people, he sought it in a place. Each day after school he would walk to the abandoned stone quarry three miles from his home and descend a narrow footpath down the sheer face of a hundred-foot limestone cliff to reach a secluded woodland pool. It had been his and his father's favorite hideaway. Here his father had taught him to fish, how to build a campfire, how to read the signs of the wilderness, how to cope with what each knew without voicing it was a desperate loneliness in their lives.

One evening at nightfall, a few weeks after his father's funeral, he sat in silent contemplation beside the water's edge, oblivious to an approaching storm. Suddenly, the sky darkened, the rumble of nearby thunder intruded on his thoughts. Jarred to reality he started up the footpath. He had climbed a third of the way when total darkness enveloped him. Near panic, whipped by a wind-driven rain, he clung to the side of the cliff, fearful that at any moment he might lose his grip and be hurled onto the rocks below. Then, in the distance, a bolt of lightning rent the sky, illuminating the trail for a split second. He loosened his grip on the stones, climbed a few feet and stopped. Minutes later the lightning flashed again. And again he groped his way upward, foot by precarious foot, anxiously awaiting each flash. An hour later he reached the top, exhausted, but safe.

In later years, pondering that frightening experience, he realized that he had drawn on it often in meeting the challenges in his life. Now, it was time to drawn on it again. What had happened to *Cobra One?* The answer was eclipsed in darkness. To find it he could only follow the trail wherever it led, groping his way, watching for the lightning—those flashes of insight that would lead him out of the darkness.

He gathered the material from the desk to lock it in the field safe. Near the bottom of the pile General Bartholomew Sabin's personnel file lay open. The general's command photo stared up at Ward. Even in that impersonal photograph Ward could feel the intensity of the man.

Tomorrow he would meet Sabin.

Perhaps tomorrow the lightning would begin to flash.

8

IT was a scene to give men pause. The vast mesa that comprised Kirtland's southern extension was a seemingly endless sea of sage and firebush ranging in a dazzling crazy-quilt of desert colors from the amethyst Manzano Mountains on the east to the distant, azurine horizon on the west. Clearly visible over a hundred miles to the southwest, two-mile-high Whitewater Baldy Peak pierced a cloudless sapphire sky. Even to the ever-practical Ward the panorama was striking. Except for a single discordant note. Sprawled over twenty acres just below the crest of the hill where he was driving was a stalag-like compound surrounded by a high wire fence punctuated by perimeter guard towers every three hundred yards. A roadside warning proclaimed:

ATTENTION!
Restricted Area Ahead
Quickseal Clearance Required
NO UNAUTHORIZED PERSONNEL BEYOND THIS POINT

Inside the compound, far to the rear of a cluster of smaller buildings, were two giant aircraft hangars. A tarmac connecting the hangars extended through a track-mounted gate in the security fence to a concrete airstrip that stretched like an alabaster ribbon for five miles across the desert floor. *Cobra One's* private runway, Ward mused.

Ward parked in a slot marked "Official Visitor" and entered the guardhouse. A security policeman took his identification card and fed it into the slot of a computer terminal. Within seconds the monitor lit up with a photo-image identifying MAJOR JONATHAN WARD and a listing of the major's security credentials. The SP returned Ward's ID card along with a numbered red badge with an alligator clip. "Sir, you must wear this in plain view at all times while inside the compound. Cameras are not authorized inside the compound. Nothing inside the compound may be taken out. All persons are subject to search on exit. Surrender your badge here when you leave."

Ward clipped the badge to his uniform blouse. "Where will I find General Sabin?"

"Building One, sir."

Thirty-nine-year-old Brigadier General Bartholomew Sabin was a tall man with the sinewy build of a dedicated distance runner, which, indeed, he was. He kept his body toned with a five-mile cross-mesa run each dawn, and twice that distance each evening, rain or shine. His diet consisted of white meat, fresh fruit, raw vegetables, whole-grain breads, plain yogurt, skim milk, and water. Red meat was deleterious. Alcohol was taboo. Tobacco was abominable. Beneath short-trimmed flaxen hair, his iceberg-blue eyes reflected the air of a man who knew himself to be superior to most. A barely visible scar creased the top of his left cheek, just below the eye. He was, in the words of one gushing member of the Officers' Wives' Club, where Sabin was an insatiable topic, "criminally handsome."

As Ward entered Sabin's office this morning, precisely on time, the general left him standing while he casually signed some papers. Another officer, seated near Sabin's desk, eyed Ward intently. Ward glanced at the staring officer and he diverted his gaze.

Sabin placed the pen in its holder and looked up. Ward saluted. "Major Ward, sir."

Sabin returned the salute crisply and nodded toward an empty chair.

Ward sat.

The office was decorated with an impressive array of mementos and paraphernalia. A huge zebra skin, mounted on a red-velvet backing, was spread-eagled on the wall behind Sabin's desk. On each side of the trophy were groupings of ebony-framed photographs: Sabin with rifle beside the downed zebra; Sabin with rifle beside a downed bull elephant; Sabin with rifle beside a downed water buffalo. There were others, but Ward passed them over. On the opposite wall were photographic evidence of trophies of another kind: Sabin receiving a medal from William Westmoreland; Sabin receiving a medal from Nguyen Van Thieu; Sabin receiving a medal from Nguyen Cao Ky; Sabin receiving a medal from Richard Nixon. Ward knew from the records what *that* award was. He shifted his eyes to the rows of rainbow-hued ribbons on Sabin's blouse. It was there, rightfully preceding the others, a sky-blue field adorned with tiny white stars. The Congressional Medal of Honor. Signifying that this handsome young general was a bona-fide American hero.

Sabin sat ramrod straight in his chair, his hands resting lightly on the armrests. With no gesture toward introduction he said, "Lieutenant Colonel Hadley is here at my invitation."

Ward nodded toward the short, stocky colonel. *So you're my deposed predecessor in this miserable affair?*

Ward began, "General, I . . ."

"I'm not finished," Sabin snapped.

Ward noted the smirk on Hadley's face.

"I am opposed to the purpose of this meeting," Sabin said. "I am particularly opposed to your involvement."

Certainly to the point, Ward thought. He said, "May I ask why?"

"Reopening the crash investigation is an affront to my credibility . . . and to Colonel Hadley's. As for you, you are not rated. The intricacies of the XR-Twenty-One-Hundred program are difficult enough for the most experienced pilot to fathom. To entrust the investigation to an unrated officer is folly. It will require my people to interrupt vitally important work to educate a layman. I've made my position clear to General Burnside. Since he sees matters differently, I suggest that there is only one reasonable course left to you."

He paused, obviously expecting a reaction.

Ward remained silent.

Sabin continued: "Study Colonel Hadley's report. It's thorough and it's accurate. It accomplishes all that anyone can hope to accomplish in the matter. Endorse it and get this thing over with. It would be in the best interest of us all, you most of all."

It was a blatant attempt at intimidation. Instead, Ward felt anger. He'd been shanghaied into this damned job. He'd been threatened if he didn't do it right, now he was being threatened if he did. Moreover, he resented Sabin's arrogance—the presumptuous claim of technological superiority. It was an echo from Ward's past. He recalled the Kamchatka signal and the self-righteous engineers who had tried to muzzle him. He'd had enough of it.

"General, you're right . . . I'm not a fly-boy."

Sabin's eyes narrowed at the parochial slur.

"On this turf," Ward said, "I *am* a layman. A layman forced into a job I didn't ask for or want. I, too, have important work to do. Too important to have to take time away from it to correct someone else's mistakes."

Hadley coughed.

Ward continued. "But like it or not, pilot or not, I've got the job. For your information, I *have* studied Colonel Hadley's report. All day yesterday and most of last night. At this moment I don't know if I share your or General Burnside's opinion of it. No matter, he's ordered me to put it to the test. And until *he* calls me off I intend to do just that."

The air was electric. Ward considered that he might have gone too far, but he didn't care. If the whole damned thing fell apart at this moment, so be it.

Hadley stared hard at the floor, unwilling to look at either man.

For a long moment Sabin's expression remained unchanged. Then he nodded. "It appears that we understand each other. I insist, though, that you include my objections in your report."

It wasn't the reaction Hadley had expected and his face showed it.

Ward, too, was surprised. It was an unexpected retreat. Despite his anger, he felt a surge of relief. "Agreed," he said.

Sabin leaned forward on his desk. "Very well. How do you intend to proceed?"

Ward proceeded with an overview of what he already knew from the multitude of reports he had read. That the XR-2100 was a first generation Stealth-type aircraft designed to be blind to radar detection. That the aircraft's purpose was photographic and electronics reconnaissance. That it incorporated an advanced-design navigational computer called *Stargaze*. That *Stargaze* worked like the name implied—the computer "read" the stars, up to fifty at a time, using one major star as a "lockstar." That by constantly monitoring the lockstar's position in relationship to the other stars, *Stargaze* could position the XR-2100 precisely on any pre-programmed flight path.

"In other words," Ward asked, "*Stargaze* could fly the plane?"

"Yes," Sabin confirmed.

"All functions . . . takeoff, landing, fuel consumption, course corrections . . . complete control?"

"Absolute control . . . even to operating the reconnaissance equipment."

"And the Pacific flights were to test this control?"

"Yes."

"Then how, if *Cobra One* was under *Stargaze* control, could the accident have been pilot error?"

Hadley shifted in his seat.

Sabin said, "Major Crowell took control away from *Stargaze*."

"How do you know that?"

"The computer has two control settings: STARGAZE and PILOT. When *Cobra One* was salvaged the control was found in the PILOT position, showing that Major Crowell had taken manual control of the plane."

"Yet, you found no malfunction . . . no reason for him to have taken control."

"None whatsoever."

"What about the flight recorder? Did it indicate a problem? There's no mention of it in Colonel Hadley's report."

"There was no flight recorder on *Cobra One*."

"I don't understand. I thought that was an Air Force requirement."

Sabin shook his head. "The XR-Twenty-One-Hundred is a covert-operation aircraft, with all that implies. It's light-years ahead of anything flying today. The chances of it being brought down over unfriendly territory are virtually nil. Yet, it *could* happen, like the U-2 over Russia in 1960. In that incident the pilot should have taken a termination capsule and set the plane to explode. He didn't, and both he and the plane fell into Russian hands. That embarrassment proved the wisdom of omitting flight recorders on covert aircraft. In the worst of circumstances, it would reveal too much about the aircraft's capability to the wrong people."

Ward was taken aback by Sabin's emotionless, matter-of-fact condemnation of Pilot Gary Powers' refusal to kill himself and blow up the U-2. The general was deadly serious.

Ward said, "Then you have no reservations about blaming the accident on Major Crowell?"

"None at all."

"No problem with the conclusion that he just went beserk . . . then flew *Cobra One* a thousand miles across the Pacific before it crashed?"

"None. A thousand miles is inconsequential for the XR-Twenty-One-Hundred—approximately twenty minutes. And pilot panic isn't an unheard of phenomenon."

"Even in one so rigorously tested as Major Crowell?"

Sabin's jaw firmed and Ward knew that he had hit a sore point.

"A system failure, I agree," Sabin said. "Unfortunately, as rigorous as it is, our selection process is not infallible."

In the give-and-take so far Sabin hadn't budged an inch. Yet, despite the rocky beginning, he was being cooperative. Ward didn't want to lose the initiative. "All right . . . for the sake of discussion let's suppose we agree that Major Crowell was at fault. There has to be a rational explanation for his sudden failure. Shouldn't the investigation have been widened to try to determine that? Was he ill, on drugs, being cuckolded, badly in debt? There's no mention in the report of Crowell's outside associates . . . or his family. Why?"

Hadley leaned forward. "I . . ."

Sabin silenced the colonel with a raise of a hand. "The investigation was kept in bounds on my order. What real purpose would have been served otherwise? The question raised by the crash of *Cobra One*, as is true in most aircraft accidents, was a simple one: Was it the fault of the plane or the pilot? All evidence supports the conclusion that it was not the fault of the plane. With that determined, why carry the investigation endlessly forward? I must caution you that you are dealing here with a highly classified project, with an imminent vital mission to be performed. It is in the national interest to conclude the investigation and get on with that mission."

Ward was uncertain what he'd heard. "An *imminent* vital mission? How can that be a factor with the aircraft out of commission?"

Sabin and Hadley exchanged glances. Then Sabin looked at Ward quizzically. "I assume, Major, that you're aware that there is a *Cobra Two?*"

Cobra Two? There was no mention of a second plane in anything he'd read. MacWatt hadn't mentioned it . . . or any impending mission. Ward felt like a fool. Sabin was, indeed, educating a layman.

"No," Ward shook his head, "I wasn't aware of a second plane."

"I see," Sabin said pointedly. "I presumed that you would have been better briefed."

There was nothing to say, so Ward remained silent.

"*Cobra One* was the prototype," Sabin explained, savoring the effect of this surprise on Ward. "*Cobra Two* is the first production model. For all intents, they were built at the same time. The design was that good. Following the accident, *Cobra Two* was grounded briefly by order of the Secretary of the Air Force. After it was determined that *Cobra One* was not at fault, the grounding order was lifted. Nothing has changed that—not even General Burnside's determination to reopen the investigation. *Cobra Two* will proceed with the mission."

It was an unsettling turn of events and Ward wasn't certain what to make of it. MacWatt had emphasized that finding the cause of the accident was "of greatest urgency." Why? Ward wondered now. What's the damned urgency if the aircraft has been cleared for operation? What the hell is this new investigation all about? If the Quickseal mission—whatever that is— is scheduled to proceed despite the crash, what purpose is being served? He would have something to say about this to MacWatt. In the meantime, be damned if he'd go one step farther in the dark.

"General," he said. "I'd like to know about *Cobra Two*'s mission."

Hadley looked up sharply. "Major, that mission has no bearing on what happened in the Pacific . . . none at all. You have no requirement for that information." The colonel wiped the palms of his hands on his trousers.

Ward didn't know whether to regard Hadley—*this sweating toady*—with contempt or pity. "Colonel, I can get the information from you in this office or in General Burnside's office. Either way, I intend to know a lot more about what's going on before I continue with this investigation. And I remind you, it's my responsibility now to determine what has a bearing on what happened in the Pacific."

The blood drained from Hadley's face. "Well . . . I . . . uh . . ." He looked at Sabin pleadingly.

Sabin allowed the colonel to squirm for several more seconds. Then, without comment, the general rose and went to a map case on the wall. He pulled down a map of the area extending from the Mediterranean Sea to the Caspian Sea. Prominently centered was the Persian Gulf. Sabin made a broad gesture over the region. "You recognize this, of course."

Any schoolchild would in this day and age, Ward mused. "Of course."

"The Middle East is the most volatile area in the world. It's a misfortune of geography that the lifeblood of Western industrial society—oil, of course—lies beneath these otherwise useless lands. Historically—despite the more noble-sounding rationalizations—wars have been fought for access to energy sources. That axiom is a basic foundation of our global strategy. So, too, is it of the Soviet's. For years they have systematically exploited the Middle East. In recent months they have become bolder. They've moved into Afghanistan. They've manipulated Iraq into attacking Iran. They'll move to occupy the major oil producing countries anytime they believe they can do so with impunity. Not so much for their need, but to deny ours. We must never allow that to happen. It's imperative that we know all their troop and transport movements in the region. We can accomplish that, to a high degree of success, through the use of satellites and covert agents. But there's an urgent need for closer, pinpoint reconnaissance. The XR-Twenty-One-Hundred was designed and rushed through production to fill that need."

He paused. "Now, what I'm about to reveal is extremely sensitive. It must not become a part of your report."

Ward nodded, with a mental reservation to make that decision for himself.

"In just a few days," Sabin said, "the Defense Department will announce the deployment of four AWACS aircraft to Saudi Arabia. The cover story will be that they are being sent at Saudi request to bolster their defenses. In fact, they are advance Quickseal units."

"The same AWACS that took part in the Pacific tests?" Ward asked.

"The same. They'll fly radar patrols in Saudi Arabia to reconcile the Soviets to their presence. Then, in October, three C-5A cargo aircraft from the deployed unit will return stateside ostensibly for supplies and personnel rotation. One will divert to Kirtland. It will on-load *Cobra Two* and fly it to a secret compound near Cairo. From there, *Cobra Two* will fly night infrared and electronic intercept reconnaissance flights"—he indicated the sortie routes with his hand—"over Iran, Iraq, Afghanistan, Abadan, the Persian Gulf, and the southern regions of the Soviet Union. The AWACS positioned in Saudi Arabia will monitor these penetrations."

"How," Ward asked, "if *Cobra Two* can't be detected by radar?"

"By coded signals transmitted continuously from the plane."

"Ah, yes . . . like Crowell did in the Pacific."

"Exactly."

It was a bold program, Ward admitted. "And this was to have been Major Crowell's mission?"

"On *Cobra One* . . . yes."

"And on *Cobra Two?*" Ward asked.

Sabin returned to his desk and sat down. "That will be Colonel Hadley's assignment."

Ward looked at the colonel with a new awareness, and, for the first time, with a degree of respect.

Ward thought over what he had learned. The meeting had been enlightening. Sabin, for all his early bluster, had been forthcoming. But the puzzle remained a puzzle. "General, I'd like to look around the compound, maybe talk to some people, take a look at *Cobra One* . . . and *Two.*"

Sabin nodded. "Colonel Hadley will escort you."

Hadley stood and Ward did too. The two officers saluted and left.

In the hallway Hadley stopped and groped in his pocket for a cigarette. "God, I'm dying for a smoke. You don't dare in his presence, you know." He offered the pack to Ward.

"No, thanks."

Hadley lit up, took a deep drag and exhaled slowly. He was shorter than Ward, and a bit beefy. His thinning brown hair and worry-lined face made him look older than his age, which, Ward knew from the records, was 37.

Hadley drew hard on the cigarette again, coughed, and exhaled. "Look, uh, whatever you want to see . . . any way I can help . . . just ask." The antagonistic Hadley of Sabin's office had vanished.

Ward thought about that. He recognized that the colonel was Sabin's whipping boy. He'd seen the relationship many times on many bases, and had never understood it. "He must be one hard-assed bastard to work for."

Hadley made no reply.

Ward sensed that the colonel's silence didn't stem from any sense of loyalty to his boss. He waited. After a while he said, "Colonel, I have a lot to do, and not much time."

"Oh . . ." Hadley stubbed the half-smoked cigarette in a nearby receptacle. "I'm sorry . . . yes . . . yes. This way."

Walking at a brisk pace he led the way down the long hallway to the courtyard, toward the Quickseal hangars.

9

BRIGADIER General Bartholomew Sabin sat in his office in somber reflection. Ward had not been cowed. Indeed, his demeanor bordered on arrogance. At other times, in other circumstances, Sabin would not have tolerated such hubris in a junior officer. But under the present circumstances the major was a man to be reckoned with.

The general pushed an intercom button.

"Monitor Room," a gruff voice responded.

"This is General Sabin. Who's speaking?"

"Sergeant Holmes, sir."

"Sergeant Holmes, Colonel Hadley is escorting an officer through the compound. I want to know everywhere they go, who they talk to."

"Yes, sir. Photos, sir?"

"Yes. And Sergeant . . ."

"Yes, sir?"

"The next time I call this number I don't want to have to ask to whom I'm speaking. Do you understand?"

"Yes . . . yes, sir. Sorry, sir."

Sabin switched off the intercom.

On a far wall a command photo of Major General Louis Burnside stared down at him. He eyed the photograph with mixed emotions. Burnside had been a brilliant R&D commander. *Had* been. But events had swept past him, and his contemporaries. McCollum, for example. The Chief of Staff and Burnside were of the same mold. Holdovers from an outmoded era. They should have been put out to pasture years ago. If it were my decision, Sabin mused, it would be done now, without remorse.

He had been born to make hard decisions, he reflected. And he'd never allowed emotion, never permitted anyone, to sway him from his convictions . . . from his destiny.

Suddenly, in his mind's eye he saw his father as plainly as if the old man were standing there in the room with him.

"No . . ." he uttered in a hoarse whisper, "not even you . . ."

The war clouds that rolled ominously out of Europe that April 1941 held little threat for 36-year-old Karl Sabin. Newly widowed, father of an infant son whose mother had died in childbirth, Karl was also the sole support for his 62-year-old mother, Hannah. Both his age and his domestic responsibilities insured him against the draft that was depleting the ranks of younger and less encumbered men in Carbondale, Illinois.

It was not a situation to Karl's liking. For years he had been seeking a way out. A way out of a marriage that had gone sour. A way out of a stifling, no-future job as a junior clerk in the town offices. His wife's pregnancy, after ten barren years, reduced him to despondency. A baby would be the final link in the intolerable chain binding him to a life of utter despair.

Instead, the baby provided Karl's salvation.

Unexpectedly, after her grandson's birth, and her daughter-in-law's untimely death, Hannah Sabin stepped into the role of mother, as well as grandmother, with great delight. Karl took heart. His deliverance was at hand. Two months after his son's birth, solemnly declaring that he could not stand by idly while others bore the burden of arms, he left little Bartholomew to the care of Hannah and joined the Army. At the induction center he allotted all except a few dollars of his pay to Hannah. Then, breathing a sigh of relief, he marched off to do his duty to God and country.

After basic training he was assigned as a rifleman to the Far East Command in the Philippines. His troopship docked at Manila on November 2, 1941. A week later he joined the small

American garrison at Laoag, on the northern tip of Luzon. One lazy morning the following month he awoke to find his country at war. Three days later, on December 10, 1941, a Japanese assault force swarmed ashore on Northern Luzon, overwhelming the meager American forces there. Karl's fighting days ended before they began.

For six months he rotted in a filthy, unsheltered prison stockade near Laoag. Then, in June 1942, he was herded with 150 other POWs into the cramped hold of a cargo ship and transported to Japan. There he was put to work at slave labor, laying railroad tracks across the length and breadth of Honshu.

The ordeal saved his life. Despite the privations of his lot, and the sometimes brutal ministrations of sadistic guards, as a working POW he received rations commensurate with his work. Relatively well-fed, forced to perform rigorous physical labor, he developed a rock-hard body—and a determination to survive. For the first time in his life Karl Sabin respected himself.

The racking toil continued without letup for three years. Then, in midsummer 1945, there was a noticeable change of attitude among the Japanese guards. Their bellicosity waned, the work load slackened. The Empire was losing the war.

One morning in August the POWs awakened to find that their guards had walked away from their posts. A dozen other guards, unaware of their comrade's desertion, were asleep in their quarters. The POWs raided the arsenal, armed themselves, then prodded the sleeping guards awake. All but five were taken to the gate, booted in the ass and told to go home. The POWs lined four of the remaining guards, loathed for their sadistic treatment of their prisoners, against a barracks wall and shot them. The fifth guard, a brutal sergeant who had bludgeoned two sick POWs to death with a rifle butt, they tossed into a deep pit of human excrement known in the camp as the "honey pot." With grim determination they took turns pushing the sergeant's head back beneath the slimy feces each time he bobbed, gasping and pleading, to the surface. After fifteen minutes the hapless man's struggles ceased and he sank to the bottom of the pit.

On the last day of September 1945, Karl Sabin returned to Carbondale a celebrity. Four hundred people jammed into the train station to greet "The Hero of Luzon," the soldier who had earned the distinction of being held prisoner of war longer than any other from the state.

At the forefront of the throng, Hannah Sabin grasped her son to her breast with genuine affection. At her side a tow-headed, unsmiling youngster clutched desperately at Hannah's dress, visibly displeased at her display of affection for someone other than himself. With a flourish, Karl lifted four-year-old Bartholomew and kissed him mightily. Then, to the delight of the news photographers, he sat the startled boy astride his shoulders. Deeply moved, the crowd cheered this bittersweet reunion between son and father who had voluntarily, and self-lessly, left his loved ones to answer the call to duty.

It was a new world for the one-time Carbondale junior clerk. *That*, Karl promised himself, he would never be again. One evening, while he was considering his options, a trio of local businessmen visited him. There was a vacancy on the city coun-cil, they reported, created by the death of the incumbent. It was to be filled by special election in November. Why didn't Karl stand for the office? He could count on full support from the business community.

Karl agreed on the spot. In November he was elected on the Democratic ticket with the largest majority in Carbondale his-tory.

He held office for three terms, gaining experience and influ-ence. In 1952 he decided it was time for bigger things. He entered the race for state senator. Billed throughout the district as "The Hero of Luzon" he won hands down. By 1956 he was considered unbeatable in state politics. In the summer of that year he purchased a large antebellum house in an affluent sec-tion of town, hired a cook and maid (over Hannah's outraged objections) and settled comfortably into the role of Democratic Sachem of Southern Illinois.

As Karl's reputation spread, so did his son's. A diligent stu-dent, active in sports, Bartholomew Sabin had matured into an unbeatable, and unusual, combination—an athlete-scholar. Tall, spindly, with golden hair and penetrating blue eyes, the hand-some boy shattered every standing scholastic and track record in the Carbondale Elementary School System. In his freshman year at high school he set the state cross-country and mile track records for his age. Liked by his peers, despite a tendency to aloofness, he was equally popular, and more at ease, with adults. Older men found his poise and determination a welcome offset to the frivolity they saw in others of his age. Mothers of the fortunate girls he dated—and he played the field—were as enraptured by his breathtaking good looks as were their heart-stricken daughters.

The charismatic combination of Karl Sabin, popular state senator, and Bartholomew Sabin, rising star athlete, had not gone unnoticed by the state's Democratic hierarchy. One afternoon in September 1956, Bartholomew arrived home to find several men in conference with his father. Karl beckoned to his son. With the air of a novitiate introducing someone to the Pope, Karl said, "Bart, I'd like for you to meet Mister Adlai Stevenson."

The distinguished-looking man with the recognizable face smiled and extended his hand. "My pleasure, Bartholomew. I saw you capture the indoor-mile record on TV last week. You were in a class by yourself."

"Thank you," Bartholomew said without emotion. He excused himself to go to his room to study.

That evening at dinner Karl tried to make small talk with his son. Their relationship had never been warm, although Karl had tried. He blamed it on his extended absence during Bartholomew's formative years and prayed that the boy would eventually grow closer to him. For he had grown to love his son dearly, and yearned for his approval.

Karl said, "Mister Stevenson thinks you'd be an asset on the campaign trail this fall, Bart."

Bartholomew cut a piece of chicken with his fork. "I don't understand."

"You and I, together. You know, Senator Sabin and his popular athlete son . . . that sort of thing. If Adlai beats Eisenhower this time it could mean bigger and better things for the Sabins."

Hannah Sabin snorted. "Hmph! I wouldn't be gathering any eggs before the hen cackles if I was you. Folks aren't about to put Ike Eisenhower out of office for a pinko like Adlai Stevenson."

"Shush, Mama," Karl chided. "We're well aware of your fascist sentiments. Adlai Stevenson's a fine gentleman. Besides, this conversation is between Bartholomew and me."

"Hmph!"

Karl looked back at his son. "It would mean a couple of rallies in Chicago . . . perhaps short visits to Rockfort, Peoria, Decatur . . . places like that. I'd do the speech making. All you'd have to do is wave . . . and smile for the ladies"—he gave a wry wink—" like I hear you're quite adept at doing."

He waited.

Bartholomew didn't respond.

"Well?" Karl said finally.

Bartholomew shook his head. "No, Dad."

Karl sucked in his breath. "Would you mind telling me why?"

Without looking up Bartholomew said, "I just don't want to."

Karl started to press the issue, but saw Hannah shaking her head in disapproval. They ate the remainder of the meal in silence.

In February 1959, two days after Bartholomew's 18th birthday, 80-year-old Hannah Sabin died peacefully in her sleep. Bartholomew was devastated. For three days following the funeral he remained in his room, taking neither food nor drink. He emerged on the fourth day, his face a drawn mask of despair. He stopped at the breakfast table for a glass of milk. "I've got to get back to school," he said to his father.

With heavy heart Karl realized that during these last few days was the first time he'd ever seen his son display passion.

Since the beginning of Bartholomew's senior year, Karl had tried to feel his son out about a choice of careers. Bartholomew had remained noncommittal. Now, as graduation approached, Karl raised the issue again. "Political science would be a natural. Yale perhaps. Even Harvard. They're not exactly giants in the sports world, but with a degree like that behind you, and my influence, this state could be your oyster. And that would only be the beginning."

Bartholomew said, "I should have told you, I suppose. I've applied for a presidential appointment to the Air Force Academy."

"The Air . . ." Karl was flabbergasted. "But . . . you've never mentioned a military career."

"Grandmother and I talked about it."

Karl felt an old hurt. Once again Bartholomew had discussed a vital issue with his grandmother, but not his father.

"We considered Annapolis," Bartholomew said, "but I want to fly, and the Air Force offers more for a pilot."

Karl recognized that his son was serious. "Well . . . it's a surprise, but if that's your choice . . . A presidential appointment though? That's a bit run-of-the-mill. I can get you a direct appointment easily. In fact, I'm having lunch tomorrow with Senator . . ."

"No, Dad. I have to do it my way."

As always, Karl mused. There was no point in arguing.

In May 1959, Bartholomew scored the highest grade ever recorded in Illinois on the competitive examination for a presidential appointment to a military academy. In June he entered the Air Force Academy at Colorado Springs with an appointment from President Dwight Eisenhower.

At Christmas he came home on leave. During dinner the first evening Karl announced a surprise. "I had a call yesterday from Boston . . . Senator John Kennedy. He's going to take on the Republicans next year . . . and he's going to win. He wants me to announce . . . *for governor*."

Bartholomew ate in silence.

"Did you hear what I said, Bart? Governor! I've already tossed my hat in the ring. It will be an unbeatable ticket." He looked across the table, his face beaming with pride. "How'll that sit with your friends out there at the academy, huh? Bart Sabin, son of Governor Karl Sabin . . . the old Hero of Luzon."

Bartholomew pushed his plate away angrily. "For God's sake, Dad . . . stop it!"

"Wha . . . ?"

"Don't you see what you're doing?" Bartholomew snapped, his voice strident with long-concealed bitterness. "Don't you realize how embarrassing this has been all these years? Jesus Christ, Dad! You're no hero. You were a prisoner of war. You surrendered! If you were a hero you'd have been dead for eighteen years!"

Stunned, Karl couldn't believe what he'd heard. Then, in blind rage, he rose and reached across the table and slapped his son a resounding blow in the face. "Who . . . the hell . . . do you think . . ."

His voice choked off and his knees turned to jelly. He slumped back in the chair.

Bartholomew's eyes welled with tears. He raised his hand to

the stinging welt on his cheek. Then, without a word, he rose and went upstairs, got his unpacked bags and left the house.

In a daze, Karl remained seated at the table until midnight. Twice he lapsed into wracking sobs. It had all been for naught.

Next day, without explanation, Karl Sabin withdrew his name as a candidate for governor. He dismissed the household help, locked the doors of his home, and refused to receive visitors. Four months later, an emaciated, shattered recluse, he died at age 55. His doctor blamed heart failure. It was the nearest medical explanation for a broken heart.

Bartholomew returned to Carbondale to see his father buried in a grave between the mother Bartholomew never knew and the grandmother he adored. At the end of the graveside service he laid his hand for a moment on Hannah Sabin's tombstone. Then he left Carbondale, never to return.

In June 1963, Bartholomew graduated as a second lieutenant from the Air Force Academy. In a class of 489 he ranked number one.

By 1965, the United States was deeply involved in Vietnam. That summer, Lieutenant Bartholomew Sabin was assigned to Saigon with duty as a forward air controller. During the next twelve months he flew 109 treetop-level missions in a slow-moving, single-engine L-19 Cessna, targeting enemy positions with smoke flares for the deadly mach-two F-4C Phantom fighter bombers. Twice wounded by ground fire, he returned to the states in 1966 with two Purple Hearts and the rank of captain.

For three years he chafed in a desk job at the Pentagon, volunteering monthly for return to combat. In 1969 his wish was granted. Promoted to major, he was assigned as commander of the 618th Tactical Fighter Squadron at Da Nang. He was 27.

An exacting leader, he tolerated no laxity and demanded full measure from every man in his unit. One rule was inviolable: he would order no mission he wouldn't fly himself. Strict, at times overbearing, he was nonetheless respected by his fellow pilots. To his seniors he was recognized as a comer destined for flag rank.

One day Sabin received a call from the division commander. "You're getting a new hand tomorrow, Major. Ngo Minh himself. He's quite impressed with your record and wants to fly a mission with your unit. Quite an honor."

It was an honor Sabin would gladly have forgone.

Highly respected, with an excellent combat record, 41-year-old Air Vice Marshal Ngo Minh was second in command of the South Vietnamese Air Force. Flamboyant in personal life, an iron-willed professional in the air, he was widely regarded as a pilot's pilot. He was also an astute politician with presidential ambitions. The presence of such a prominent national hero on the mission could be a distraction. With no alternative but to accept the situation, Sabin assigned himself the role of keeping an eye on Ngo Minh and ordered the other pilots to simply do their jobs.

The five F-105 Thunderchiefs that struck an oil depot near Hanoi next morning did so with precision accuracy. On the last sortie, Ngo Minh, with Sabin close on his right wing, zeroed in on the sole remaining storage tank with a steady barrage from his 20-millimeter Gatling. The tank erupted in a ball of flame. Ngo Minh set his plane on its tail and zoomed straight up. At that moment the radio crackled: "Dog One and Two . . . missile coming in!"

Sabin evaded sharply starboard, Ngo Minh to port.

"He's hit!"

Sabin turned to see Ngo Minh's plane falling from the sky.

"This is Dog One," Sabin radioed. "Keep him in sight. Watch for a chute."

The Americans dived toward their stricken ally.

Suddenly, Ngo Minh's plane leveled.

"He pulled it out! He's heading for the coast."

For twenty minutes, with experienced skill, the Air Vice Marshal nursed his crippled jet southward. Each precious passing moment decreased the miles to homebase. Then, all at once, the smoking plane yawed starboard and spun violently earthward. Once again, barely 300 feet above the trees, Ngo Minh got the jet's nose high, its wings level. But it had flown its last flight. Keeping his gear up, Ngo Minh pancaked hard into the ground, losing one wing and the canopy on impact. The fuselage plowed headlong across a flat plain, ripped through a thin stand of saplings, and came to rest at the edge of a small lake. The remaining wing tank burst into flames.

"No one could survive that," Dog Three called.

Sabin swept low over the burning plane for a closer inspection. Through a break in the black, roiling smoke he saw Ngo

Minh pull himself over the side of the cockpit and fall heavily to the ground. The downed pilot pulled himself across the dirt on his belly, hand over hand, away from the burning plane. At the edge of the lake he stopped and lay unmoving.

"He's bad hurt," Dog Four called.

Ngo Minh lay at the bottom of a hill that rose between the lake and a thick forest. Several figures bearing guns emerged from the forest and started over the hill toward the downed plane.

"Shit! There's a Cong unit in those woods."

"Let's discourage them," Sabin ordered.

In tandem, the F-105s zoomed low, sweeping the edge of the forest with machine-gun fire. The emerging figures scurried back into the woods.

Dog Three called, "We need rescue in here, fast."

"Negative," Sabin responded.

"Sir . . ." Dog Three argued, "that's the Air Vice Mar . . ."

"Break it off!" Sabin said sharply.

Dog Three shut up.

Sabin considered the situation. If that Cong unit had bazookas, or any artillery, a rescue helicopter would be a sitting duck. He wouldn't order a suicide mission, not even for the South Vietnamese Air Vice Marshal. He wondered if Ngo Minh was alive? If so, he must not be captured. He made a quick decision. "Dog Three . . . keep those Cong troops occupied. I'm going for a puddle jumper."

A pause. Then: "Sir, are you sure that's the way?"

"Do what I ordered. And whatever happens . . . Ngo Minh is not, repeat *not*, to be taken alive. Confirm understanding."

"Roger," Dog Three replied somberly. "Understood."

Sabin banked southward and fired full-throttle across the sky toward Da Nang. Minutes later he landed straight-in. At the end of the runway he turned and taxied at high speed toward a far apron where a Cessna L-19 "puddle jumper" was warming up for a mission. Sabin jumped from the F-105 and ran across the tarmac to the L-19. He ducked around the whirling propeller, yanked open the door and ordered the startled pilot out.

The pilot, a lieutenant, stared at Sabin incredulously.

"Out, dammit!" Sabin grabbed the young officer by the arm and pulled him from the cockpit. Dumbfounded, the lieutenant watched as Sabin taxied the commandeered plane to the runway and took off.

Forty minutes later Dog Three spotted a tiny aircraft skirting the trees. "Here he comes. Let's clear the way."

While the F-105s laid down a barrage, Sabin landed the L-19 on the plain near Ngo Minh's burning jet. Ngo Minh lay among some reeds at the water's edge. Sabin taxied to within fifty feet of the water and stopped while still on solid ground. He locked the brakes, left the prop turning and jumped out. He ran to Ngo Minh's side. Ngo Minh's eyes were open and he held a pistol in his hand. The Air Vice Marshal raised his head feebly. "Major . . ."—he coughed and fought for breath—". . . you are a fool. But . . . a very brave fool." His head fell back to the ground and he moaned.

At that moment Dog Three zoomed low, rocking his wings frantically. Sabin looked up. Just below the crest of the hill two Cong soldiers who had braved the barrage were running toward Sabin with raised rifles. Sabin grabbed the pistol from Ngo Minh's hand and sprawled flat on his stomach. There was a sharp crack; a bullet kicked up dirt near Sabin's ear. He steadied the pistol with both hands and waited. Seventy-five feet away the Cong soldiers stopped foolishly to take aim. Sabin fired and one of the soldiers collapsed. The other rushed headlong down the hillside toward Sabin, wildly firing his rifle point-blank. Sabin waited. At thirty-five feet he took aim and squeezed the trigger. The bullet tore away the left side of the Cong soldier's head. He crumpled and rolled lifelessly down the hill, coming to a stop two feet from Sabin.

Sabin scanned the skyline. There were no other soldiers in sight. He pocketed the gun, grasped Ngo Minh by the arm and leg and tossed the little man over his shoulders. Ngo Minh screamed in pain. Ignoring the screams, Sabin raced to the L-19 and threw the wounded Air Vice Marshal inside. Sabin climbed in and revved the engine. Just then a larger group of Cong soldiers reached the hilltop. The L-19 rolled across the plain in a hail of rifle fire. The door-window shattered and a bullet hit Sabin high on the left cheek, ripping through flesh and bone. Blood gushed out, blinding him. Unable to see, he pulled the L-19 into the air by instinct, grabbed a handkerchief and wiped his right eye clear. He wadded the handkerchief into a compress and held it over his left eye throughout the agonizing flight home. He landed on the main runway, cut the engine, and fainted from pain and blood loss.

In May 1970, in an impressive White House ceremony, President Richard Nixon presented newly-promoted Lieutenant Colonel Bartholomew Sabin with the Congressional Medal of Honor "for service above and beyond the call of duty" in his daring rescue of Air Vice Marshal Ngo Minh. As the President placed the ribbon-held medal over Sabin's neck, Ngo Minh rose slowly from a nearby wheelchair and lifted his hand in salute. As Sabin returned the salute crisply, photo bulbs flashed. That night Air Force PR officers worked overtime to assure that the stirring photographs hit every major newspaper in the country. The Air Force's "Golden Boy" was hailed as a popular and attractive hero.

Despite his new status, it was an embittered Sabin who returned from his second tour of Vietnam. His contempt for the mismanagement of the war was intense. At the same time he harbored a grudging respect for the Communists. They were, he was convinced, determined to subjugate the world. And who was to stop them? He grimaced at the thought of a long string of effete American political leaders: Truman, who, despite his feisty image, disbanded the greatest military force the world had ever known, then challenged but eventually kowtowed to the Reds in Korea; Kennedy, who in 1961, advocating that a balance of power would foster world peace, unilaterally slowed American technological advances to allow the Soviets to catch up; Johnson, who craved victory in Vietnam, yet needlessly sacrificed American lives by refusing to unleash the full force of military power at his command.

Suicidal idiocy!

Still, it was not too late. It was insane to attempt to match the Communist nations militarily on a man-for-man basis. Salvation, Sabin was convinced, lay in regaining and maintaining technological superiority—*and the disciplined will to use it*. With any assignment his for the asking, he entered graduate studies at the Air Force Institute of Technology. Imposing a sixteen-hour workday on himself, he finished a four-year course in three, graduating in 1973 with a doctorate in aeronautical engineering. That summer, when most of his academy classmates were pinning on the gold leaves of major, 32-year-old Bartholomew Sabin pinned on the silver eagles of a full colonel.

He was assigned to USAF Intelligence (A2) with carte blanche orders to go where he wanted, when he wanted, to evaluate the free world's air forces. He flew the globe studying armaments and tactics. And in only one country did he find that rare combination of martial power and iron-willed determination that met his exacting standards—the Republic of South Africa.

At the invitation of General Jan Kruger, Sabin remained as a guest of the South African Air Force for four months, traveling extensively throughout that vast country, assessing defenses, evaluating tactics, flying their aircraft—even joining his host on safari.

"It helps one to know oneself," said Kruger of the hunts.

Sabin took to blood sports with relish. On his first large-game kill—a bull Cape buffalo that charged to within forty feet before Sabin dropped him with a single shot from a borrowed Weatherby Mark IV—he felt an exhilaration he'd known only once before. It was the same heady sensation he felt that day on the hillside in Vietnam when he shot the two Cong soldiers. Nothing else, not even aerial combat, equaled this cathartic, almost sensual release of emotions.

It was on another hunt, a fly-in safari a week later in the Eastern Transvaal, that Sabin's globe-trotting paid off.

The night was brilliant, the sky ablaze with stars, the mountain air a refreshing change from the humid coast. Sabin and Kruger sat beside a low campfire, nightcap in hand. In the offing porters were packing gear. Kruger, a rugged, thickset man with a heavy walrus mustache and a penchant for the wild, lowered his cup and sighed. "Life gets no better than this, Bart. A pity we must break camp. But Dayan is arriving in Cape Town tomorrow night. We have several ongoing matters to discuss."

Sabin recognized a cue when he heard one. It was well known to A2 that South Africa and Israel shared research and development information, particularly on nuclear weapons. Sabin said nothing.

Kruger continued: "They have a new approach to this radar

avoidance thing, you know. Some way of burnishing the fuselage skin. Highly promising. Something like your Stealth engineers are working on, eh?"

Sabin smothered his surprise. How had the South Africans learned about Stealth? He could guess: the Mossad. Israeli technical-intelligence agents were among the best in the world. There was more to this conversation than after-hunt chitchat. Sabin waited.

"They've been unable to develop it fully," Kruger said. "Nor have we. But with the proper research facilities . . . like at your Edwards Air Force Base . . ."

"General Kruger," Sabin interjected, "I have the impression that I'm being courted as the sole patron at a closed auction. But I'm not sure what I'm supposed to bid . . . or bid on."

Kruger laughed. "You live up to your reputation, Colonel. Direct and to the point. All right, as they say in your country, 'down to brass tacks.' "

Kruger pulled a slim leather case from his jacket and offered Sabin a cigar. Sabin declined. Kruger lifted a burning stick from the campfire and lit up. "Bart, we know how close you are to developing an aircraft that will be immune to radar detection. But you have not made the final breakthrough yet, eh? We can provide that breakthrough. With refinement . . . modifications your people are surely capable of, our data could save you a year . . . perhaps two . . . of research."

"And in return?"

Kruger puffed his cigar. "Four months ago you launched your *Cyclops Two* satellite from Cape Canaveral. It so happens that *Cyclops* orbits certain parts of the world—our somewhat unstable northern neighbors—from where we are most anxious to garner a continuing flow of information. We want access to *Cyclops*. Not finished reports, mind you. But directly from the satellite. We have the necessary tracking stations. All we need is the code to trigger *Cyclops* into transmitting the data, and the key to decipher it. Give us that and we give you the data your Stealth project so desperately needs."

"The Israelis are aware of this?"

"Yes."

Sabin was hesitant. It was an enticing offer, but one with potentially dire political consequences. "General, you know the restrictions on our dealings with South Africa. I can't even visit here in uniform. Our government—Congress certainly—would never agree to the arrangement."

Kruger knocked the ash from his cigar. "We don't expect you to ask them."

Sabin thought on it. "How can I be certain your data is worth it?"

"Fair question. Suppose you make a quick trip home. Bring back one or two of your Stealth people. Let them decide. If we have what you need, the deal is on. If not, no hard feelings, eh?"

Sabin made the trip. Five days later, in Cape Town, the chief Stealth engineer agreed that the Israeli-South African scientists had, indeed, made a major breakthrough. The deal was struck. Sabin provided Kruger with the codes to *Cyclops*. There were no records made of the under-the-table transaction. It was strictly an A2 matter.

Following his South African coup, Sabin was rewarded with a challenging new job. Plans for a Stealth-type reconnaissance aircraft were underway at Edwards Air Force Base. The plane would incorporate an advanced state-of-the-art navigational system called *Stargaze*. Sabin was assigned to head the project.

Progress on the plane, designated XR-2100, was slow. Work faltered on the wing. Hundreds of designs were tested and discarded. Nothing attempted by the score of engineers working on the project would meet the stringent Stealth design yet support the plane's required payload. The Air Force considered scrapping the program. For the first time in his career Sabin faced failure.

Late one night he went to the wind-tunnel laboratory alone. For hours he pored over computer readouts on the failed wings, checking figures against a small scale mock-up of the XR-2100. The problem lay in the airflow between the wing and the horizontal tail stabilizer. Suddenly, inspired, Sabin removed the wing and stabilizer from the mock-up and transposed them on the fuselage—wing to the rear, stabilizer forward.

He studied the weird configuration. "I wonder . . ."

He pushed the intercom button to the laboratory night duty officer. "This is Colonel Sabin. Have Doctor Van Atton report to the wind tunnel."

"Now, sir?"

"Now!"

They worked through the night, devising and revising designs based on the transposed wings and stabilizer. At dawn Van Atton agreed. "Colonel . . . I think you've done it."

Next day, a wind-tunnel test on a full-scale mock-up confirmed that Sabin's design worked in theory. But would it work in flight?

In November 1977, the prototype XR-2100, callsign *Cobra One*, rolled out of a secreted hangar at Edwards. Observers, restricted to high-ranking officers and civilian engineers, watched as the test pilot emerged from a climate-controlled van that pulled up alongside the plane. By his own decision, the space-suit clad test pilot was Colonel Bartholomew Sabin.

For the first hour Sabin maneuvered *Cobra One* across the sunbaked ancient lake bed that made up the Edwards test strip, taxiing, turning, revving to near takeoff speed then stopping, getting the feel of the controls. At last he pulled to the downwind end of the runway. Suddenly, the massive rocket-jet engine emitted a thunderous roar; seconds later the afterburner ignited. Trailing a sheet of flame behind, *Cobra One* leapt forward along the runway, gained rapid momentum, then lifted effortlessly into the dry desert air.

In the viewing stand an Air Force colonel, a former test pilot and current astronaut, said to a colleague, "That part was easy. But with that bird's configuration, getting it back on the ground in one piece is going to take some doing."

Three minutes later Sabin leveled at 34,000 feet, dipped the nose slightly, passed through Mach-1, then pulled the nose high again. At 80,000 feet above the Pacific, the sky above him an ebony dome, he passed through Mach-3. *Cobra One*'s skin temperature registered 635°F. Still, the plane soared with the grace of an eagle, responding to Sabin's gentle touch as if man and machine were one. As the speed indicator clicked off a mile every two seconds Sabin was elated. The sky—no, *the universe* was his. His creation *lived*, and it exhilarated him.

On the ground a loudspeaker kept observers in tune with Sabin's transmissions. An hour from takeoff he called that he was bringing the plane home. The former test pilot nudged his companion. "Now comes the real test."

Approaching the coastline Sabin slowed to subsonic speed. As he crossed the mountains to Edwards he could see the crash crews strung out along the runway. He lined the nose of the plane with the strip and eased off power. Suddenly, there was a violent shudder. *Cobra One* dipped sharply, then yawed, banging Sabin's head hard against the side of the cockpit. Only his foam-cushioned helmet kept him from being knocked unconscious. Addled, he jammed the throttle forward and sucked oxygen deep into his lungs. He regained control a hundred feet above the ground.

On the second approach the plane went into the same violent maneuver. This time, wary, Sabin pulled out at once.

A voice came over the radio: "Colonel Sabin, this is General Teasdale. What's happening up there?"

"I'm losing stability on approach," Sabin replied to the Air Force Deputy Chief of Staff. "Severe buffeting."

The exchange came through the loudspeakers.

The skeptical astronaut said, "I told you."

General Teasdale said, "Colonel, don't hesitate to eject if that becomes necessary."

Sabin's voice boomed through the speakers: "Negative!"

Sabin considered options. He would not abandon the XR-2100. But what was causing the problem? Rapidly, his mind a computer now, he mulled the wing-stabilizer design. The small swept-wing, although displaced behind the forward stabilizer, had been buoyed sufficiently during takeoff. But at the reduced landing speed it was losing that buoyancy. Why? His mind raced through all he knew about wing design, all he'd learned at the wind-tunnel laboratory. Then—an idea. *Perhaps* . . .

He radioed: "Coming in again."

For the third time *Cobra One* approached the runway. On the ground tension mounted. For some reason Sabin was maintaining air speed. Then, inexplicably, he pulled the plane's nose high into the air. Observers gasped. The astronaut exclaimed, "What the shit?!" Then, understanding, he jumped to his feet. "My God! It just might work!"

Nose high, tail down, *Cobra One* moved through the air belly forward, like a duck flaring for landing on a pond. The nose-high attitude and the increased landing speed forced a steady rush of air beneath the wing. For a full minute the plane seem-

ingly floated forward over the runway at that precarious 45°
angle. Then, ever so gently, it settled and the rear gear touched
down. Observers held their breaths. For a half mile *Cobra One*
rolled in that upright position, then, as if in slow motion, the
nose sank with the grace of a wafting feather, and the main
gear touched down.

Throwing decorum to the winds, the distinguished observers
cheered themselves hoarse.

Three months later the Air Force founded a new test unit to
prepare the XR-2100 for operation. To be homebased in New
Mexico, the unit was designated *Quickseal*. And with the birth
of Quickseal came new glory for Sabin. On his 37th birthday
he was promoted over the heads of 409 more-senior colonels
to the rank of brigadier general. Along with his silver stars he
was given the job of organizing and directing Quickseal.

And it had gone well, Sabin reflected, until Major Peter Crowell
proved unworthy and lost control of the finest aircraft ever
developed.

Now, there was this damnable business with Major Ward.
A nonrated officer. A nonflyer given unjust authority to pass
judgment on a project—on men—he could never understand.

Sabin slammed his fist against his desk. "Damn Burnside!"

He sat back and forced himself to regain control. He had
never allowed emotions to cloud his judgment, he must not
now. Ward was an obstacle, true. But Sabin had dealt with
obstacles before.

And I will deal with this one, he vowed.

Of that he had not the slightest doubt.

10

COBRA TWO stood in the center of the giant hangar like a prized thoroughbred stallion instated in a private stall, majestic, proud. Nothing Ward had heard or read had prepared him for the actual sight of the plane. It was larger than he had envisioned, the size of a DC-9. Its coal-black skin, bearing no identifying numbers or lettering, was pockmarked with millions of tiny pores, machine-etched and precisely spaced, Ward knew, to obliterate incoming radar signals. At the front, behind a wide flat nose that drooped almost to the floor, two horizontal stabilizers gave the awkward-looking craft the appearance of a monstrous hammerhead shark. Near the tail, a thin, unbelievably small swept wing appeared too fragile to support the massive fuselage. Ward was reminded of a World War II plane jokingly referred to as "the flying prostitute." It had no visible means of support.

Lieutenant Colonel Hadley released a hatch at the bottom of the fuselage and motioned to Ward.

Ward climbed the hatch ladder into a maze of dials and gauges. He eased himself into the pilot's seat and looked around the cockpit. Just above his head was a long black box flush-mounted to the ceiling. The box was a maze of coded computer keys. Centered among the keys was a red switch covered by a guard plate. The switch positions were marked PILOT and STAR-GAZE. Ward realized he was looking at the heart of the XR-2100.

The cockpit was cramped. Hadley stood on the ladder with his head protruding through the floor. "It's programmed through that small slot . . . there, on the right." He pointed to *Stargaze*. "You simply feed the program in there and lock it in place. Like the computer on the lunar landing module."

"A tape program?" Ward asked.

"Micro-disc. No larger than a postage stamp. You could inscribe the entire Encyclopedia Britannica on one disc."

"It's done here, in the compound?"

"Yes . . . in the blockhouse."

"For all coordinates . . . the whole globe?"

"Sure. It's not that difficult. We fly missions against mock targets. Dallas is Moscow, for example. Phoenix is Berlin, Denver is Teheran. The flight simulator in the blockhouse can interpolate flight data from those sorties to any point on earth. Accurate within a hundred feet."

Ward gave the cockpit a final look. "I'd like to see *Cobra One*."

The aircraft in the other hangar was a shambles of parts scattered around the football-field-size floor. The wing, in two parts, lay in one corner, the stabilizers in another. The gear and pilot controls in yet another. Only the fuselage remained in one piece. Two long rows of tables bore the disassembled components of the plane—radios, radars, altimeters, gauges, meters, dials. One large table bore the disassembled *Stargaze*.

"The plane was hardly damaged in the crash," Hadley said. "But we broke it down, bolt by bolt, to try to determine what happened."

"You did it all here?"

"Here . . . and the electronic components in the blockhouse, on the flight simulator. If a component works OK on the simulator it works OK on the plane."

"And it all checked out."

"Every item," Hadley confirmed.

High in one corner of the hangar a tiny red light on a TV

camera blinked on, catching Ward's attention. He had noticed the same thing in the other hangar. "I see we're being monitored."

Hadley glanced at the camera. "I, uh . . . guessed we might be."

"Are we being voice recorded too?"

"No. But be warned . . . all the phones are bugged. Loose talk, you know."

They went to the blockhouse next. Several people, civilian and military, men and women, were busy at tables, desks, blackboards, desk-top computers. In the center of the room was a mock-up of the XR-2100 cockpit.

"It's a standard Air Force flight simulator," Hadley explained, "modified for Quickseal. It's controlled by the master computer . . . there. All the flight programs—the discs—are checked here. In effect, we fly all missions here before we fly them in the air."

"And Crowell trained here?"

"Absolutely. The simulator is available twenty-four hours a day. Peter was religious about it."

"Then the problem he encountered . . . whatever it was . . . should have been caught here."

"Yes . . . if it'd been an equipment problem."

A defensive answer, Ward mused. He looked Hadley in the eye. "Colonel, do you truly believe that Peter Crowell, a pilot who you say was religious about his training, simply lost control of that plane?"

Hadley broke off the gaze and fumbled for a cigarette. "It, uh . . . all points to that."

He lit the cigarette nervously. "Would you like to see the simulator in action?"

Ward shook his head. "Maybe later. Right now I'd like to get started with the others. Engineers, maintenance types. I'll need a place to work."

"You can use my office."

"That's not necessary. Just a table and a chair somewhere . . ."

"No. I insist." The colonel led the way back to Building One.

For the next three days, working through the weekend, Ward

interviewed all the people that Hadley had interviewed during the original investigation. He uncovered nothing to refute the colonel's conclusions.

Yet, he reflected the following Monday afternoon in his quarters, there were things that disturbed him. Sabin's attempt at intimidation, for one, followed by the general's absolute cooperation. And Hadley. What was it about the nervous colonel? Antagonistic, even belligerent, at first, then, out of sight of his boss, eager to please, overly helpful. Volunteering information, like the bugged phones—insisting that Ward practically usurp his office. It was not the posture of a man sure of his loyalties.

Still, none of that meant progress.

What next?

He went to the kitchen and got a Coors. He brought it back to his desk and looked at the locked field safe with a dreary sigh. Should he start again from the beginning? What else? He opened the safe and started to pull out the pile of documents when his eye fell on a cassette. Crowell's mayday recording. He pushed the documents aside and grabbed the tape. He inserted it in the recorder on his desk and set the machine to play. A voice came through the speaker: "MAYDAY . . . COBRA ONE . . . STARGAZE MALFUNCTION . . . OUT OF CONTROL . . . MAYDAY . . . MAY . . ."

Ten words, fading on the last one. The only words Ward had ever heard Major Peter Crowell speak.

Ward flipped the recorder to rewind and played the tape again.

"Shit," he said.

Something wasn't jibing. He played it again, this time trying to put everything else out of mind. He had analyzed thousands of tapes and often his ear would pick up something that his conscious mind wouldn't register right off. Some anomaly, at the subliminal level, that would sometimes drive him to distraction. His solution: isolate himself, listen to the tape repeatedly, until whatever it was that was registering on his subconscious would take shape, form, meaning.

Now, he realized, his subconscious was trying to tell him something about the Crowell tape.

He took a swig of beer, reset the recorder and played the ten-word mayday message again. And again. And yet again. On the eleventh playback he heard it.

11

LIEUTENANT Colonel Elwood Hadley lived with his attractive, brunette wife and their gangly teenage son on an elm-shaded street in a secluded section of base housing. Generally reserved for higher-ranking officers, the street was commonly referred to by younger officers and enlisted men as "menopause lane." Aptly descriptive in the case of most residents, it was not so for Elwood and Dee Hadley, both in their mid-thirties. They owed their good fortune in the zealously guarded hierarchy of military housing to a sycophant base commander. Upon learning that the Quickseal unit would be commanded by the Air Force's most publicized hero, the commander decreed that all General Sabin's officers be domiciled one rank above their actual pay scale. Hadley was assigned to full-colonel quarters.

It was a status relished by both Hadleys. For Dee, it meant day-to-day association with ranking wives, the true shakers and movers in the close-knit military social whirl she so dearly loved. For Elwood, it offered backyard camaraderie with senior officers who could foster his career.

And on this Monday afternoon Elwood Hadley's career was very much on his mind.

He sat in his quarters, his fingers entwined around an on-the-rocks martini, his third since arriving home a half hour before. Deep in thought, he stared at the drink, oblivious to his wife's running dialogue from the opposite chair.

"It was a shameless display," Dee Hadley was saying, "right there in the airport lobby . . . in front of God and everybody. She actually kissed him. Not a simple buss on the cheek either, from what I hear. The general wouldn't even take her to the plane. Beth Quartermaine has it on the best authority that she's leaving him for good. Beth says it has been coming on for years. The Quartermaines were stationed with the Burnsides in Iceland, you know. Beth says that Eileen and MacWatt were lovers then. It started in Japan . . . that's where they met and first got it on, during the Korean War . . . just before she married the general. Beth says she heard that MacWatt actually introduced them. Beth says that Eileen recognized a rising star and hitched her wagon to it quick. That didn't stop the affair though. She and MacWatt kept a room at one of the small inns in Fukuoka. Can you *imagine?* Around all those foreigners, too."

Hadley continued to stare at his drink.

"Elwood . . . you're not listening."

"Huh? Oh, I'm sorry . . . what did you say?"

"I said, Can you imagine?"

"Imagine what?"

Dee Hadley frowned in exasperation. "What Beth Quartermaine said . . . about Colonel MacWatt and Eileen Burnside being longtime lovers and all."

"Oh, crap, Dee!" Hadley made an angry gesture, sloshing some of his drink on the rug. "No, I can't imagine it. And I don't believe it. Colonel MacWatt's not that sort. Even if he was, Mrs. Burnside isn't. She's a decent and generous lady— everything, in fact, that Beth Quartermaine is not. You must quit listening to all that absurd Wives Club rot."

His vehemence startled her. What *had* gotten into him lately? This wasn't the first time recently that he'd flown off the handle at something she said. It wasn't like him. He used to be so easygoing. So . . . manageable.

She got up and got the pitcher from the bar.

"Well . . ."—she refilled their glasses—"Beth Quartermaine has little call to criticize anyone. The *way* she carries on around Bartholomew Sabin. Like a bitch in heat. Honestly, I do believe she would drop her pants in the middle of the club ballroom if he asked her to." She breathed a deep sigh. "Of course . . . a lot of wives have the hots for Bart Sabin . . ."

"Do you?"

"Huh . . . do I what?"

"Have the hots for General Sabin?"

"Oh . . . Elwood!"

She thought it best to change the subject. She replaced the pitcher on the bar and sat down. "I wasn't going to bring this up until after dinner . . . but Dickie's in trouble again at school. He's been hanging out with that Wilson boy, and the Narc reported them for smoking pot in the locker room. It'll probably mean another suspension . . . unless you can reason with his counselor again. And you'll just *have* to talk to Dickie tonight. He won't listen to a word I say."

Silence again.

"Elwood . . . did you hear?"

"What?"

"Dickie's in trouble at school."

"Well for Christ's sake why didn't you tell me?"

"I *did* tell you," she reproached him. "Just now."

She waited.

"Elwood . . . what *is* the matter?"

He downed the remainder of his martini and stood. "Hon . . . I, uh, have to go back to the office for a while. Don't count on me for dinner. I'll get a bite at the club."

"Elwood . . ."

He bent and kissed her on the forehead. "I'm sorry. I might be late."

He drove to the nearest guard gate and dialed a number. No answer. He pulled out onto Gibson Boulevard and drove to the east side of the base and parked in front of a sprawling building with a sign above the entrance that read: OFFICERS OPEN MESS. He looked at his watch. 7:10. The club would be crowded. Perhaps that was best. He entered the foyer and walked straight to the bar. The darkened room was packed with younger officers, their wives, girl friends, all trying to converse above the ear-rending beat of a rock trio performing on a rear dais. Hadley waited for his eyes to adjust then looked around. He didn't see who he was looking for. He went past the bar to the dining room. Most of the tables in the spacious overlighted room were occupied. He spotted Major Ward sitting alone at a table near the decorative water fountain in the center of the room.

Ward sipped a draft beer and studied the menu.

"May I, uh, join you?"

Ward looked up, surprised to see Hadley. Ward motioned to a chair.

Hadley sat down and rummaged for a cigarette. "I think we should talk."

"Oh?"

The colonel lit up and glanced around the room furtively. "Not here. Look . . . could we . . ." Suddenly his face drained of color. Ward followed his gaze and saw that General Sabin had just entered the dining room. The general was walking toward them.

Hadley stubbed the cigarette. "Oh, Christ!" It was a cry of despair.

Sabin stopped at the table and Hadley stood up. Ward rose too. Sabin glanced from one to the other curiously. "I thought you didn't like dining at the club, Colonel."

"Sir . . . I was . . ."

"I phoned him," Ward said. "There're things about his report I need to discuss."

"I see," Sabin said. "Do you think this is the proper place to discuss such matters, Major?"

"No, sir. We were just getting ready to go to my quarters."

After a long moment Sabin nodded. "Very well." He left.

They sat back down. Hadley took a deep breath. "Jesus . . . thanks, Major."

"Don't mention it." Ward finished his beer. "Shall we go?"

In the parking lot Hadley eyed Ward's staff car hesitantly. "Where did you get it?"

"Colonel MacWatt assigned it to me."

"No . . . no, let's take mine."

Good God, Ward thought, he thinks the car's bugged. He said, "Whatever you say."

Hadley drove. Ward sat in silence, waiting. After a couple of miles Hadley said, "I'm no fool, you know. I've been fooled, maybe. But there's a difference."

"I'm not sure I know what you mean."

"About Crowell. Hell, everyone knows that if there's no

equipment failure found after a crash you check out the pilot thoroughly. Even General Sabin wanted that . . . *demanded it* . . . at first."

"At first?"

Hadley paused. "Look, don't get me wrong. He's the best officer I've ever served under. With Sabin what you see is what you get. He's self-assured . . . maybe self-righteous. But he's fair . . . firm, but fair. Ironclad control. But that night at the command post on Johnston Island, when *Cobra One* went down . . . well, he flipped. Blew his stack. That plane was his brainchild. He designed it, was the first to fly it. He trained Crowell and me . . . did you know that?"

"No, I didn't."

"At Edwards. No one could have done it better. He picked us out of forty pilots he tested. He made Crowell chief pilot. By rank it should have been me. But I'm not bitter. Crowell was the better pilot. I know that. Sabin did too. He thought the sun rose and set on Peter Crowell. Until that night. Then his attitude changed . . . but fast. After it was certain that *Cobra One* was down Sabin flew into a rage. There was absolutely no way the problem could be with the plane . . . *his* baby. The fault *had* to be Crowell's. He appointed me investigating officer on the spot. Ordered me to tear Crowell's life apart . . . said everyone knew he was having personal problems anyway. I could bring in the OSI if necessary. I got the message. He didn't come right out and say it, but I understood. I was to bring in a report putting full bame on Peter."

"And you did."

"Yes . . . but without a proper investigation to back it up."

"No argument. But why the hell did you do it, if Sabin gave you free rein?"

They were driving near the flight line. Hadley waited until the takeoff roar from a C-141 subsided. "After we returned from Johnston Island to Kirtland, Sabin called me to his office. General Burnside's tech advisor was there . . ."

"Coffman?"

"Yes . . . Coffman. They had the crash evaluation report showing there was no problem with the plane. Sabin told me there was no use expanding the investigation . . . to just wrap it up based on the crash eval report and find pilot error."

"He *ordered* you to find pilot error?"

"Ordered . . . suggested . . . what's the difference? I knew what he meant."

"Dammit, Colonel . . . command interference in an official investigation is a serious offense. You had Sabin by the balls."

"Ha!" Hadley snorted. "No one . . . and I mean *no one*—gets General Bartholomew Sabin by the balls. You might keep that in mind, Major."

He let the point sink in.

"Besides," he continued, "who was my witness? Coffman? That's a laugh. Anyway, his presence made it pretty damned obvious that General Burnside wanted things expedited too. I almost had a hemorrhage when Burnside rejected my report."

He began to whine. "Christ . . . now I'm caught between two hard-nosed generals, both of them pissed off at me. It's not fair. I tried to do what was right . . . what was expected of me. Now what's going to happen to me?"

Ward had no answer.

They drove in silence. After a while, his voice a plea, Hadley said, "Look . . . the Air Force is all I know. I'm not an academy grad, like Sabin. Or an engineer, like you. I'm a line pilot. That's all I've ever been. At my age I wouldn't have a snowball's-chance-in-hell on the outside." He took out a cigarette and pushed in the car lighter. "What I'm trying to say . . . I've got ony two years 'til retirement. If there's anything I can do to set things straight . . . to help General Burnside. Well . . . you know what I mean."

Ward knew what he meant. Scared shitless of both generals, not knowing which would eventually emerge on top, Hadley was trying to stake out a position on both sides of the fence.

"Did you try to reason with Sabin?" Ward asked.

Hadley raised the lighter to his cigarette. In the darkness the red glow gave an eerie hue to the colonel's distressed face. "I told him that the final report might look better if I interviewed at least a couple of people involved in Crowell's personal life. Sabin shot it down. Said it would jeopardize Quickseal."

Sabin's stock warning, Ward mused. "But what's his point? Why all the goddamned rush to get the investigation completed?"

"That's pretty obvious. He's determined to get *Cobra Two* into the Middle East quick. To vindicate his pet project. It's an obsession. He simply can't face failure. As long as the investigation is ongoing there's a possibility that the plane's airworthiness could be questioned anew. He can't stand the thought of that possibility, however remote."

"So . . . you went along."

"Yes."

"Even though it puts *your* life on the line . . . if there *is* something wrong with the plane?"

"Major . . . there's nothing wrong with that plane!"

It was the only point on which Hadley had not vacillated and by now Ward was convinced that the colonel sincerely believed it.

Ward thought over Hadley's revelations. "What did Sabin mean about everyone knowing that Crowell was having personal problems?"

"His wife. Crowell moved back on base—alone—several weeks before we went to the Pacific. He wouldn't talk about it. But I could tell that it was eating him. I suppose Sabin could too. He should have pulled Crowell off as chief pilot right then. But he didn't."

And *that*, Ward mused, was the fatal error. He wondered if he should mention Crowell's mayday recording? He decided not.

He said, "Crowell's records show that he lived near here somewhere."

"In the Jemez Mountains. Are you, uh . . . thinking about going there?"

"What else? I'm getting nowhere fast sticking around here. Besides, you were well acquainted with Crowell. If I read you correctly you're pretty positive that something in his private life may have affected his performance of duty. That leaves me little choice."

"I, uh, guess not. But, look . . . it's your idea. OK?"

"Sure," Ward said reassuringly. "It's my idea."

They drove back to the club. Ward stood for a moment watching Hadley drive away. Strange man, strange conversation.

He started for his car then noticed a gnawing sensation in his stomach. *Hell, I haven't eaten.*

He turned and went back into the club.

12

AS she did each morning, Janet Crowell stirred awake just as the sun's first lemon rays began to probe the sky above perennially snowcapped Old Baldy Peak. She had gotten into the habit of early rising as a young girl, when she first moved with her parents to Tres Pinos. There were always chores to be performed on the 600-acre ranch, minuscule as it was by New Mexico standards. There was stock to tend, hay to be hoisted to the barn loft, fences to be mended, stalls to be cleaned. During the early years her father and two hired hands did most of the hard work. Then, as his experiments, and the growing demands for his expertise, kept him away from home more and more, the responsibility for the ranch fell upon Janet and her mother. After her mother's untimely death, many of the ranch functions that once-vicacious lady had cherished were simply disbanded. The hired hands were dismissed. Still, there was much to do, and Janet insisted on doing her part. Even later, during her years at the university, she chose to live at home, rising each morning in time to do her share of the work before driving seventy miles into Albuquerque to attend classes. She loved Tres Pinos that much.

On this morning she lay for a long while looking out her

bedroom window. A dense sea of mighty pines, blue spruce, and gold-leaf aspens spread beyond sight across the craggy hill-side bordering Tres Pinos' broad grassy meadows. Since she first looked upon the scene from that window twenty years before, on her seventh birthday, it had remained her favorite view.

She kicked back the covers and stood. When she dropped her gown she caught a glimpse of herself in the mirror. She was a tall girl, with a slender, sensuous body. A body that should have pleased any man, she thought with a wrench of her heart. Instinctively, she looked at the photograph on her dresser. A silver-framed likeness of a handsome young man in uniform smiled back at her. "Oh, Peter . . . Peter . . ." she moaned. "Why . . . ?"

From her bathroom she heard stirrings downstairs. She finished washing, gave her frizzled, golden hair a quick swipe with a brush, then dressed in faded jeans, a long-sleeve denim shirt, scuffed western boots. When she got down to the kitchen her father, in pajamas and robe, was sitting at the table thumbing through last night's *Albuquerque Tribune*. He had started the coffee. It was the only thing he was reasonably good at in the kitchen.

She kissed him lovingly on the cheek. "Morning, Dad. Eggs?"

"Fine," James Moslin replied.

She studied him silently while she cooked. He had aged so much lately. His hair was grayer, the lines in his face more deeply etched. After all these years he still missed mother terribly. She thought of Peter again and wondered if it would be that way with her?

She set his plate before him. He laid the paper aside and began to eat. "Have you given any further thought to that call last night . . . from, what was his name again?"

She poured coffee for both of them and stirred milk into hers. "Major Ward. Yes . . . I think I'll meet him."

He buttered a piece of toast. "I just hope you're doing the right thing. Sometimes it's best to let sleeping dogs lie."

"I know. At first I was doubtful. I thought all this dreadful business about Peter was settled. But Major Ward says there're still some unresolved questions. If they're about Peter . . . if there's *anything* that could help me understand . . ." Her voice broke off.

He put a hand atop hers. "All right. It's just that I don't want to see you hurt more."

She squeezed his hand. "I know. But . . . I don't think there's much more that can hurt me now."

He ate a moment in silence. "Is he coming here?"

"No. I have to run into town anyway. I might be late."

"You'll be here for dinner?"

She gave him a wry look. "Who's cooking?"

"Father Dan," he said triumphantly.

She smiled. "Then I'll make it a point to be here."

He returned her smile with a heavy heart. He loved her deeply and was glad for the exchange about Father Dan. He was grateful for anything these days that brought a smile to his daughter's face.

On this sun-drenched autumn day most of the luncheon crowd at the Albuquerque Hilton had forgone the inside dining areas in favor of the large outdoor courtyard enclosed by the hotel's sprawling, fortresslike structure. They sat at umbrella-canopied tables situated at random around an astroturfed patio. Noonday conversations were accented by the hurried comings and goings of brightly uniformed waiters and waitresses bearing food and drink.

Jonathan Ward had taken a table near the pool. He looked at his watch. Mrs. Crowell had left things hanging. But if she was going to show up she should be doing it soon.

At a nearby table a young man in his late teens or early twenties rose to leave. He leaned down and kissed the cheek of an older woman he had dined with. His mother, Ward guessed. He remembered once, years before, seeing one of his boyhood friends kiss his mother. A volunteer gesture, of the boy's own volition. Why? Ward had wondered on that occasion. He wondered the same now, but, with the knowledge of passing years, understood that his attitude revealed far more about him than it did about his boyhood friend, or the young man at the next table.

He put the thought out of mind.

Several people were swimming in the pool or sunbathing alongside. Ward's attention was drawn to one dark-haired, coppertoned girl stretched out on her stomach on a striped beach towel. She had loosened the strap of her bikini bra and her breast was visible almost to the areola. There was something familiar about the girl. An image that brought him pleasure—and pain.

Susan.

He had first seen her, too, he recalled, beside a swimming pool, one Saturday afternoon shortly after she moved into her apartment above his in Suitland, Maryland. They had struck up a conversation; he learned that she had a thirteen-year-old son, was separated from her husband, was enchantingly lovely. The following evening he invited her to one of the endless series of parties that punctuated the social life of the singles group that made up the bulk of the tenants. In quick succession they became friends, dates—lovers.

The physical initiative had been Susan's. One evening, at another of the parties, she stood, took his hand and said, "Come with me."

She led him outside to a large floral garden bordered by giant spiraea bushes. She ducked low and pushed aside the draping branches of one of the shrubs and beckoned him to follow. She stripped to the buff and helped him do the same. And there, on the softened ground beneath that flowering canopy, with the sounds of their friends' gaiety in the offing, they made love for the first time. It was audacious. Crazy. Mind-blowing. And because of that, all the more pleasurable.

Thereafter they held their trysts in his apartment. And it was there, one afternoon, that an unsettling thing happened.

They were making love. In a moment of intense fervor Ward felt Susan's body stiffen. He opened his eyes to see her staring up at him fearfully. Losing his ardor he rolled to one side. "What . . . ?"

She sat up on the side of the bed and began to put on her clothing. "I . . . don't know . . ." Her voice wavered. "You got . . . you weren't making love, Jon. You were . . . doing battle."

It was the only explanation she could give. And she refused to see him for several days. When at last she did, and they entered lovemaking again, timidly at first, then with abandon, the image of that puzzling afternoon was always in his mind. He performed. It was good. But it was never again great. Never again the same.

He was poor at introspection. But afterward, when recalling

that experience, he wondered what the hell had gone wrong? He had had many women. Far more than most men, he realized without braggadocio. Yet most of the others—no, *all the others*, he realized with a start, never having focused on it before— had been one night stands. Once they had satisfied his passion they became objects of scorn. The quicker he got them out of his bed . . . out of his life . . . the better.

Except for Susan. With her he had attempted a sustained relationship. And it had been working. Or so he thought, until that morning a few days ago when she broke the news about her husband wanting a reconciliation. Even then she made it clear that she was Ward's—if he wanted her enough to marry her. And he had panicked.

A sustained relationship? He laughed without mirth. He wondered if he was capable?

He glanced up at the double glass doors leading from the hotel lobby out onto the courtyard. A hostess was pointing to his table. A slender blonde woman dressed in denims and rawhide boots nodded thanks to the hostess and started toward him. Ward put his reflections aside and stood so the woman would see his uniform.

She stopped at the table. "Major Ward?"

"Yes. Please sit down, Mrs. Crowell."

He had expected an older woman. Someone nearer her husband's age, mid-thirties perhaps. This woman was in her late twenties at the oldest. She was attractive, in a windblown sort of way. Her honey-blonde hair was tied in an unkempt ponytail. Her face was devoid of makeup. Her lips were chapped. Her nails, at the end of slender, well-tapered hands, were unevenly filed. All that, plus her seedy attire, gave her the appearance of one who was unconcerned with her looks.

"I wasn't sure you'd come," he said.

"Neither was I. Your call was . . . well, quite unexpected. I thought everything had been settled. Now . . . frankly, I'm curious."

He tried to keep the conversation low-key. Briefly, he explained the circumstances of the renewed investigation and his role in it. She listened with interest. "There are still some unanswered questions," he said at last. "I'm afraid they center on Major Crowell."

"In what way?"

"On whether he should have been flying the mission that night."

"I . . . don't understand. Peter was an excellent pilot. You surely must know that from his record. Anyway, what he did or didn't do on duty was none of my affair. I don't see how I can help."

He wondered how to approach the next subject. Something in her demeanor, in her manner of speaking, revealed a vulnerability that belied her hardened appearance. It also revealed a deep-seated tension gnawing at her being.

Ward said, "Look . . . have you eaten? I'm starved."

She shook her head. "I'm not hungry. But please, order for yourself. Maybe I'll take a drink . . . a Bloody Mary."

He ordered chicken salad and a draft beer for himself and a Bloody Mary for her. When the waiter left, Ward said, "I should forewarn you . . . some of my questions are of a personal nature. Of course, you're under no obligation. But I hope you understand, there's a lot at stake."

She got a quizzical expression on her face. "Personal nature?"

He might as well get it out in the open. "Mrs. Crowell, an officer who worked closely with your husband has raised the question of his state of mind in the days preceding the crash. This officer believes that Major Crowell suffered from depression severe enough to have affected his performance of duty. He has suggested that the depression stemmed from something in the major's personal life. Now, whether this officer is right or wrong, I don't know. But if there is the slightest possibility that he's right, it could help determine the cause of the crash once and for all."

She was silent for a long moment. "Major, you say that there is a lot at stake. Are you free to tell me what?"

"At the very least, a general officer's judgment in not grounding your husband. At the worst—the life of another pilot."

The waiter brought their order.

She stirred the Bloody Mary with the celery-stalk swizzle. "I couldn't bear the thought of another person dying if something I might say could prevent it."

"Then you'll help?"

"I'm not sure I can. But, yes . . . I'll try." She took a sip of her drink. "What is it you want to know?"

Rapport.

Ward smiled his thanks. He picked up his fork. "Do you mind?"

"Please . . . go ahead."

He started his lunch. The chicken was delicious, the lettuce fresh and crisp. He wondered where the hell they got fresh lettuce in this desert? "Mrs. Crowell, do you know of anything that may have been preying on your husband's mind?"

"I, uh, don't know. Perhaps . . . I'm not sure where to start."

"Wherever you like. Take your time."

She took a breath as if to gain composure. "Peter and I were married right after I graduated from the university. He was stationed at Kirtland. The following summer—that was four years ago—Peter was transferred to Alaska. We lived in Anchorage."

"Do you know what Peter did there?"

"No. He never talked about his work."

Ward knew. Crowell had flown covert photo-mapping overflights of Soviet naval facilities in the Far East.

Janet Crowell continued: "After two years Peter was reassigned to Kirtland, to a unit called Quicksilver . . ."

Ward didn't correct her. It wasn't important.

"We decided not to live on base this time. We'd been having . . . some problems." She didn't elucidate. "We moved to Tres Pinos."

"Tres Pinos?"

"My family home in the Jemez Mountains . . . a small ranch. Tres Pinos is Spanish for *Three Pines.* Peter and I thought we could work things out there . . . away from the base gossip mills. Peter loved the ranch. He was a California boy, but he preferred New Mexico—the high country, even talked about us living at Tres Pinos when he retired. But his enthusiasm didn't last. Isolation wasn't the answer. He grew moodier each day. One morning he just moved out. He went back to Kirtland."

"A permanent separation?"

She shook her head. "I don't think he really wanted that. He came back most weekends. I could tell he was still interested in our marriage . . . in me. But he was . . . cold. In the final two months before he left for the Pacific he seemed to be living deep within himself. He spent most of the time at Tres Pinos helping my father with chores. In a way I was glad that he was going away for a while. I thought it might help us both. Instead . . . he went off and died."

Her hazel eyes misted and she took a large drink from the Bloody Mary. "I was shattered. I couldn't help feeling that somehow I was responsible . . . that somehow I'd failed him."

So far she had described only the tip of the iceberg. Ward wondered if she was, perhaps unconsciously, being protective of her husband's memory. He had to smoke out the issue, whatever it was. "Mrs. Crowell, was there another woman in your husband's life?"

"No," she replied evenly. "I would have known."

"Was he drinking . . . , on drugs?"

She gave a derisive laugh and shook her head.

"Was he ill?"

She didn't answer this one as quickly. "Not in any way you might mean."

"I don't understand."

She was clutching her drink so tightly that her fingers appeared bloodless. He sensed that her openness thus far to him— a total stranger—was symptomatic. She was craving to speak of these things, to talk through the burden. Perhaps in an effort to understand it, to bear it. "Mrs. Crowell . . . would you like to go somewhere more private?"

She shook her head. "The first part of our marriage was wonderful I want you to know that we took so much pleasure in each other went everywhere did everything together then after those first two fantastic years . . ."

It spewed out in rapid-fire staccato, an anguished torrent of words. Suddenly, she caught herself. She looked up, embarrassed. "I'm . . . sorry."

He was torn by mixed emotions. She was withdrawing into herself just when she was on the verge of getting to the heart of the matter. But her guard was down. She was vulnerable. Now he must take advantage of that vulnerability while it lasted. He felt a sense of disgust. But he had no choice. He gave her an encouraging smile. "Please—after those first two fantastic years?"

She looked at him, not unwarmly, but without returning the smile. Then, more composed, she said, "After we'd been in Alaska for several months, Peter decided that we should have a child. He loved children, wanted so much to be a father. His own father died when Peter was a boy . . ."

Ward felt an empathic pang of remorse.

"I was overjoyed at the prospects of a baby, of course." She said it as if every woman in the world would have felt the same. "We planned it so carefully. Peter made charts of the best times, that sort of thing. He even bought a book of names to choose from.

"After a few months, when I didn't get pregnant, he began to tease me for being barren. He tried to make a joke of it, but I could tell he was anxious. I detest going to doctors. But I did . . . a specialist in Anchorage. He told me there was nothing wrong with me. He suggested that Peter come in for an examination.

"Peter was appalled. Said the fault *had* to be mine. He grew angry, accused me of staying on the pill behind his back. I'd never seen this side of his nature. It was if I had become a threat to his manhood. After that, things just went downhill for us. I tried to keep our relationship alive. Tried to . . . initiate things. But that only made him angrier. After a while, he simply lost all interest."

"You mean he was impotent?"

She nodded. "And that's how things stood when we came home."

Sterility and impotence. Now Ward understood her earlier reluctance. Even though her husband was dead, she had wanted to shield him from this revelation.

After a while Ward said, "Do you know much of your husband's life before you were married?"

"Only what he told me. His father was a minister. After he died Peter lived with his mother until he went into the Air Force, right after college. His mother died when he was in Vietnam."

"Did he ever speak of the war?"

"Not to me. He did with my father. They were there together, you know. That's how I met Peter, when he came to Tres Pinos to visit Dad."

Ward didn't know. "Your father was a military man?"

"No . . . a professor. At least he was, before he started private experiments. He's a horticulturist."

Horticulture? Ward thought. *In Nam?*

"Did your father approve of your marriage?"

"Very much so. He was heartsick when Peter and I returned from Alaska so down with each other. I tried to spare Dad's feelings, but one night I broke into tears and told him everything. He was terribly distressed . . . couldn't even discuss it further. He left the room crying. I was unprepared for that. We've never talked about it since."

She stared unseeing at the empty glass she still clutched in her hands, her thoughts on the visions in her mind.

Ward was intrigued. Here was a new facet in Major Peter Crowell's life, perhaps in the course of the investigation. "Mrs. Crowell . . . do you think your father would talk to me about your husband?"

She looked up. "Dad? I . . . don't know. It's difficult for him to talk about Peter, even to me."

Ward insisted. "I think it's worth a try."

She thought a moment. "What time is it now?"

He looked at his watch. "One-ten."

"I have a couple of more errands to run. I could meet you here at two-thirty and you could follow me home. No promises though." She eyed his uniform. "You'll need more than that blouse. It gets cold in the mountains."

He drove back to his quarters and taped his recollection of the meeting while it was still fresh in his mind. He locked the tape in the safe, then went to his bedroom, hung his blouse in the closet and grabbed his heavy wool uniform sweater and zip-up jacket. He was at his car when he thought of MacWatt.

He went back inside and dialed MacWatt's office.

"The colonel has stepped out for a while," Ann Lucero answered. "Would you like for me to page him?"

"No," Ward replied. "Just tell him that I've talked with Mrs. Crowell and am on my way to talk with her father. I'll report in when I get back."

"I'll see that he gets the message."

Ward hung up. He sat by the phone for a moment, wondering if he was off on a wild goose chase?

Then he remembered the mayday tape.

He left to meet Janet Crowell at the Hilton.

13

MAJOR General Burnside shoved the letter across his desk to his deputy. "Special courier at noon—marked 'eyes only.'"

Colonel MacWatt noted the imprint beneath the official Air Force seal at the top of the stationery: *Office of the Chief of Staff.*

MacWatt read:

Major General Louis Burnside
Cmdr, AFRTC
KAFB, NM 87115

Dear Lou:

As you know, in three weeks I will be sending the President a list of brigadiers I am recommending for promotion to major general. I've received a lot of pressure from some Moguls on the hill who want Bart Sabin's name on that list. The cheerleading is superfluous because I've always considered him one of our finest officers. All of which, quite frankly, prompts this letter.

I have just taken another look at your latest efficiency report on Sabin. Your special categories support my opinion of him. But I detect a certain reticence in your subjective evaluation. It's nothing I can put my finger on, but

I know you well enough to suspect that something is bothering you about this officer.

Lou, you've been closer to Bart Sabin these past two years than anyone else in a command position. If there's something I should know about him that isn't in his records please let me know at once. Of course, it will remain between you and me.

By the way, if your decision to postpone your retirement means you're staying on board indefinitely it will mean a third star. And I intend to fly to Kirtland to do the honors myself.

My love to Eileen.

Best regards,

Walter G. McCollum
Chief of Staff
United States Air Force

The penned signature above the typed name read simply "Gip." At the bottom of the letter, in the same handwriting, was added: "PS: I will expect to hear from you within the week."

MacWatt laid the letter back on Burnside's desk without comment.

Burnside rose and stood beside the large blue flag with two silver stars denoting his rank and peered out the window at distant Mount Taylor. "Mac . . . am I that damned obvious?"

"No," MacWatt replied. "I've detected it, but I've known you a long time. So has Gip McCollum. But it's not obvious."

Burnside returned to his chair. He massaged his left arm a moment then picked up the letter: "This is a man's career, Mac . . . his life. And not just *any* man. Hell, Bart Sabin's not my cup of tea on the social circuit, but that has nothing to do with his professional competence."

"No sir."

Ann Lucero entered with coffee. She gave one cup, black, to Burnside and set the other, creamed and sugared, beside MacWatt.

Burnside pulled a bottle from his desk drawer and laced his

coffee. MacWatt had never seen him do that on duty before. Burnside offered the bottle. "Sorry, bourbon's all I've got."

MacWatt made a face and declined.

Burnside took a swallow of the spiked coffee and sat back. "Mac . . . no holds barred . . . what's your gut feeling about Bart Sabin?"

"Is this talk to be general to colonel, or Lou to Mac?"

Burnside chortled. "I've never known it to make a hell of a lot of difference . . . but, Lou to Mac."

MacWatt took a swig of coffee and shifted heavily in the deep leather chair. "Bart Sabin is brilliant, arrogant, humorless, dedicated to his profession. He inspires great devotion or great hatred. He's one of the most martial-minded officers I've ever known. I don't like him. Nonetheless, he *is* a shaker and mover. In another era I could see him as a field marshal."

" 'Field marshal' is disturbing."

"It wasn't meant to be flattering."

Burnside sat in thought.

MacWatt asked, "And your gut feelings?"

Burnside said, "I see Sabin as ambitious, fearless, a hell-for-leather combat officer. He's an authoritarian, a ruthless decision maker, extremely confident of his superior wisdom. He's fiercely competitive but just as fiercely disciplined. And he won't demand anything of a subordinate that he won't undertake himself. There's not more than one in ten thousand officers with those qualities."

"Then what's the rub?" MacWatt asked.

"Yes," Burnside repeated thoughtfully, "what is the rub?"

Burnside's countenance turned wistful. "I guess it's a sign of growing old, but lately I've been doing a lot of thinking about the past. The flag's gone up and down the pole many times since that night in Itazuke when you saved my butt from a midnight swim in the Korea Strait. Remember?"

"I remember a lot of things about Itazuke, Lou."

"Those were the golden years, Mac. We'd whipped the Huns and the Japs. We were standing tough to the Reds in Korea. We were on the side of the angels. We could wear the uniform into any bar from Maine to California and be treated to drinks."

The wistful look faded. "Well, that's gone now. Nam turned the dream into a nightmare. But there's a disturbing new mood in the country, a backlash to the nightmare. There are people in positions of power—political mossbacks, perhaps—who look upon Nam as a failure of will. In their view, the loss of the war, the pardoning of the draft dodgers, the Panama Canal Treaty, the current fiasco in Iran—just to name a few—are all the handiwork of the same gutless ilk.

"Now, what's all this got to do with Bart Sabin?" He pointed to McCollum's letter. "Gip mentions the pressure he's getting to promote Sabin. Well, I happen to know it's not just Sabin. And it's not just happening in the Air Force. Across the board, Young Turks, military and civilian, are being eased into positions of authority while more moderate officers are being eased out. Gip says I'm due for a third star. That means a kick upstairs. That'll put Bart Sabin here"—he slapped the arms of his chair with force—"in this chair. And *that*, Mac, is the rub. Bart Sabin, riding herd not only on Quickseal, but on Blue Bonnet, Straw Man, Pony Boy—all the rest. The most advanced and destructive weapons systems being developed. *What is it* about that that disturbs me so?"

It was not a rhetorical question. It was a plea for help.

"Perhaps," MacWatt suggested, "it's because you know the difference between a mossback and a Nazi."

Burnside pursed his lips. "Ah . . . the field marshal analogy again."

"No holds barred . . . remember?"

"Yes . . . as long as it doesn't get out of this room."

Burnside let out a weary sigh. "I sure didn't need this on top of . . . everything else. How's the *Cobra One* thing progressing, by the way?"

"Major Ward called in. He talked today with Crowell's wife. He's on the way now to interview her father."

"Professor Moslin," Burnside commented.

"I don't know why," MacWatt said, "but Ward seems to be trying different angles."

Burnside was pleased. "It's a hopeful sign, Mac . . . a hopeful sign. Anything will be better than that ridiculous Hadley report. I intend to have further words with the good colonel once this is settled."

And *that*, MacWatt knew, meant that Lieutenant Colonel Elwood Hadley's days in uniform were numbered.

Burnside picked up McCollum's letter. "You know, Ike had

conflicting emotions about Patton. Remember: *'If you've got to go, you want Patton leading the way. But you never want Patton deciding whether or not you've got to go'?'*

MacWatt smiled and nodded. Burnside had misquoted. It wasn't Ike's assessment of Patton, it was John Kennedy's assessment of General Curtis LeMay. MacWatt let it stand.

"Perhaps it boils down to that," Burnside said. "Like them or not, agree with their philosophy or not, we need the Sabins . . . just in case we have to go."

"Perhaps."

Burnside swiveled in his chair and locked the McCollum letter in his safe. "Well . . . the monkey's on my back, and I'll have to make a decision one way or the other, soon." He kneaded his left arm again.

"You keep doing that, Lou . . . you feeling all right?"

"Doing what?"

"Rubbing your arm."

"Oh . . . no . . . I feel fine. I just slept on it wrong."

He stood and stretched his lanky frame then stepped across the office to the washroom. "Mac," he called back through the open door, "it's been a long day. How about letting an old buddy stand for drinks at the club? Glenlivet . . . for old time's sake."

"You're on," MacWatt called back.

Burnside took the pill case from the medicine chest and swallowed two red capsules with water.

"What do you hear from Eileen?" MacWatt asked.

Burnside stepped out of the washroom. "I expect her to call tonight. God . . . I miss her." He took his coat down from the rack and there was a faraway look in his eyes. "You know . . . I couldn't have made it without Eileen. I love her so much . . . I've never been able to put it in the right words to her. But, even now . . . after all these years, I . . ."

Suddenly he looked over at MacWatt and reddened. "Well, for God's sake . . . how about that, Mac? Getting mushy at my age." He slipped his coat on. "You ready?"

MacWatt pushed himself out of the chair. "I'm ready. And Lou . . ."

"Yes?"

"The drinks are on me."

14

THE woman emitted a gutteral cry and dug her fingers deeper into the man's shoulders. For the second time in five minutes her pretty face contorted, her body convulsed. "Oh-h-h-h . . ."

Willing himself free from superhuman control the man permitted himself release.

Chests heaving, bodies gleaming with perspiration, they lay side by side on the wide bed.

How can there be such happiness? Ann Lucero wondered. She mouthed a silent prayer of thanks to Eros, the god of love. *Madre de Dios . . . forgive me!*

Hastily she prayed again, begging forgiveness for praising a false god. She crossed herself. Had she committed a mortal sin? Venial? She decided to worry about that later. She turned on her side and laid her head on the man's broad shoulder. "That was marvelous. I'm so . . . happy."

"And I am happy," Bartholomew Sabin replied.

As she had so often during the past weeks Ann wondered anew what angel of destiny had brought this golden man to her arms? Even now, lying nude beside him, she flushed recalling the fantasies the first sight of him had evoked in her mind that day he reported for duty at Kirtland, two years before. Two years during which he had been so near, and yet so far.

General Bartholomew Sabin, desired by every woman she knew, yet, to her knowledge, possessed by none. On his visits to General Burnside's office his rare exchanges with her had been crisply businesslike. She realized that he thought of her—if he thought of her at all—as an efficient civil servant. Nothing more.

Then, barely a month ago, he stopped at her desk and complimented her on a new dress she was wearing for the first time that day. Flustered, she made some inane reply about over-indulging herself. He smiled—it would have melted the heart of a Celtic witch—and they continued to chat. Astonishingly, he asked her if she were free for dinner that night.

"Why . . . yes," she lied (for she was quite popular) and made a mental note to conjure up some story to tell her previous date for that evening. She agreed that Sabin should pick her up at her apartment at seven.

They dined at the Officers Club. He was gallant, solicitous, witty—charming characteristics that belied his formidable reputation. They ended that first evening in her apartment—in this very bed—and he had kindled emotions in her that she never knew existed.

Why her? From all the women he could have had?

She asked him about that once, after one of their frequent assignations. He grew reflective. He admitted (she thought without vanity) that he recognized the affect he had on women. But there was no depth to most women he knew. He desired a woman of intelligence—a woman with whom he could be intellectually, as well as physically, compatible. Then, too, his position dictated discretion.

On that occasion he had lifted her hand and kissed it. "All that, I found in you."

She was deeply flattered.

But on this late afternoon her thoughts were not on the intellectual aspect of their relationship. She raised on one elbow and gazed upon the full length of his body. It was the most magnificent male physique she'd ever seen. Muscle and bronze. She placed the tip of her finger lightly on his flat stomach and traced smaller and smaller teasing circles downward through a patch of golden hair to his loins.

Bartholomew Sabin lay passive under the urgent ministrations of that probing hand. Ann Lucero's lust was insatiable. He wondered about that, as he had wondered about it in others at other times. Slaves to passion. He could understand lust for power—position. But the lust of the flesh? It was debilitating. It could detract one from one's destiny. How often he had seen men of promise destroyed by their inability to control the urgency of their glands.

Imbeciles!

Still, like any exploitable human weakness, sex could be useful. He could be virile when the occasion demanded. And there were women, he knew full well, to whom rank and power were equated with eroticism. He suspected that Ann Lucero was as captivated by the stars on his uniform as by those in her eyes.

Her hand became boldly demanding.

He rolled toward her and gently kissed the lobe of her ear. "Ann . . . there's something I've been wanting to ask . . ."

"Anything, my darling."

"It's rumored that I'll be replacing General Burnside soon . . ."

"Oh . . ." It wasn't exactly what she'd expected.

"It's based on solid information. He's such a unique man . . . a great officer. He's certain for promotion. That will mean a move up. I hope when that day comes—when I take command— that you'll stay on as my confidential secretary."

She was elated. "Oh, yes. . . . I will."

They kissed. "I'm so very glad," he said.

He lay back. "Frankly, I hope it's soon . . . for his sake. I'm quite concerned about him. He's beginning to show a certain . . . strain."

"I know. Lately he seems so . . . driven. I do what I can to ease things for him."

He kissed her again. "I'm sure you do. I just hope he's not losing his judgment."

Her hand stopped its manipulation. "I don't understand."

"Oh . . . rejecting Colonel Hadley's investigation, for example. It was a poor decision, not well thought out. And it's causing a lot of unnecessary pressure on us all . . . General Burnside included. This new major . . . Ward—he's competent enough in his own field. But he's sorely unqualified to replace

Colonel Hadley. I simply don't understand General Burnside's rationale. Surely he should see that an outsider can do little more than exacerbate the problem."

Ann's ardor subsided. She rolled back to her side of the bed. "I'm afraid we shouldn't discuss this," she said warily. "I *am* his confidential secretary you know. He trusts me . . . Oh, darling. I hope I haven't offended you."

Sabin rolled toward her. "On the contrary. I respect you all the more."

He lowered his lips to her breast and ran his hand slowly down her body. He probed, gently, expertly. She responded with a quick tremor.

Suddenly he lay back, withdrawing physical contact. She let out a gasp of frustration and looked at him questioningly.

"You must understand," he said. "I'm concerned for his welfare. Deeply so. I'll do all in my power to protect him. I hope others feel the same responsibility. Colonel MacWatt, certainly, should be on guard. He *must* keep Ward on a tight rein . . . not let him stray afield."

"Stray afield? In what way?"

"Carry the investigation beyond those bound by a Quickseal clearance. That could be devastating. A clear breach of security. I fear there would be severe repercussions."

Ann bit her lower lip. "Oh dear."

"Is something wrong?"

She turned her head on the pillow and looked at him. "Major Ward called this afternoon. He's going to question Major Crowell's wife . . . and her father."

Sabin sucked in a deep breath and let it out slowly. "I see."

"Darling . . ." she asked anxiously, "is there *anything* you can do?"

He lay back, his eyes on the ceiling. "I . . . don't know. Perhaps."

For a long while he lay in silent thought. Then, unexpectedly, he reached for his watch on the nightstand. "I'm afraid I must go."

"Oh-h-h . . . so soon," she said.

"Unfortunately. I'm committed to one of those boring Junior-Officer-Council dinners. You understand?"

She tossed her arms around his neck. "I guess so . . . but, not just this minute. Please."

He allowed her to pull him down to her. "No"—he owed her this much—"not just this minute."

Senator Nathan Beaumont pulled up a chair beneath the crystal chandelier in the dining room of his spacious George-town townhouse. With practiced care he boned and sliced the broiled chicken breast into bite-size pieces, spooned pilaf and steamed green beans onto the plate, then placed it lovingly in front of his wife. "There you are, my dear."

"Thank you, Nathan."

Mary Jane Beaumont picked up her fork with her thin left hand and began to eat. For seventeen years, since that tragic day in Virginia when, following the hounds, her mount had failed to clear a hedgerow and fell crashing down upon her, Mary Jane had been confined to a wheelchair, her legs and right arm paralyzed. Ever since, despite the rigors of high office, Nathan Beaumont had dedicated every nonworking moment to her. At affairs of state, or at an occasional command per-formance at the White House, the distinguished white-maned senator could be seen wheeling his wife before him as joyously as a newlywed escorting a beloved bride. Even on his overseas junkets, which, compared to those of his colleagues, were in-frequent, he managed to take Mary Jane along, paying her expenses from his own pocket rather than charging them to the public till. In Washington, where fidelity was a rare com-modity, the senator's devotion to his crippled wife was legend. A legend that was reflected at the polls. In a Democratic state where he, a staunch conservative, was returned to office each six years with a comfortable majority of the votes, his share of the female vote was even more lopsided. He appreciated the fact but didn't boast of it. He would have been just as devoted with or without the approval of his distaff constituents.

Dinner completed, the senator left the dining room to the care of Albert, his houseboy, and pushed Mary Jane into the parlor for her nightly glass of port. He poured the wine, made certain the television remote control was at her left side, and excused himself to go to his den.

"Homework, Nathan?" She sipped her port.

He nodded. "Nothing changes. I must get things in order if we are to have time to enjoy ourselves in Johannesburg this Christmas."

"I'm so looking forward to that. The Krugers are such gracious hosts."

He bent and kissed her frail cheek. "And I, my dear."

The den was a small book-lined room just off the parlor. Senator Beaumont settled at his desk and unsnapped his attaché case, just as the private-line light on his phone began to blink. He picked up the instrument and pushed the blinking button. "Yes."

"Senator, about that appropriations bill you questioned. There will be nine line items."

"Thank you."

He hung up and uttered a mild oath.

There was a Wyeth on the wall behind his desk. He pulled the hinged painting aside to reveal a wall safe. As he did each time he unlocked the safe, he vowed to find a better concealment. It was the first place any burglar would look.

He opened the safe, removed a sheet of paper from an envelope and unfolded it on his desk. The paper was printed with a checkerboard-type grid.

"Nine items," the senator repeated.

He ran his finger across the top of the grid five spaces then down four. The resultant intersection revealed a seven-digit number. He committed the number to memory and locked the paper back in the safe.

He took a roll of quarters from his desk and stepped back into the parlor. His wife was engrossed in an Australian movie on PBS. He said, "I've got to go out a minute. I'm completely out of pipe cleaners."

His wife turned down the sound. "Why not send Albert?"

"No . . . the air will do me good. I won't be long. You'll be all right?"

"Surely. Don't forget your coat, dear."

In the garage he walked past the new Continental Mark VI and got into a weathered, eleven-year-old Ford. He'd purchased the Ford soon after his Senate colleague, John Stennis, was mugged and shot by a two-bit hoodlum only blocks from Beaumont's home. In Washington it was imprudent to flaunt one's wealth or position after sundown.

He drove through the darkened suburb quickly. He despised D.C. at night. Like most American cities nowadays it was a cesspool of crime. The predictable result of nearly five decades of fuzzy-headed left-wing ideology, he thought bitterly. *Damn them!* Roosevelt. The ACLU. Bleeding heart judges. Thugs released time and again to rob, rape, prey on decent people at will.

He spotted a lone black man standing beneath a streetlight and checked again to make sure the car doors were locked. His mind turned to the racial makeup of the capital . . . the despicable situation in the schools. Just this week he'd lost another top aide who—unlike all those liberal senators and congressmen—couldn't afford the cost of a private school for his children. With ironic amusement the senator thought of a comment J. Edgar Hoover once made to him during one of their frequent lunches together at the Mayflower: "Integration is based on the theory that if the mule and the thoroughbred drink from the same trough, the mule will someday win the Kentucky Derby."

The senator had laughed. Hoover hadn't. He had not been making a joke. Nonetheless, the story got big laughs in the Capitol Hill cloakrooms. But you had to be more discreet about things like that these days. *Remember Earl Butz.*

On 34th Street the senator approached an all-night shopping center. In the middle of the well-lighted parking lot was an island of pay phones specially installed to be used from an automobile. He pulled up to one of the phones and took the roll of quarters from his pocket. He rolled down the window, took the phone from the hook and dialed 1-505 and then the seven-digit number he'd committed to memory.

Gerald Coffman sat in his car beside a rural phone booth on Rio Grande Boulevard in Northwest Albuquerque. From time to time Coffman raised his eyes from the map he was ostensibly studying and glanced at the phone. Suddenly the phone jangled. Coffman jumped from the car and picked it up before the second ring. "Hello!"

There was a sound of coins being deposited. Then a familiar voice said, "Calm down and tell me what's so important."

"The new boy is talking to the professor."

Short silence. Then the voice asked, "To what extent?"

"We don't know," Coffman said nervously. "He phoned in this afternoon. Said he was going to talk to the wife and her father. We just found out about an hour ago."

"I see. You were right to call me. Keep on it. In the meantime, our friend insists on coming stateside to take delivery personally. *You must keep things on schedule*. Understand?"

"I . . . yes."

"Anything else?"

"No."

The phone went dead in Coffman's ear.

Senator Beaumont started the car. He despised these James-Bondish shenanigans.

He pulled back onto 34th Street, his mind replaying the information he'd just received from Coffman. Did it require action? The chances of Professor James Moslin being a threat at this late date were practically nil. He'd been out of things since 1972. There'd been many changes—many innovations—since then. Yet—*a nagging yet*—Moslin's daughter had married Peter Crowell. That made Moslin the only Delta Group member with a link—however innocent—to Quickseal. Coffman had made a point about Major Ward's reputation for tenacity. How ironic it would be if after all the planning, all the preparation, a johnny-come-lately junior officer should sabotage things. The senator shook his head. It was too much to risk. Nothing, no one, must be permitted to interfere now.

The senator turned at the next intersection, circled the block and drove back to the shopping center. This time at the phone island he dialed a number in Tucson.

An unfamiliar voice answered.

Senator Beaumont said, "Tell Mister Smith that Mister Kole is calling."

Moments later a resonant voice with a decidedly un-Smith-like accent came on the line. "Smith here."

"I'd like to pick up my option."

There was a pause. "Mister Cole, you say? Is that with a C, like in *cat?*"

"No . . . with a *K*, like in *kangaroo*."

"I see. Very well, Mister Kole. When would you like the option dated?"

"As soon as possible."

"I'll take care of it."

Senator Beaumont placed the phone back on the hook and looked at his watch. He'd been gone almost an hour. He started the car and headed home. He decided against working any more that night. The Australian movie should be over by now. He'd challenge Mary Jane to a game of backgammon. Backgammon gave her so much pleasure.

He speeded up.

It was getting late and Senator Beaumont wanted to be with his wife.

15

THE imposing fieldstone and oak house stood on a pine-sheltered knoll facing a broad grassy meadow. At one corner of the two-story structure three ancient ponderosas towered above all.

Tres Pinos, Ward thought.

He parked in the circular driveway beside Janet Crowell's white Chevy pickup. Nearby were a new GMC Carryall and a battered blue Dodge. Ward eyed the Dodge. In the East a car like that would be rotted with rust. There was none on the Dodge. A plus for the desert, Ward reflected.

But could this still be the desert?

Since leaving the main driveway at San Ysidro he had followed the white Chevy northward along a serpentine mountain road through an infinitely changing panorama: picturesque villages, precipitous annato cliffs, tumbling crystalline streams, steaming hot springs. All framed by an endless backdrop of pines, aspens, birch, spruce, fir. It was difficult to believe that this rich mountain greenery bordered the arid plain he'd left scarcely thirty minutes before.

Janet beckoned. He zipped his jacket—there was a sharp bite to the air—and followed.

Inside the house the decor was birch, knotty pine, mohair

and leather. Richly patterned Navajo rugs of different colors and sizes accented floors and walls. In the great-room an over-size stone fireplace emitted warmth and the pungent aroma of burning piñon. Two objects mounted above the fireplace caught Ward's eye. One was a near-life-size oil painting of an attractive blonde woman seated in a fan-backed basket chair. In that pleasant Nordic face Ward could detect genetic features that had passed from mother to daughter.

The other object was a framed *Time* magazine cover bearing the photographs of three men and the legend: NOBEL COUNT-DOWN: *Three in the Running.*

"Hi, Dad . . . Father Dan," Janet called out.

Ward turned. He hadn't noticed the two men seated across the room at a low coffee table. On closer inspection he saw that they were sorting trout flies. One of the men, Ward recognized from the *Time* cover, was Professor James Moslin.

At Janet's introduction, her father—his hair was grayer than in the photo, Ward noted, but his hazel eyes were just as clear—nodded without rising. "Janet called about your visit, Major. I'm afraid it's a waste of your time."

The other man flashed a welcoming smile. Without waiting for an introduction he rose and took Ward's hand warmly. "Don't be put off by my brusque friend, Major. He's been buried in these hills so long he's forgotten his manners. I'm Father Dan Espinosa. Are you a fisherman by any chance?" Father Dan's deep voice was rich with the lyric accent of his Castilian forebears.

Uncharacteristically, Ward took an instant liking to this smiling priest with the cinnamon skin and the coarse black hair. "No . . . I'm afraid not."

"Ah . . . sad, sad. You are missing one of life's greatest pleasures, my boy. Which, I might add, Jim, we are about to do also . . . if we don't get to that stream pronto."

Father Dan picked up his tackle box.

Moslin grabbed a rich-looking sheepskin coat from the couch, slipped it on, then pulled a blue knit cap down around his ears. Father Dan eyed the sheepskin coat wistfully, then glanced forlornly at his own frayed Navy-surplus pea jacket. "Ah, if it were not for my vows of poverty, I'd abscond with that coat, indeed I would."

The two older men and Janet smiled at what Ward knew must be a standing joke.

Father Dan turned to Ward. "You will stay for dinner, Major? Fresh trout, I can assure you."

Ward glanced at Moslin.

Father Dan said, "Well, Jim . . . don't just stand there. Tell the young man he's welcome."

Moslin nodded. "Yes . . . certainly."

Laden with gear, but walking with a spirited gait that belied their ages, the priest and the professor followed a well-beaten path across the fields to the faraway deep woods that sheltered the ranch's finest trout stream.

Ward turned up his collar against the biting chill of the high country. He had read a sign in one of the villages that proclaimed 7,000 feet altitude. And that was well before the final climb to Tres Pinos. Now, he was strolling the grassy meadow that stretched for a half mile from the house to the base of a high cliff that bounded the north side of the property. It was kill-time for him. He wanted to get on with the business that brought him here. But until Moslin returned from the stream there was nothing better to do.

At his side, hands thrust in the pockets of her denim jacket, Janet was talking about Father Dan. "He's terribly outspoken at times, and a bit presumptuous. But he's a prince of a man. Always pouring oil on troubled waters . . . that sort of thing. Dad's never been religious, but I don't know what he'd have done when Mother died if it hadn't been for Father Dan. He didn't know us personally . . . we're not Catholic . . . but he drove up from Jemez Springs that afternoon, and he stayed through the night, talking with us . . . praying. It's the only time I ever saw Dad pray. I've never forgotten that."

She stooped and picked up a stone and threw it straight and true toward a flock of ravens that were feeding on carrion in the field. The birds gave a raucous cry and lumbered into the air.

She returned to her subject: "Their friendship grew from that night. They're almost inseparable now. Father Dan's semi-retired . . . he's in his seventies . . ."

"Seventies?"

She nodded. "He doesn't look it. He's been here, in the

mountains, forever. Dad has his research here. They enjoy the same things—good books, long conversations, fine food, fishing. *Always* fishing. They compete like schoolboys. Who can tie the best fly? Or cast the best line? Or land the biggest trout? They'll be on the stream everyday now, until the freeze."

A shot sounded in the near distance. Ward looked up in surprise.

"Hunters," Janet said without breaking stride. "They're sighting in their rifles, getting ready for the season. They come here from all over the country."

She paused. "Peter saw opportunity in that."

"Oh?" Ward's interest picked up.

"He talked of turning Tres Pinos into a resort. There're excellent trout waters on the ranch, and other prime streams within walking distance. Deer are so plentiful they're a nuisance. Several large elk herds feed near here. The woods are full of upland grouse, wild turkeys."

"Peter was a sportsman, then?"

"Not really. He was thinking of our future. He knew I could never live anywhere but here. Dad was interested too. They even drew up plans for cabins, along the base of the cliff . . . over there. Then . . . Peter's death ended the dream."

After a moment she said, "He's here, though. I scattered his ashes from the cliff, the Friday after he died. I . . . thought he would have liked that."

They walked in silence. She kept her eyes on the path. From time to time Ward glanced at her. They were casting long shadows now and the waning sun had turned her hair to amber honey. He'd never known a woman like her. A woman who brought grace to jeans and boots, who drove a pickup truck, who talked knowingly about trout waters and prime streams and deer and elk and upland grouse and wild turkey. A woman who absolutely knew her place—if not her purpose—in life. He wasn't quite sure what to make of it.

At the east meadow they approached a string of corrals and a huge barn. There were no animals. She led him into the barn and pushed a wall switch.

He stared in awe.

"My father's laboratory," she said.

The barn had been converted to a giant greenhouse. A large

section of the south-exposed roof had been replaced with Plexiglas. Standing in three rows on a tiled cement floor were thirty long tables, each boardered at the edges to hold soil. An intricate system of plastic water pipes, fans, humidifiers, growing lamps and timing devices was connected to a computerized central control panel. The control panel was not operating.

Ward walked among the tables. Only a few bore visible signs of plant life. He ran his finger into the soil of a couple of the plant-bearing tables. It was dry and powdery. This laboratory, for whatever purpose it served, was being sorely neglected.

As if reading his mind Janet said, "I'm afraid he hasn't spent much time here lately."

"He built all this?"

"He designed it . . . they built it for him."

"The university?"

She shook her head. "The government. He works on a yearly grant . . . ninety-five thousand last year . . ."

"Jesus! *For this?*"

For a moment her face went blank. Then, her eyes flashed fire. "My father is a brilliant scientist! He's accomplished great things . . . breakthroughs in food production . . . plant protein . . . high altitude yields . . . he . . . he doesn't get one damned cent more than he deserves!"

He was startled by the vehemence of her defense. He had been indiscreet, had overstepped his bounds. Nothing new for him. Why then, this time, did he regret it so? "Look . . . I'm sorry. I didn't mean to imply anything . . ."

She flipped off the light. "We'd better get back."

Moslin and Father Dan, aprons in place, were hunched over the kitchen sink cleaning trout. The priest's eyes sparkled. "Ah, there you are, Jonathan . . . may I call you that? Major is so formal."

"Please do."

"Good . . . good. Look here, Jonathan." He pointed to a dozen large trout. "Ten rainbows, two fine browns."

Janet said, "I'll be in my room."

Ward watched her until she reached the stairs. He cursed his ignorance in the greenhouse, hoped it hadn't spoiled things here for him . . . before they even began. He decided to make the best of it while he could. He turned back to the men at the sink. "Professor, if we could talk for just a few minutes . . ."

Moslin worked the entrails from a trout's belly with his thumb and held the fish under running water. "Major, really, there's nothing I can tell you that you don't already know."

"I realize it's a long shot," Ward persisted. "But I understand you knew Major Crowell in Vietnam, and that you had almost daily contact with him here just before he went to the Pacific. You must have gotten some insight into his state of mind during those last days."

Moslin laid the cleaned trout aside and picked up another. "I knew Peter in Vietnam, yes, and did see him often during his last days. There was nothing extraordinary about it. We had some plans for Tres Pinos and were working on them. There's simply nothing more of importance to tell you."

Father Dan paused in his chores. "For Heaven's sake, Jim . . . quit talking to the young man with your back turned. Here"—he took the trout from Moslin's hand—"mix Jonathan a drink, go to the living room, talk. I'll call when dinner's ready. If nothing else, explain how you're responsible for the chemical devastation of that poor country. Confession is good for the soul."

Moslin shot the priest a mean look. With no graceful way out he removed his apron, washed his hands and turned to Ward. "Bourbon and water?"

Ward was a beer man, but he felt the need for something stronger. "Fine."

Moslin mixed the drinks and led the way to the living room. He lowered himself wearily onto the couch. Ward took a chair near the fire. The room was lighted by the fire-glow only.

"What did he mean, 'chemical devastation'?" Ward asked.

"I'm sure you have detected by now, Major, that my good friend Father Daniel Espinosa talks too damned much." Moslin took a healthy drink from his glass. "I was in the defoliation program. Dioxin . . . Agent Orange . . . I'm sure you've heard all about that?"

"The program, yes . . . your participation, no."

"It was an on-again-off-again thing. I went there first in sixty-five, at the request of President Johnson. There were some unexpected problems . . . my work in horticulture was widely known. He invited me to the White House and persuaded me that I could—should—be of service. He was quite adept at that sort of thing, you know."

"So I've heard . . . what kind of problems?"

"I can't discuss that. Anyway, it has nothing to do with your purposes."

Ward let it pass. "And that's when you met Major Crowell?"

"Not on my first tour. Later . . . in the summer of seventy, as I recall. Peter was a pilot in the program. I used to sit in on the debriefings . . . that's how we met. He liked my stories about New Mexico and I invited him to visit. Frankly, I never expected to lay eyes on him again. Then, he was assigned to Kirtland and came to see me. You know the rest."

Ward sipped his drink. "Did you approve of him marrying your daughter?"

Moslin's jaw tightened. "I'm not sure that's any of your business."

There was an uneasy silence. Then, as if in afterthought, Moslin said, "Yes . . . I was pleased. Janet was happy. That's very important to me. And Peter took great interest in Tres Pinos. I saw a future for them here."

"Did he ever talk to you about his work at Kirtland?"

"No. Peter was tight-lipped about that."

Unlike Father Dan, whose ebullience subtracted years from his age, Moslin's solemn mien gave him the appearance of a man beyond his fifty-seven years. Ward wondered if the professor was being evasive or reluctantly cooperative? He decided on another approach. "What was Peter's and Janet's relationship when they came back from Alaska?"

Moslin snorted. "I'm sure you know the answer to that, Major, or you wouldn't have asked."

"You weren't concerned?"

"Surely I was concerned. But it wasn't my business. All marriages hit sour notes now and then. People have to work out their problems for themselves. There's nothing abnormal about that."

Ward sat forward. "If I understand Janet correctly"—his voice betrayed his skepticism—"Peter wasn't interested in working out their problems. He moved back on base, he virtually ignored her, he spent most of his time at the end with you. Now, Professor, do you honestly look upon that as normal?''

Moslin looked at Ward for a long moment. Then he rose and went to the window and gazed out over the darkened ranch. ''Major, you are a guest here at my daughter's request. I accept that. But I deeply resent the tone of your . . . your interrogation.'' He turned to face Ward. ''During Peter's last days—and keep in mind, no one realized they were going to be his last days—his interest was in the ranch. I spent time with him, yes. He had plans for Tres Pinos—plans for himself and for Janet. I was helping with those plans. Whatever you may have inferred from what Janet has told you, the simple fact is that Peter was working for *their* future. There was nothing sinister or devious about it. And I suggest that it's time for you, and those you represent, to recognize that fact and let him rest in peace.''

The glow from the fireplace set sinister shadows dancing around the room. In that dim light Ward could make out the anguish in Moslin's eyes. In speaking of Peter Crowell the professor was speaking from the heart.

Strangely, Ward felt an enormous burden lift from him. He'd blown it. First with Janet, now with her father. He had tried to tell MacWatt that he was the wrong man—that he was no investigator.

Well, I gave it my best shot.

He was done with it. If MacWatt and Burnside didn't like it they could get themselves another boy. He was washing his hands of it. He was through with chasing down wild-ass rumors, with badgering bereaved people.

He set his unfinished drink on the coffee table and stood up. ''I'll be leaving now, Professor. Thank you for your time. Would you please tell . . .''

Moslin wasn't listening. His eyes were fixed on something beyond Ward. Ward turned to see Janet descending the stairs. She had changed into rich-looking tan woolen slacks and a matching camel's hair sweater that outlined a comely figure the denims had denied. Her feet were adorned in brown pumps. Her hair was brushed into a thick golden fall behind her shoulders and her lips were lightly glossed. The soft illumination from the fireplace fell gently upon her, revealing an image of haunting loveliness, a glow of reawakened vitality.

Before anyone could speak, Father Dan's voice boomed out from the kitchen: "Soup's on!"

Moslin's stony countenance vanished. He went to his daughter, held her at arm's length while he gazed upon her fondly, then kissed her tenderly on the cheek. Grasping her hand in his he turned to Ward. "Major . . . please join us for dinner."

The rustic ranch-oak table was laden with a platter of trout poached in pungent spices, French-style green beans with almonds, creamed pearl onions, steamed small new potatoes, cheddar-and-pineapple salad on a bed of fresh romaine. Standing beside the table, the sleeves of his dark-blue turtleneck sweater pushed above his elbows, Father Dan beamed over his culinary offering.

At the sight of Janet, the priest clasped his hands joyfully. "By all that's holy, just look at you, my child. Jim, we must have young men at our table more often."

Janet flushed. "Oh . . . Father Dan!"

Moslin held his daughter's chair. "Dan, I swear your mouth is as big as your gluttony."

"No, Jim," Father Dan admonished. "Gluttony is a sin. But a hearty appetite—now there's a gift from God."

They all laughed.

Ward ate heartily, pleasantly surprised at how delicious fresh-caught trout could taste. Following Father Dan's instructions he boned a fish and bit into the succulent firm white meat. He nodded approvingly. "Father, I don't understand how you've escaped marriage."

Father Dan laid back his head and roared with laughter. "Good! Excellent! I must mention that to my Bishop." Then, pointedly: "And you, my son?"

Ward gave a puzzled look.

"Are you married, Jonathan?"

"Oh . . . no."

"Your family?"

Ward shook his head. "None."

"Sad . . . perhaps."

Father Dan stood up suddenly. "Oh, my. I almost forgot."

He went to the refrigerator and took out a bottle of Rheinhessen—Dalsheimer Burg Rodenstein 1975. He retrieved three frosted glasses from the freezer and set them before his friends. "An excellent vintage. German wines must be drunk within their first ten years, you know."

He filled the glasses and set the bottle near Moslin.

There was no wine glass for Father Dan.

The priest returned to his chair, noting the question in Ward's eyes. "I am an alcoholic, Jonathan."

"Oh?"

"Indeed, it was the affliction that brought me to this fabulous Jemez country. Let's see . . . I was fifty-one . . . that was twenty-two years ago. Our order has a retreat at Jemez Springs, sort of a last resort for sodden priests. Most certainly, that's what I was—a whiskey priest, in desperate straits, ill in body and soul, at the end of my rope. I took the waters and prayed. Sweated through delirium tremens and prayed. Gradually, with our Dear Lord's grace, I learned anew that I need no other crutch in this life than Him. Here, in the serenity of these great mountains, I felt a nearness to God that I have felt nowhere else. I petitioned the Church to allow me to remain here, doing whatever task needed doing. To my everlasting gratitude, the petition was granted."

Ward glanced at Janet and her father. They continued to eat. Ward realized that this story had been told at this table before.

"Since then," Father Dan said, "I have spent my time counseling others in the unfortunate state that I was in." His eyes gave a mischievous twinkle. "And . . . in trying to teach a certain professor emeritus how to fly-fish."

"Ha!" Moslin retorted.

In the camaraderie of the table Ward had put the purpose of his being at Tres Pinos out of mind. Only minutes before he had vowed to put it out of his life. Now, he wondered if he dared bring the conversation around to Peter Crowell. He decided to give it a shot. "Janet tells me that Peter wasn't a fisherman."

"No," Janet confirmed.

"Never had a pole in his hand," Moslin added.

"Oh, but he did," Father Dan refuted.

Moslin and Janet looked up at the priest quizzically.

"Didn't he tell you?" the priest said.

"Tell us what?" Janet asked.

"A most unusual occurrence. I suppose I should have mentioned it. There was no binding confidentiality . . . still . . . a priest . . ."

He hesitated.

Janet said, "Father Dan . . . please."

Father Dan nodded. "Peter came to my cabin at Jemez Springs one morning. This past . . . July . . . yes, that's when it was. Let's see, he wouldn't have been living at the ranch then?"

Janet shook her head. "No."

"Yes . . . I see. He wasn't in uniform, but he must have driven up from the base. I was on my way to Guadalupe Creek, wanted to test some nymphs I'd tied the night before. I was surprised to see Peter. He asked if he could go along, said perhaps I could give him some pointers. Of course, I was delighted.

"We took the old logging road along the west side of the stream, up to the stone tunnel . . . you know the place, Jim."

Moslin nodded. Like his daughter he was deeply interested in this strange narration.

"I pointed out the best pools. Peter made a few halfhearted casts. By then I realized that fishing wasn't the reason he'd come to see me.

"I'd packed a lunch. We shared it sitting on a fallen log beside the stream. He was quiet. I tried to make conversation . . . to get at what was on his mind. Then, quite unexpectedly, he asked, 'Father Dan, do you believe there is a God?' "

Janet gasped. "Peter asked *that*. Of you?"

"He did. I assured him that there was, indeed, a living, caring God."

"But . . ." Janet sputtered. "Peter *never* discussed religion . . . never gave God a second thought."

Father Dan reached over and patted Janet's hand. "Forgive me, my dear, and please don't take offense. But I don't believe any of us knew Peter as well as we might have thought. I'm convinced that he not only thought about God, he was obsessed with Him."

"Oh-h-h."

Moslin looked at his daughter with concern. "Dan, I'm afraid this conversation is a bit too much."

"No!" Janet exclaimed. "I want to hear . . . all of it."

Father Dan hesitated. "Are you sure, my dear?"

"Yes . . . yes."

"Very well. But if it becomes too disquieting . . ."

"Yes . . . I understand."

Father Dan nodded. "Peter was the son of a minister. Such children bear an unjust burden from the beginning, among their young peers certainly. Sometime during his youth, after his father died, Peter apparently rebelled against his religious up-bringing. It's not uncommon. He probably felt no remorse so long as his principles were without real challenge. Then—and I have no idea where or when—something happened to bring Peter face to face with his conscience. It threw him into a deep personal . . . and spiritual . . . crisis."

The priest shook his head sadly. "I've seen it happen so many times. I should have recognized the signs in Peter. Nevertheless, that day on the stream, it became clear. Peter mentioned my alcoholism, the depth of depression he'd heard me speak of. I knew at that moment he was identifying with my earlier spiritual anguish. Then, he asked an even more puzzling question: 'Father, will God forgive a person who forfeits his life to destroy a great evil?' "

All eating had ceased. Janet was staring at the priest. Moslin's eyes were fixed on his plate.

"A great evil?" It was Ward who posed the question, his mind racing back over all that he knew of Major Peter Crowell.

"Yes. I asked Peter to please phrase his question in more specific terms. He asked if I knew the story of Colonel Von Stauffenberg?"

"Von Stauffenberg?"

"Wolfsschanze." Moslin uttered the word.

"Wolfsschanze," Father Dan confirmed. "In World War Two, Colonel Von Stauffenberg placed a concealed time bomb beside Adolf Hitler at a map table at Wolf's Lair—a command post in Poland. Von Stauffenberg left the bunker before the bomb exploded. Hitler changed positions at the table and was spared. Von Stauffenberg was later executed. Peter theorized that if the colonel had stayed and manually triggered the bomb, Hitler—a 'great evil'—would have perished and the war would have ended sooner, saving countless lives. Of course, Von Stauffenberg

would have died by his own hand. And there was Peter's point.
Would God, he asked me, have forgiven Von Stauffenberg?"

"And . . ." It was Ward now who was urging the priest on.

Father Dan replied, "What was a moral dilemma for Peter
was not, of course, for me. I told him that an act of self-
destruction removes one from God's presence—denies one
access to Heaven. He looked at me for a moment—such a
sad, heartrending look—and he said, 'And where, Father, is
Heaven?' "

Father Dan's voice trailed off, his mind's eye on the scene
he was describing.

Her voice a hoarse whisper, Janet asked, "And . . . you told
him . . . what?"

The question brought Father Dan back to the present. "Why,
I told him the truth, my child. I told Peter that Heaven lies just
on the other side of death."

"And Hell," Moslin said softly.

"Yes," Father Dan agreed. "And Hell."

Ward stopped on the porch and zipped his jacket to the collar.
The night had a frigid edge and he could see his breath in the
moonlight. At his side, oblivious to the cold, Janet apologized
for the ruined dinner: "I didn't know . . . I need time to think."

"It's all right. Janet . . . do you by any chance have a recording of Peter's voice?"

"Recording? I don't . . . Oh, yes . . . in Alaska we made a
Christmas tape for Dad. Why?"

"I'd like to borrow it. It's more than mere curiosity, I assure
you."

She went back into the house. In a couple of minutes she
returned with a cassette. "Whatever it is, you'll let me know?"

"I promise."

He drove down the winding mountain road as fast as he
dared. The car clock read 8:45. He could be at Kirtland by 10:30.

Twenty miles from the ranch he came to the little village of
Jemez Springs. He spotted a pay phone in front of a general
store. He stopped and dialed the operator and asked for Colonel
MacWatt's quarters number at Kirtland, collect.

Moments later he heard MacWatt's gravelly voice accepting
the call. "Ward?"

"Colonel . . . I'm on my way back to the base. Have Colonel Hadley meet me at the Quickseal compound at eleven. Tell him to be prepared to work through the night."

"You on to something?"

"I'm not sure. Maybe."

"Anything you can tell me now?"

"No. I'll explain later."

"All right. Hadley'll be there."

Ward ran back to the car and sped away, his mind assiduously replaying the scene at the dinner table. So far, it was the only thing that made sense.

He pushed the accelerator closer to the floor.

Was his hunch right? Right or wrong, he vowed he'd know before this night was over.

16

THE man signed the registration form "Tom Beck" and pushed it across the glass counter to the porcine woman.

She shifted slightly on her stool and glanced at the name. "How many days will you be staying with us, Mister Beck?"

"Three."

"Full hookups?"

"Just electric and water. I'll be going in and out. I'll use the central dump."

She made the notations on the form.

He handed the woman three tens. With practiced economy of motion she leaned slightly toward the register, deposited the tens and gave him four dollars change. He adjusted his steel-rimmed glasses as she pointed with her pen to a laminated map taped to the counter. "You're here. Follow this paved road around the building, past the pool. You'll find space thirty-one in the second row on your left."

"Is there a phone nearby?"

"There're two in front of the office—right here—and a booth at the northwest corner of the pool."

"Thank you." He pocketed the change and left.

At space 31 he leveled the truck, plugged into electricity and connected the water hose. Inside the camper he threw his fleece-lined jacket and wool cap onto the cab-over bunk. He boiled water, made tea and set it on the dinette to steep, then slumped wearily onto the couch. Laying his glasses aside he rubbed his eyes hard with his fists. He'd been on this job for a full month now. This was the eighth Albuquerque trailer park he had registered at during that time. Each under a different name, a fake address, a change of license plates. He wondered how much longer it would last? Well, there were many more campgrounds in the city. He would have preferred staying in the mountains, but night temperatures there were often below freezing this time of year. Overnighters were scarce. He couldn't take the chance of drawing attention to himself. Even though his six-year-old three-quarter-ton Ford and nondescript bed-mounted camper were like dozens of others seen in the Jemez every day. Hunters sighting rifles. Fishermen stretching the season. There was no better rig for anonymity in New Mexico. But, ever cautious, he kept the odds in his favor by leaving the mountains each night to return to the city, changing parks every third or fourth day.

He flexed his legs beneath the table and stretched his arms to relieve aching muscles. He was a short, heavyset man with a prominent paunch and thinning hair. At fifty-one he was beyond his prime, and he knew it. But it was a secret he shared only with himself. To others he was tops in the business. He disliked drawn-out jobs, like this one had turned out to be. But for a thousand a day he wasn't going to complain. That was high dollar in any language.

Still, there were regrets. He had missed Petie's birthday—again. It was his sixteenth and they had planned to spend the day at Catalina. Of course, Marge would explain. He had no complaints about Marge. She had raised the boy right. Petie had developed into a bright young man with a firm sense of direction. And Marge had been fair about visitation privileges, even after she remarried. But then, Beck had been generous with Petie's support, adding an occasional five hundred here, a thousand there, to be put into Petie's account for medical school. It was far more than the courts had decreed. But the thought of his son made Beck's chest swell with pride. He didn't begrudge a penny.

He spooned a large dollop of raw honey into the hot tea and

sipped it slowly, letting the savory hot brew warm his overtired bones. Then, with a sigh, he put the steel-rimmed glasses back on and took a flip-top notebook from the pocket of his flannel shirt. Scanning the notes he mulled the stake-out for that day. The activities had been fairly routine. At midmorning Blondie had left in the white pickup. Bluecoat arrived in his rattletrap Dodge at 3:30. Bluecoat and Sheepskin left the house with fishing gear at 4:17, taking the meadow path to the wooded stream.

Beck chuckled. You could almost set your watch by *that*.

He flipped back a page and frowned. He had overlooked the entry just before 4:17. It was a new wrinkle. At 4:01 Blondie had returned with a man following in another car. A government car, it appeared—and the man was wearing an Air Force uniform. Even with binoculars the distance from the top of the cliff to the house was too far to make out the man's rank. But there was an officer's insignia on his hat. From 4:30 to 5:49 Blondie and Air Force strolled around the ranch, spending some time in the barn. Bluecoat and Sheepskin returned to the house at 6:00. Blondie and Air Force joined them there at 6:15. They were all still there when surveillance ended at nightfall.

Beck looked at his watch: 8:02. Still an hour before he called in his report.

He rose and lit the propane oven and took a TV dinner out of the freezer. Salisbury steak. He eyed the package with disgust. When this job was over, he promised himself, he would spend a month in L.A.'s finest restaurants. He pulled back the foil covering the meat and vegetables, left it over the dessert, and shoved the tray into the oven.

There was a small black-and-white television on the counter next to the stove. He cranked up the roof-mounted antenna and turned the set on. A local newscaster was saying into the camera: ". . . announced today that four United States Air Force AWACS aircraft will be sent to Saudi . . ."

Beck switched channels. There was a movie about an all-woman orchestra in a German concentration camp. Beck frowned. He detested war stories. The next channel was airing *Three's Company*. Beck was delighted. John Ritter cracked him up. He watched until his meal was ready.

At 9:05 he cleared the stove and table, donned his jacket

and walked to the pay phone beside the pool. He readied change and dialed a number in Tucson. On the fourth ring a voice answered: "Yeah."

Beck deposited the required coins. "Get Smith."

After a moment a resonant voice with a distinct accent said, "Smith here."

"Not much new," Beck began. "An Air Force officer . . ."

"Skip it," Accent cut in. "The option's been picked up. Twenty-four hours. Can you deliver?"

Beck paused. As always at moments like this he felt the adrenalin surge through his body. An exercised option meant a $50,000 bonus. Beck calculated hastily. *Whatever happens to me, Petie's medical school costs would be assured.*

"Twenty-four hours?" he said.

"That's affirmative . . . can you deliver?"

"Yes." Beck hung up.

For the first time in weeks his body was suddenly devoid of aches and pains. Now *he* was in charge.

Twenty-four hours. Tomorrow.

He returned to the camper and made sure that all shades were drawn. From the long cupboard above the sink he took down an aluminum case. Inside was a Winchester Model 70 bolt-action .30-06 rifle. Nothing fancy. The kind of gun any hunter might be sighting-in this time of year. He thought of the distance from his vantage point atop the cliff to the embankment near the stream where the meadow gave way to the woods. Four-hundred-fifty yards. It was his clearest, closest view. He had sighted the rifle for that distance, using a 180-grain, lead-tipped load, the day after he'd measured it. And he'd checked the rifle for accuracy each day afterward. He lifted the gun to the light and checked the settings on the four-power Bushnell scope. They were in order. He laid the gun back in the case with a sigh. There was a time when he could have done it with open sights.

He put the case back in the cupboard, then reached beneath the mattress of the cab-over bunk and pulled out a large manila envelope. Inside was a sketch with penciled notations of distances between the cliff top and various sites on the property. He knew them by heart. He laid the sketch aside and took out a 9 × 12 glossy black-and-white photograph. A studious middle-aged man stared benignly from the picture. He looked harmless enough. Beck wondered what he'd done? Gang member on the outs with his clan? A debt welcher? Fink? Businessman whose partner wanted to collect insurance?

"Christ!" he said aloud. "I *am* getting old." Such thoughts were unprofessional—and dangerous.

He sat down at the dinette and studied the photograph again, to fix even more definitely in his mind that image that he already knew so well. At the bottom of the picture someone—Beck guessed Smith had done it—had printed in large block letters: JAMES MOSLIN.

Beck glanced from the face to the name then back to the face.

"Sheepskin," he uttered softly.

17

ELWOOD Hadley, wearing civilian slacks, a pullover sweater, and a discontented smile, made a point of looking at his watch as Ward entered the guardshack at midnight, an hour late. "What's so damned important?"

"I'm not sure," Ward responded. "Let's go find out."

Without further explanation Ward cleared through the guard post then led Hadley on a brisk walk across the deserted Quick-seal compound to Hangar One. Inside, he threw a switch illuminating the disassembled *Cobra One*. He went directly to the salvage table holding *Stargaze*, picked up the control keyboard and turned it bottom-up. "It looks like it's made of two separate modules."

"So?"

"How were they tested?"

"On the flight simulator. Like I said, if a part works there it'll work on the aircraft. They checked perfectly."

"Separately, or as a package?"

"Separately." Hadley's voice registered impatience. He was in his bailiwick now. "Christ, Major . . . what are you getting at? You know how electronic units made up of separate modules are tested."

"You didn't test the housing?"

"Housing? Major, it sounds to me like you're getting a little nitpicky."

Ward grasped the keyboard firmly. "My business is picking nits, Colonel. Let's go to the simulator." He nodded toward the end of the table. "I'll need that tool kit."

With a disgusted shake of his head Hadley grabbed the kit and followed.

In the blockhouse Ward entered the XR-2100 cockpit simulator and removed the *Stargaze* keyboard installed there. He set the unit aside and replaced it with the keyboard salvaged from *Cobra One*. "Now . . . how do you fire this baby up?"

Hadley showed how to simulate engine start, takeoff and level flight. Ward leveled at an imaginary 55,000 feet and got out of the simulator. "Where's the monitor?"

Hadley led to a desk-size console and manipulated several touch-sensitive buttons. Instantly, a monitor in the center of the console began to display a series of vectors and grids. Precisely and unerringly, the monitor produced an exact replica of the pre-programmed *Stargaze* flight path *Cobra One* flew on its final doomed flight from Johnston Island.

Hadley looked up smugly. "Perfect. You satisfied?"

"Perfect," Ward agreed. "Except for one thing."

"What thing?"

"I set the selector switch on PILOT. The monitor should be reading blank—not showing the plane under *Stargaze* control."

"Wha . . . !"

Disbelieving, Hadley hurried to the simulator. The selector switch was firmly locked in the PILOT position. Hadley's face drained of color. "Oh . . . shit-t-t-t!"

"I couldn't have expressed it better," Ward said.

Hadley slumped in a chair, his face a mask of incredulity.

Ward entered the simulator and retrieved the *Cobra One* keyboard. He grabbed the tool kit and took all to a nearby table. Four screws held the PILOT–STARGAZE selector switch in the housing. He removed them and pulled the switch box out and studied the wiring where the switch box joined the housing. He nodded knowingly: "Come here."

Like a man in a trance, Hadley rose at Ward's beckoning and went to the table. Ward pointed with the screwdriver. On a small terminal strip three color-coded wires were connected to three color-coded screw clamps. With a notable error. Although the black ground wire was correctly connected to the black clamp, the red and white wires, which should have connected to like-color clamps, were instead crosswired to opposite color clamps.

Hadley began to curse: the salvage engineers, his own inadequacies, cruel fate. He regarded Ward with mixed emotions of bitterness and admiration. Then, in a flash of insight, another incredible truth struck him. "But . . . he flew perfect intercepts against the first three AWACS. *He had to know!*"

Ward touched the tip of his nose with a finger. "On the button, Colonel."

Utterly bewildered now, unable to grasp the meaning of it all, but sensing his career in ruin, Hadley lowered his head and groaned. "No . . . it's all too . . . what does it mean?"

Ward reassembled the keyboard. "I don't know. But one thing's for sure: Until we *do* know, you must not mention this little puzzle to *anyone*. Understand?"

Hadley pulled a handkerchief from his pocket and wiped his palms. "Yes . . . yes, whatever you say."

"Good. Now, help me get all this stuff back exactly like it was. I've still got another visit to make tonight."

Colonel Robert MacWatt, draped in an ankle-length blue bathrobe over purple flannel pajamas, occupied the couch like a disgruntled beached whale. His overlong graying hair resembled an unmade bed. His Brillo-pad eyebrows (woe to the barber who tried to put shears to them) defied any known law of order. Roused minutes before from a sound sleep, the colonel stared up at Ward as one might stare at a man who had just taken leave of his senses.

"He *planned* it?!" MacWatt sputtered. He wiped his mouth on his sleeve.

"I'm convinced of it," Ward replied calmly.

"On the basis of some piss-assed fishing story? Told by an over-the-hill preacher . . . who you say can't even hold his liquor?" MacWatt snorted. "Major, sounds to me like you're wading in a deep sty without boots."

Despite himself, Ward smiled. "Will you let me explain?"

MacWatt looked at the time. 2:00 AM. He thought about the Glenlivet in the bar but decided not. "I think you better," he grumped. He stood up and flopped in frayed house slippers toward the kitchen. "First, I'm putting on a pot of coffee."

Ward looked the place over. The apartment was spacious and well-appointed, as befitted the senior colonel on the base. A regal Icelandic rug of virgin wool adorned the floor of the living room. An ornate teakwood bar, handcarved in the Pescadores, stood in one corner. Behind the bar an exquisite Japanese shoji screen depicting cranes in flight graced the wall. Beside a well-worn leather chair, a large Taiwanese mahogany drum, its goose-skin head covered by glass, served as a table. Under the glass was a black-and-white photograph of two young men seated at a bistro table with a beautiful blonde girl. The photo bore the legend: *Bamboo Club—1951.* Ward recognized the men as MacWatt and Burnside. He didn't recognize the woman.

The most eye-catching feature in the room was the books. Well-thumbed, they adorned rows of shelves on the walls, stood in crowded corner bookcases, lay in piles on the floor beside the couch and chair. The titles revealed that MacWatt's tastes ran to biography, history, oriental art, world-class cooking, classical novels. All in all, Ward concluded, it was the ambience of a discriminating but melancholy man.

MacWatt's voice boomed from the kitchen: "In here."

They sat at the dining table next to a bay window. With the first few sips of coffee, which he had sugared and creamed to the consistency of a milk shake, MacWatt's disposition began to improve. "Chicory," he boasted. "From New Orleans. Grind it myself."

Ward tasted the coffee, which he'd asked for black, made a face and reached for the sugar.

MacWatt laughed.

"It wasn't just the priest," Ward said, adding a second teaspoon of sugar to the cup. "There were other things. Things that made no sense . . . until I heard Father Dan tonight."

"Such as?" MacWatt prompted.

Ward picked up his spoon and tapped it slightly on the side of his cup. "Know what that is?"

"It's a goddamned coffee cup. What the hell do you think it is?"

"A-sharp," Ward said. He reached across the table and tapped MacWatt's cup. A different tone ensued. "B-flat."

He put down the spoon and pointed to his ear. "Perfect pitch. I detect things in sounds that other people don't. Things I sometimes don't realize I'm hearing . . . until I concentrate. That's what happened the other night. I listened to the mayday tape. Are you familiar with voice analysis?"

"No . . . well, some. There was an article in *Reader's Digest*."

"It's an applied science. Police use it. Ma Bell, to trace obscene callers. A person's voice is like a fingerprint. There's not another like it in the world. But there's a difference. Fingerprints don't change. Voice patterns do . . . under certain conditions."

"Like?"

"Stress. In a desperate situation some people can control physical panic. But no one can control his voice stress in a desperate situation. No matter how in-control they might sound the stress patterns are evident to someone who knows how to detect them. And that's what's wrong with that tape. There's no desperation stress in that voice. It's the voice of a deliberate person engaged in a deliberate act."

Something jarred MacWatt's memory. *Burnside*. The general once asked pointedly if MacWatt had listened to the tape.

"Are you sure about this?" MacWatt asked.

"I even checked it tonight against a recording of Crowell's voice in a normal situation. We can have both tapes analyzed, voice prints made. But I'm positive what the results will be."

MacWatt nodded. "What else?"

"Crowell's state of mind. His private life was a shambles, his marriage was on the rocks—he couldn't even get it up with his wife. He was driven by dark thoughts of God knows what—no one who knows him can explain them. Then he reveals to Father Dan that he's thinking self-destruction. Hell, the man was a walking time bomb."

MacWatt huffed, "Then why didn't he just blow his damned brains out?"

"Exactly," Ward agreed. "Or why didn't he just dive *Cobra One* into the sea? Why attempt a landing on a Godforsaken reef? A landing the plane survived—and which he should have."

"Maybe he started a dive then chickened out."

"Uh huh. Or—he was dead before *Cobra One* went down."

He'd slipped it in. But it was pointed and MacWatt sensed that he was serious. "You'd better explain that one."

"Remember the Navy report on Crowell's body? His helmet visor was open, he had a glove off. Why, if he was actually flying an out-of-control plane, would he take a glove off? It didn't make sense. Until I started thinking about something else in that report. Crowell's lips and tongue were discolored. The corpsman attributed that to water exposure. But it's also a symptom of something else—cyanide poisoning."

MacWatt's eyes narrowed in skepticism.

"That would explain everything," Ward said. "The discoloration, the open visor, the missing glove. He needed a free hand to do something that would have been difficult with a glove on. Like reach in his pocket for something small—something available to all covert operations pilots . . ."

"A termination capsule," MacWatt interjected.

"Yes. Hadley told me that *Stargaze* is similar to the computer used in the NASA moon landing program. That means the pilot has the option of temporary in-flight re-programming. I'm convinced that's what Crowell did. He made the three runs on the AWACS, then erased the remainder of the program that was on the chip. He declared mayday, then punched a new program into the computer's internal memory, where it would be erased when the power went off. He instructed *Stargaze* to fly to Kingman Reef, descend to wave-skimming altitude and slam into the long west shoal. It would have all the appearance of an accident during an attempted emergency landing. I figure that from his last known position the flight took twenty-six minutes. He didn't have the fortitude to stare death in the face that long— to sit idly while the reef loomed up. Who would? So, he turned that nasty business over to *Stargaze* and took the capsule. Neat, efficient. He expected his body to be shattered. No body, no autopsy, no discovery of the poison. But, there was a flaw in his plan."

"Well, that's heartening. What?"

"*Stargaze*. It did its job too well. It didn't slam the plane into the reef. During those last few seconds, while *Cobra One* was approaching the reef, something happened—wave swells most likely—that caused *Stargaze* to sense an altitude below twelve feet. At that level the computer is pre-programmed to land the plane. It lowered the gear, flared the plane and brought it down on the water. *Cobra One* skipped across the lagoon like a flat rock and settled onto the bottom against the south shoal."

"Along with Crowell's *unshattered* body," MacWatt exclaimed with a note of triumph. "So, tomorrow we get an exhumation order and see if this farfetched theory of yours holds up in the light of day."

Ward shook his head. "Too late. Janet told me she scattered Crowell's ashes Friday morning after the crash. Trace it back. He crashed and was in the water overnight. His body was recovered Tuesday and remained aboard the salvage vessel that night. Wednesday it was picked up by a helicopter and flown to Hickam Air Force Base. It was immediately transferred to a cargo plane bound for Kirtland, arriving that night. It was cremated in Albuquerque Thursday. No autopsy. No one along the line thought of questioning the Navy corpsman's finding of death by drowning."

MacWatt struck the table with his fist. "Damn!"

He thought for a moment. "But haven't you overlooked something? If your theory's correct, *Stargaze* had to be flying that plane. Salvage proved that Crowell was flying it."

"Yes. And that bugged the hell out of me until I thought it through. Now, did salvage really prove that Crowell was flying the plane? Or did they merely prove that the selector switch was found in the PILOT position, *indicating* that he was flying the plane?"

"Huh?"

"For my theory to be correct, someone would have had to tamper with the selector switch, so that it was actually in the *Stargaze* mode when the switch was set in the PILOT position, and vice versa. And that, Colonel, is exactly what was done."

He revealed his discovery that night in the Quickseal compound. "There's no mystery about who did the rewiring. Crowell flew perfect attacks against the first three AWACS using *Stargaze*. To do that he had to manipulate the switch—had to know it was crosswired. He did the wiring himself."

MacWatt stood up. "To hell with the time."

He went to the living room and returned with a bottle of Glenlivet. He refilled his cup with coffee and laced it with Scotch. Ward did the same.

Cup in hand, MacWatt paced the floor, his head bowed in thought. He had been skeptical. But as the incredible story unfolded, punctuated by Ward's precise, analytical evaluation of events, the colonel found himself edging reluctantly, but surely, toward conviction. There were still holes in the theory big enough to fly a B-52 through. Indeed, in the fading shadow of what was slowly becoming known, what was still unknown loomed ever larger.

MacWatt turned. "All right. For the sake of argument let's agree that all you've said so far is true. That Crowell wasn't just plain nuts. That he took great pains . . . made elaborate plans to deceive us. Why? Why go to all the trouble? What was he trying to prove? What 'great evil'—to use the preacher's words—did Crowell destroy by destroying himself? Do you have an answer to that?"

Ward didn't.

MacWatt said, "Then I suggest that at this point we are faced with a more perplexing problem than a mere aircraft accident."

Ward saw no reason to comment.

MacWatt sat back down at the table. It was decision time. "Major, you've done a hell of a job. I'll arrange for you to brief General Burnside first thing tomorrow. He'll prepare an outstanding efficiency report for your records. As for the rest . . . well, I reckon you were closer to the mark when we first discussed the investigation than I was. It *is* a case for the OSI. I'll see to it . . ."

"The shit you say!"

MacWatt stopped short.

Ward's eyes flashed. "Colonel, you forced me into this mess but by God you're not going to force me out. No damned pinstriped gumshoe is going to come in now and fuck up the works."

Taken aback, MacWatt nonetheless found it difficult to suppress a bemused smile. Was this agitated major—this now avid protagonist—the same officer who had protested so loudly when chosen for this assignment?

Ward leaned across the table. "Look . . . I said I didn't have the answer. But I think I know who does."

"The preacher?"

"No. He's been level all the way. Moslin's the one who's stonewalling. I'm sure he knows more than he's telling. If the key to the riddle exists, that's where we'll find it. And I think I know how to do it." He sat back. "Two days . . . OK? Without a word to anybody. Grant me that. If I hit a dead end . . . then the OSI."

MacWatt pondered it carefully. Sitting on what they knew for forty-eight hours could be dangerous. Still, he owed something to Ward. Furthermore, who, professional investigator or not, was more capable to do the job?

MacWatt nodded. "Two days."

18

TOM Beck awakened at dawn from a fitful sleep. Twice during the night he had climbed down from the overhead bunk to relieve the urgent spasms in his bowels. Now, he pushed back the covers and sat wearily with his feet dangling over the side of the bunk. An enormous belch rose from his gut and he swallowed hard against the gall that soured his throat. He wasn't pleased with himself. Before, in his prime, his nerves had been tempered steel. Even now, pride refused to let him face squarely that he might be losing his grip. He blamed the indigestion on last night's TV dinner.

He climbed down from the bunk and washed in cold water at the kitchen sink. There was plenty of hot water in the tank, but he needed this vigorous ritual to revive him. He toweled briskly, threw on the same clothes he'd worn for days, then fixed a breakfast of hot milk and Ovaltine. He didn't trust heartier fare this morning.

After breakfast he took the rifle from the aluminum case and loaded the spring clip with five 180-grain, lead-tipped shells. He left the chamber empty. He placed the loaded rifle gently on the bunk and covered it with a blanket.

It was still forty minutes before the campground office opened. He wondered if he should check out and get a rebate for the two days he'd paid for but wouldn't be using. He decided not. The less attention he drew to himself the better. He battened down the inside of the camper and went outside and unhooked the electric and water connections. Fifteen minutes later, well ahead of the morning rush-hour traffic, he had traversed the city and was driving north on I-25 toward the Jemez mountains. A cloudless, azure sky offered unlimited visibility. Beck uttered a prayer of thanks.

Thirty-five miles from Albuquerque he shifted the Ford into four-wheel drive and pulled off State Highway 44 onto a disused desert road. Twelve lonesome miles into the badlands he stopped at the crest of a high rise overlooking a wide arroyo. He got out, climbed down the embankment, then walked along the base of the hill until his practiced eye told him he had gone 450 yards. At a low sandhill he took a sheet of paper from his pocket, unfolded it and pinned it onto the spikes of a yucca plant. In the center of the paper was a five-inch-diameter black circle.

At the camper he got the rifle, then lay on the ground at the edge of the arroyo in a prone position. It was a close approximation to the view he would have from the cliff. He bolted a shell into the chamber. Then he fixed his steel-rimmed glasses firmly against the bridge of his nose, sighted the scope on the target and squeezed off five shots in leisurely succession. He climbed down to the yucca bush. All five shots were in the black.

He reloaded the rifle and put it back on the bunk. He drove back to the main road. His spirits began to improve and he projected his thoughts ahead to that night. He'd be finished with the Jemez—with this Godforsaken desolate state. Tonight he would be on I-40 westbound. By midnight, at the latest, he'd reach Flagstaff. There he would deliver the rifle, these ridiculous backwoods clothes, the camper and everything in it to an old acquaintance who for four big Big Ones—no questions asked—would make sure that none of it would ever be seen again. Then, a quick flight to L.A. Civilization! In three days—four at most—his fifty-grand bonus would be in his hands and he would establish a trust for Petie's education.

He glanced at the speedometer and eased up on the accelerator. It would be disastrous to get a ticket now. There was no hurry. He had time to kill. He smiled. *Among other things.*

Janet Crowell, too, arose that morning from a fitful sleep. Usually—in the past two years at least—that meant unsettling dreams. But if she had dreamt last night she didn't remember it, as she usually did. Instead, until she finally dozed off in the last couple of hours before dawn, she had stared into the darkness trying to reconcile her memories of Peter with the strange story told by Father Dan at dinner. It was almost as if he'd been describing a stranger. She had been Peter's wife. She was the one he should have been able to come to in time of anguish, the one who should have understood. She wondered if she ever had?

But her thoughts had not all been of Peter.

She went to her dresser and began putting her hair in order and wondered anew about Jonathan Ward. There was something about him. Something . . . threatening? The thought puzzled her. Was she that vulnerable? Peter had been dead for only a month. Still, he had left her . . . hadn't been a real husband to her for . . .

She threw the brush on the dresser. *Why am I thinking this way?*

With concerted effort she willed her thoughts to Jonathan's . . . to Major Ward's mission rather than to the man. It was then that she remembered the trunk. Peter's things. Things he'd left at the ranch when he moved back to the base. Evidence, she mused, that he had, perhaps, meant to come back all along. She had been unable to face sorting through them, and her father had packed everything in a large steamer trunk and stored it in the barn. There might be something there . . . some clue to help Jonathan, or her, to understand. She nodded determinedly at her mirrored image. She'd spend the day going through Peter's things. Just in case.

"And I *must* do something about my nails," she said aloud.

Jonathan Ward forced one eye open and looked at the clock beside his bed. A quarter past noon. He had finally gotten to bed at four. Now, his head was full of cobwebs, his teeth were covered with moss, his tongue wore a foul-tasting coat of crud.

Moslin's bourbon and MacWatt's Scotch. He moaned. He'd heard about the effect of booze at high altitudes. Two damned drinks and he felt like he'd been on a weekend binge.

He sat up and tried to stretch the kinks from his body. His mind was still hyped by the events of last night. He breathed deeply to oxygenate his blood and thought of Moslin. He pulled the phone to him and dialed Tres Pinos. No answer. He wondered where Janet might be?

Janet with the golden hair . . .

Now what the hell brought that on? he wondered.

He turned his thoughts to a shower—a long, steaming, hot shower. Then he'd lunch at the club and call the ranch again. And again. Until someone answered. One way or another, he was going to have another talk with Professor James Moslin before this day was over.

At five minutes past four that sun-blessed afternoon Father Daniel Espinosa parked his venerable blue Dodge in front of the Tres Pinos ranch house. He climbed the steps, gave a perfunctory rap at the door and went inside. There was no one in sight.

"Jim!"

No answer.

With a shrug, Father Dan went to the closet and took out his fishing gear. He sat on the couch and made his selection of flies for the afternoon, turning each lure carefully in his bronzed hand, studying the tie of the shank and the angle of the hackles with the same rapt attention that a meticulous jeweler might give to the study of a fine gem. He chose three lead-wing coachmen and three muskrat nymphs, all of which he had tied on Orvis premium #12 hooks. He glanced out the window and mused that some of the unsheltered pools might be quite sunny. He added a couple of pink nymphs to his kit.

The door opened. "I heard that old clunker of yours struggling up the grade," James Moslin said. He went to the closet for his gear.

Father Dan seated a Minalta reel to his eight-foot Eagle Claw rod and tightened the clamp. "Where you been?"

"Took a bite to Janet. She's been in the barn all day, sorting Peter's belongings."

"Ah . . . finally."

"She's doing it for Ward." Moslin's voice was flat.

"You were a bit cool to that young man last night, Jim."

At times Father Dan's paternalistic prying was irksome. Moslin started to retort by mentioning the consternation caused by Dan's untimely story last night. He decided against it. Tolerance of small faults was an acceptable price to pay for the friendship of a good man.

Moslin said, "I find it difficult to talk about Peter."

Father Dan changed the subject. "What do you think the stream temperature will be?"

"Low forties. But the barometers rising. They'll hit."

The stream was clear, the trout worked just below the surface, and in less than an hour the fishermen's creels were heavy. They decided to stream-clean the fish. Father Dan sat on a rock at the water's edge and laid seven large rainbows on the bank. "I see I got the biggest one . . . again."

"Oh, shut up," Moslin griped, and grinned.

Just downstream from where they sat the brook widened into a dog-leg turn where the water eddied in a large pool. Father Dan eyed the pool expectantly. "I still say there're some lunkers in there, Jim."

"Cagey ones if there are." Moslin threw a handful of entrails into the stream and a school of minnows darted out from beneath the rocks to feed on the unexpected manna. "I say it's fished out."

Father Dan grabbed his rod. "By golly, I'm going to give it a try."

The stream bed was covered by ageless round stones worn smooth and slick by the coursing water. It was like walking on greased bowling balls. Teetering precariously, Father Dan treaded the low rapids, thankful for the heavy soles on his insulated waders. Ahead in the sunlight the rippling pool sparkled like a million beckoning diamonds. Father Dan tied a pink nymph onto the monofilament leader, then cast expertly into the white water. He played out line to allow the unweighted nymph to flow with the current down around the large boulders where lurking trout were prone to lie facing upstream in wait for drifting food.

No strike.

He worked the line back across the pool with a threading motion of his left hand, raised the rod, and flipped the fly above his head several times and set it gently back on the water. The results were the same.

On the bank, Moslin chuckled. "C'mon, Dan, it's getting late. You can fish in the bathtub up at the house."

"Hmmph!" the priest snorted.

On the third cast the fly drifted beneath an overhanging branch that barely touched the water next to the far bank. Fearing a snag Father Dan gave the line a hefty tug. At that moment a geyser erupted beneath the branch and a huge rainbow trout surfaced with the nymph in his mouth. Bug-eyed, but alert, as a good trout fisherman must ever be, Father Dan tugged once again, setting the hook before the angry fish could throw it.

Moslin scrambled to his feet, almost tumbling down the embankment. "Migawd, Dan! He's a two-footer if he's an inch! Play him! Play him!"

The mighty trout sounded then broke water again and tail-walked across the pool, thrashing his head in mad fury trying to dislodge the alien hook.

There was no use trying to manhandle a fish like this, Father Dan knew. He must be played carefully, until he exhausted himself. Father Dan held the rod straight up to force the trout to expend his strength against the flexible pole. With his left hand he released or threaded-in line, countering each game thrust of the wily fish to maintain a tight slackless link between himself and his prey. It was a challenge of wit, a test of skills. And Father Dan knew he was pitted against a worthy adversary. Only when that fierce fighting heart had worn itself out could the great fish be landed.

The struggle continued without quarter. Then, after ten minutes, a barely perceptible signal flowed from hook to line to pole to Father Dan telegraphing that the fish's strength was ebbing. Father Dan glanced around. Neither he nor Moslin carried nets. How he regretted that decision now!

He had two options. He could wade further into the pool and try to gill-hook the fish with his fingers. Or he could back up and pull the fish onto the shoals. He decided on the shoals. He backed slowly, blindly feeling for footing. Suddenly, he slipped on a loose stone. He fought for balance, lost it, and fell backward into the stream. The pole slipped from his grasp. It washed with the current toward the deep pool.

"Oh! Oh!" Father Dan pushed himself to his feet and lunged through the shallows toward the pole. At the head of the pool he lost footing again and fell forward, this time submerging in frigid water.

Moslin was at his side in a second. He grasped Father Dan beneath the armpits and dragged him toward the bank.

"Jim! My pole . . . the fish!"

Moslin tightened his grip. "I'll get your damned pole. Jesus . . . you're soaking wet." He pulled the priest to dry ground.

Father Dan's teeth began to chatter.

Moslin helped him out of the sodden pea coat and threw it on the ground. He quickly removed the heavy sheepskin coat he was wearing, put it on the shivering priest and buttoned it to the neck. He replaced Father Dan's wet knit hat with his own, pulled it down hard around the priest's ears and pushed him toward the trail. "Get to the house. The fire's going . . . there're dry clothes in the closet. I'll bring the rest of the stuff."

Father Dan gave the pool a forlorn look. "If he's still on, it's my catch. Hear? My catch."

"Oh, for Chrissakes, Dan! Yes. Your catch. Now, damnit, git!"

The path wound for a hundred yards through the woodlands before opening out onto the meadow. From the edge of the clearing Father Dan could see the ranch house clearly, almost a mile away. A thick plume of smoke rose steadily from the brick chimney and wafted through the three old pines towering beside the porch. Anticipating the warmth awaiting him at the end of that long walk Father Dan drew Moslin's sheepskin coat tighter about him and increased his pace on the open trail.

Suddenly, something exploded inside his chest. His breath rushed from his body and he felt himself slammed backward onto the ground. He lay in a twisted heap, unmoving, like a broken straw doll. He tried to rise but his muscles would not respond.

"JIM-M-M . . . ! he screamed, and lay silent.

Moslin heard the shot. He was standing in midstream, bent

forward with a stick in his hand, trying to recover Father Dan's fly rod tangled in the branch overhanging the deep pool. Damned poachers! They were hunting closer to his land each year.

A fainter sound, muted by the coursing water, reached his ears. A cry? Then, still another sound—a vehicle (a truck?) racing away from somewhere atop the cliff overlooking the meadow. An icy chill gripped Moslin's spine. He stood upright and listened. Then he threw down the stick and waded out of the stream and looked toward the wooded trail. "Dan?" he called. He started up the trail in a fast walk, then he broke into a run. "DAN-N-N!"

He found Father Dan where he had fallen. Chest heaving from the run Moslin dropped to his knees and turned the priest onto his back. Father Dan's eyes were open, the corners of his mouth frothed with bloody spittle. There was a telltale hole in the breast of the sheepskin coat. Moslin shoved his hand beneath the coat, beneath the heavy shirt, and felt the hot sticky life that was pumping furiously from his dear friend's body. "Dan . . . Oh God . . . !"

Frantic, Moslin wondered what to do? A compress! He fumbled for his handkerchief. Run for help? He started to remove his boots. But surely Dan would die before help could return. Carry him on my back? *Do I have the strength?* There was no choice. *I must . . .*

As if reading Moslin's mind Father Dan focused his eyes on his friend. The priest's lips moved. Moslin put his ear close to Father Dan's mouth. There was no sound.

Father Dan's hand moved feebly toward his trousers pocket. "What, Dan . . . what?"

Father Dan's eyes were pleading.

Moslin reached into the pocket. His fingers touched a string of beads. A rosary! Understanding at last, Moslin withdrew the beads. Instinctively he held the rood to Father Dan's bloody lips. With all the strength left in his body the priest kissed the tiny replica of the crucified Jesus.

Now Father Dan's countenance softened and he looked up at Moslin again and for a brief moment the merry twinkle that Moslin had seen so often in those gentle eyes seemed to dance there once more. Then a rasping gasp rose from the priest's throat and his body jerked in a single spasmodic twitch. The dancing eyes glazed over and they fixed into a sightless stare at the setting sun.

It was done.

For a long while Moslin simply sat looking down at that now peaceful bronzed face. Finally, he reached over and closed the unseeing eyes. The first tears came when he folded the priest's hands on his chest and fixed them around the timeworn prayer beads. Then he lifted Father Dan and pulled him close. Cradling the priest in his arms, like a parent would cradle a beloved child, he rocked to and fro, weeping silently while the long shadows rose above the quiet hills and the waning sun at last disappeared from sight behind Redondo Peak.

19

WARD slammed the phone down in frustration.

"Damn!"

It was the sixth or seventh time (he'd lost count) that he'd dialed Tres Pinos in the past five hours without answer. He thought about driving to the ranch unannounced, but that might be a waste of time, and he didn't have much time to waste.

Nothing to do but call again later.

He picked up the evening paper and read the lead story again:

U.S. PLANES TO ARABIA

A Pentagon spokesman told reporters today that in response to a request from the Saudi Arabian Government the United States has instituted the temporary deployment of four Airborne Warning and Control System aircraft (AWACS) to Saudi Arabia. "The deployment is purely in support of Saudi Arabian defenses," the spokesman emphasized.

The AWACS, accompanied by 300 U.S. support personnel and three C5A Galaxy cargo aircraft, will fly directly to Saudi Arabia with mid-Atlantic refueling . . .

Ward tossed the paper aside. The story confirmed Sabin's briefing in spades.

The phone rang. He grabbed it before the second ring. "Yes?"

"Jon . . . Major Ward?"

"Janet?" There was an unsettling tone to her voice.

"Oh, Jonathan . . . can you come at once? My father wants to see you. Something dreadful has happened."

James Moslin sat on the couch facing the fire, drink in hand, an old man. His eyes were sunken deeply into their sockets. The eyelids were puffy. His face was a study in anguish. Seated at his side Janet held his free hand. She had been crying.

Ward said, "I came as fast as I could." He put his jacket and hat on the rack and took a chair facing the couch. "The sheriff has a roadblock at Jemez Springs. They suspect a poacher—a stupid hunting accident."

"It was no poacher," Moslin said flatly. He kept his eyes fixed on the flames. "He's miles from here by now."

"He? Who?" Ward asked. "Do you know who did it?"

Moslin shook his head. "I only know that he made a terrible mistake. He killed the wrong man."

"Oh . . . Dad . . ."

Moslin squeezed his daughter's hand. He told Ward about the coat exchange. "He obviously had us under surveillance. He mistook Dan for me."

It was too farfetched. "But why would you be marked for . . . something like that?"

"Assassination?" Moslin didn't quibble about the term. "That's why I asked you here. I want to tell you something . . . both of you, before it's too late. It's not a pretty story. But it's one I should have told long before this."

He drained his drink, plainly not the first of the evening, and handed the glass to Janet. "Would you?"

She rose dutifully and started for the kitchen. At the doorway she stopped and turned to Ward. "I'm sorry . . . do you . . . ?"

"No, nothing, thanks."

She returned and handed her father the refilled glass, took her place on the couch and waited.

Moslin said, "What I told you before, about my work in the defoliation program, was true. But it wasn't the whole truth. If my suspicions are correct, the whole truth—the fear that I might reveal it—has everything to do with the . . . the terrible thing that happened today. And"—he looked pointedly at Ward— "with you."

"Me? You mean the investigation?"

"Yes."

Moslin took a drink and fixed his eyes once again on the fire, as if by addressing those impersonal flames he found it easier to talk. "When I left Saigon in the summer of 1968 I didn't expect to return. The defoliation program was going well . . . Orange had proved itself. I was eager to get back to teaching. I took the same chair at the University of New Mexico that I had vacated on leave of absence to work for the government.

"Soon after the first of the year—I remember the spring semester had begun—I received a surprise visit. Doctor Lionus Greene came to see me at the school. At that time he was the Assistant Secretary of Defense for Research and Development. We had worked together earlier and knew each other well. He revealed some disturbing things about the defoliation program. Most of the experimental plants we had used years before to test Orange had turned up permanently acarpous—were producing sterile seeds. That didn't surprise me. What he told me next did.

"Beginning in the mid-sixties some of the men working with Orange began experiencing physical problems—low backaches, fever, painful urination, general malaise. Tests showed that a high percentage of these men, too, were sterile. Defense suspected Orange and immediately classified the findings 'Top Secret.' The complaining men never knew. They were told they had urinary tract infections.

"Their sterility was traced to a slight rise of temperature in their testicles. That's not uncommon. Tight-fitting, jockey-type underwear sometimes causes temporary sterility in males. Shepherds in some countries bind rams' testicles to produce the same result. But among the men in Vietnam there was a more serious problem. There was an accompanying insidious brain infection. Eventually, most of them recovered. But several died. Pathology revealed an accumulation of dioxin in their systems. There were eleven confirmed dioxin-related deaths."

"But nothing like that was ever reported," Ward exclaimed. "There've been no deaths attributed to Agent Orange."

"No. The deaths were attributed to other causes."

Ward shook his head incredulously.

Moslin said, "Greene finally got to the purpose of his visit. Defense wanted me to return to Vietnam, to work on Orange again, to isolate the infecting component and eliminate it. I could hardly refuse. I was one of the scientists responsible for Orange. Now it had turned killer. I left for Saigon the following week.

"On arrival I found a fully-equipped laboratory awaiting me. My chief assistant was already in place—Doctor Clyde Abernathy, a professor of chemistry at Stanford. First-rate reputation. Defense assigned us the codename *Delta*, under command of Major General Henry Rodale . . . you've heard of him?"

Ward shook his head.

"A brooding, single-minded man. My age, quite a bit larger. Virtually humorless. He assured me that I would have complete control in the laboratory but must keep him informed of every detail of our work. I learned that Delta was Rodale's sole responsibility. Somewhat strange, I thought, for a two-star general. But I didn't dwell on it.

"Previous Orange research concentrated on plant life. This time we worked with animals. Our approach was to expose mice, guinea pigs, other small rodents to modifications of the basic Orange formula. After some false starts the experiments progressed faster than any of us had hoped. Within six months we were experimenting on primates—monkeys and chimps. By the end of the year we had made an important breakthrough. One of the formulas, applied under rigid laboratory controls, virtually eliminated the brain fever and thus the deaths. But it still caused sterility. We waxed somewhat poetic and codenamed it *Kronus* . . ."

Ward said, "Kronus?"

Janet said, "Oh! The Titan . . . the one who devoured his children."

Moslin nodded. "I reported *Kronus* to General Rodale. He was elated. Next day, unaccountably, he ordered me to freeze the experiments at that stage and prepare *Kronus* in sufficient amounts for field testing. He planned an airdrop—aerial spray—using one of the defoliation planes. I warned him that the plan was premature—that we needed to conduct foliage tests first in the laboratory."

Moslin took a drink. "And he said: 'The tests are not to be conducted on foliage.' "

Ward said, "Oh . . . Christ."

Moslin said, "I see you're ahead of me."

"Chemical warfare," Ward said. "Human application. But . . . no deaths . . . no immediate effect. Holy shit! Slow genocide!"

Moslin nodded. "Cold, calculated, more diabolical than you may have guessed. The South Vietnamese High Command had already picked the target. Vo Lanh . . . a village of four hundred just north of Saigon."

Janet exclaimed, "Their own people?"

Moslin replied, "Easier to follow the results, they claimed."

"Did you object?" Ward asked. "Make any plea for sanity?"

The words stung Moslin. "I'm afraid that my only objection was that *Kronus* was too volatile at that stage for human experimentation. It would mean a low-level drop—less than a thousand feet. More important, the formula required an injection of a hydrogen-oxygen catalyst at the very last moment. But the precise mixture would depend on exact measurements of humidity, temperature, dew point, and a dozen other elements at the target area immediately before the catalyst was injected. That was possible only in the laboratory, I explained. Rodale overruled me. In fairness I must tell you that he gave me . . . us—I discussed it with Abernathy—the opportunity to pull out of the program at that point."

"And?"

"And . . . we didn't. We had developed *Kronus*. We rationalized that we were best qualified to assure that it caused the least harm. Looking back, I realize that our professional egos blinded us. We *wanted* to see the results of our creation. So . . . *God it was easy* . . . we became parties to the conspiracy. And . . . that's how I met Peter Crowell."

Janet paled. "Peter was part of . . . that?"

Moslin shook his head. "He didn't know. He thought he was flying a routine defoliation mission. We briefed him that it was a new Orange formula being tested against garden crops, that the villagers had been compensated. He accepted that on good faith.

"On the night of the mission Abernathy and I worked with *Kronus*—filled the canisters, made the final mix—right up until the minute of takeoff. Peter had developed a somewhat radical low-level flight plan, a fan-shaped upwind pattern to concentrate *Kronus* on the target area.

"The drop was made at midnight, the last day of May 1970. Ten days later Vo Lanh officials reported an epidemic in their village. Saigon suppressed the report, but a British journalist got wind of it and followed up. The wire services broke the story that a 'strange virus' had attacked Vo Lanh. Forty-seven villagers died. Thirty-three were children . . . under the age of ten."

Janet gasped.

Ward remained silent.

Moslin said, "Late on the night the story broke, Peter came to my quarters. He'd been drinking and I knew he had guessed the truth. He begged me to tell him that it wasn't so—that he wasn't responsible for those children's deaths. I was too guilt-ridden to lie. I didn't tell him everything about *Kronus*, but I admitted it had almost surely caused the tragedy. I tried to convince him that he wasn't responsible.

"He screamed and cursed me. He called me a fiend and murderer. Then he ran out into the night. It finally came to me that I shouldn't have let him leave in that state of mind. His quarters were about a mile from mine. I walked there—through a driving rain, I recall—but there was no answer when I knocked. I started to leave. Then, quite unlike me, I turned and kicked the door in. Peter was lying on the couch, his pilot's pistol in his hand. The gun hadn't been fired. There was an empty vodka bottle on the floor. He had passed out before he could . . . do what he had in mind. I hid the gun and sat with him through the night. He came out of it sometime in the morning hours too sick to resist my help. He began to quote Scripture—babbled about 'our sin.' I got coffee into him and tried to reason with him again about his innocence for what happened at Vo Lanh. He finally promised that he wouldn't try anything foolish. To make sure, when I left, I took the gun with me.

"Two weeks later, by coincidence I can only presume, President Nixon ordered all chemical warfare experiments halted. Delta was disbanded. General Rodale retired from active duty. Abernathy and I were surprised to learn from an Associated Press release that we had been awarded lucrative Federal grants to conduct private research. Mine was to study high-altitude winter grain yields, a subject that I had already studied to death. His was a similar make-work project in chemistry. We both recognized the truth. It was just one more deceit in a rotten, deceitful war. We were being paid to remain silent."

He turned up his glass and drained the remainder of the watery drink. "And silent I've remained . . . until now the dearest friend I ever had has paid for my silence with his life."

There was a chill in the room. Without asking, Ward got up and put two split piñon logs on the dying fire and poked the embers until the flames began to lick greedily at the seasoned wood. Moslin's mea culpa had been fascinating, at times infuriating. But where was the connection? Ward closed the fire screen and settled back in his chair. "Professor, it's an unsavory story. But I fail to see the tie-in with what happened at Kingman Reef . . . or to Father Dan."

Moslin nodded. "Bear with me . . . please." He eyed his empty glass, decided against another drink and set it aside.

"During the final two weeks I was in Saigon I made it a point to see Peter often. I felt a responsibility toward him. Despite everything, he appeared to welcome my friendship. Indeed, I sensed that I had become a father-figure to him. He seemed to have accepted my counsel about Vo Lanh—to have relegated it to some niche in his brain where he could cope with it. On the morning I left, Peter saw me off at the plane. I never expected to see him again.

"Five years later, when he showed up here, I was uneasy. But, he was a different person. Mature, confident, proud once more to be an Air Force officer. Then"—he gave Janet a soft look—"he met you. I was pleased with your marriage. The years you were in Alaska I missed you both. When you returned, and confided in me about your problems, it hurt, but I chose to stay out of it, to let the two of you work it out. Then, one afternoon, Peter forced the issue."

"I didn't know," Janet said.

"It was here, in this room. He began to question me about your past—your health . . ."

"My health?"

"Your inability to conceive. He blamed you, said he *knew* he could father children . . . because he had."

"Had . . . ?"

"A high school affair. The girl got an abortion. Peter dragged this unsavory skeleton out of his closet to convince me of his fertility. Once again, like on that rainy night in Saigon, he was pleading with me to tell him that *he* wasn't at fault . . . And I hurt him very much, I fear."

"How . . . what did you do?"

"I told him the truth about *Kronus*. A year after the attack on Vo Lanh the birthrate in the village dropped ninety-seven percent. The most dramatic single-year birth decline ever recorded. It was classified information, but Abernathy got hold of it and called me. He had performed a sperm count on himself. He was sterile. I did the same on myself, with the same results. I told all this to Peter. I told him that he was just another victim of *Kronus*."

"Oh, dear God," Janet sighed. "He wanted children so . . ."

"Peter was devastated. Then he said something I'll never forget. He said, 'God is just, Jim. We were fools to deny it.' Next morning he moved away from Tres Pinos."

Janet was silent.

Ward knew this couldn't be the end of the story, but he allowed them time for their thoughts. Finally, he prompted, "But he came back . . . often I understand."

"Weekends mostly," Moslin replied. "For reasons neither of you could suspect."

Janet looked at her father strangely.

"Peter was obsessed with *Kronus*. He questioned me in great detail about Vo Lanh. What went wrong? Could the deaths have been avoided?

"I explained *Kronus'* volatility—that because of the required precision measurements of the elements, the last second injection of the catalyst, it could be deployed with relative safety only from a flying computer. I told him that no such aircraft existed—then or now.

"And he told me about the XR-Twenty-One-Hundred and *Stargaze*."

Ward was jolted. "What?"

"In detail. *Cobra One* and *Cobra Two*. I was fascinated. An aircraft immune to radar, controlled by a sophisticated computer capable of pinpoint celestial navigation, of performing every flight function including operating the ancillary equipment. I had to agree with Peter. It was the perfect plane for *Kronus* missions."

Ward shook his head firmly. "Absurd, Professor." How far could he go? He was into a Top Secret area. Yet, what could he reveal that Crowell hadn't already? "I've seen both planes, examined them. Neither is adaptable for chemical warfare. Besides, only *Cobra Two* is operational . . . and I know its mission. Crowell was off base. Impossible."

"So I might have thought," Moslin agreed. "Except for a couple of incidents Peter told me about."

Ward started to say something. Instead, he sat back and listened.

"Peter had been flying high altitude training missions to test programs that had been engineered for *Stargaze*—each mission programmed on a single silicon chip, if I understood correctly."

He looked at Ward for confirmation.

Crowell *had* gabbed. Ward made a bland gesture. "Yes . . . correct."

"Last March Peter's commanding officer, General Sabin, assigned Peter a new mission. The Mescalero Apache reservation in southern New Mexico was the mock target. The flights were programmed for an altitude of a thousand feet—*in a fan-shaped upwind pattern.*"

Ward glanced up sharply.

"Yes," Moslin said. "A computer modification of the same flight pattern Peter had developed ten years before—for Vo Lanh."

"And . . . the second incident?"

"Two weeks before Peter went to the Pacific he flew *Cobra One* to Edwards Air Force Base for some last minute modifications. One of the other pilots took *Cobra Two* . . . a Colonel . . . uh . . ."

"Hadley?"

"Yes . . . Hadley. They were at Edwards for four days. The last night they were there Peter went to the project office around midnight to pick up some material he'd stored in the safe. He walked in on two men going over the blueprints for the modifications. One of the men was Doctor Van Atton, the chief design engineer. The other man hastily left the room. But Peter recognized him. He was Henry Rodale."

Ward shot out of the chair and began to pace. "But it doesn't make any damned sense! None of it. A ten-year-old formula that has to be treated with kid gloves, secret training flights that only Crowell flew, an over-the-hill retired general. Christ, it's out of a bad movie. It's too much to swallow."

"Maybe," Moslin said. "Still, you're left with the prospect that the man who was in charge of Delta, who had access to the *Kronus* formula, now has—perhaps had all along—access to the design plans for the XR-Twenty-One-Hundred."

Ward stopped and stared into the middle distance. "Design plans?" His eyes widened. "My God! A *Cobra Three!* But where? For what purpose? Whose babies are they trying to kill before they're even conceived?"

He looked at Moslin beseechingly.

Moslin shook his head. "I've told you all I know."

The professor rose wearily from the couch and went to the closet and took out a heavy denim jacket. "Now, I'd like to ask a favor."

Ward nodded.

Moslin said, "I think you can see now that what happened today was no accident. Someone did not want me talking to you, otherwise it would have happened before this. Pretty soon that someone is going to learn that a mistake was made—that the wrong person was silenced. I think it best that Janet and I move out for a few days. The church has offered us sanctuary. We'll go tomorrow morning . . . we'll let you know where." He fixed a knitted scarf around his neck and put the jacket on. "Tonight though, I'm going to spend one last evening with Father Dan. Will you stay here?"

Janet said, "I can go with Dad . . . if it's a problem."

"It's no problem."

Ward turned back to Moslin. "If you're so sure you're right, shouldn't you call Doctor Abernathy . . . warn him?"

Moslin buttoned the jacket. "Clyde Abernathy blew his brains out, Major . . . the day after he called me about Vo Lanh."

The bed was too soft. Ward tossed, unable to sleep. A distant vapor light at the barn gave the pines outside the window a ghostly aura. There was something else. The eerie quiet. The utter lack of sound at Tres Pinos that was nerve-racking to one accustomed to sleeping against the unabated sounds of city traffic or the interminable drone of jet engines on any Air Force base.

But it wasn't the soft bed, the ghostly pines or the deafening quiet that robbed him of sleep. His mind was in turmoil. Had he, as MacWatt had suggested, pushed into an area beyond his competence to proceed? The XR-2100 puzzle no longer centered on the crash of *Cobra One*, or Major Peter Crowell's probable culpability. There was clear evidence of a conspiracy.

Evidence?

"Shit!"

He stared hard at the darkened ceiling and shook his head in frustration. What evidence? A cross-wired navigation box? Proving what beyond the probability of a crazed pilot?

Moslin's suspicions of a hit man? Despite the professor's troublesome story about *Kronus*, who would believe his fears of martyrdom were anything other than the product of a guilt-ridden conscience?

All else was hearsay. Crowell said this, Crowell saw that. The unsubstantiated and unsubstantiatable testimony of a dead man. A man whose mind was warped, who plotted death and succeeded.

Conspiracy? By whom? Who was lying, or at least not telling the whole truth? Sabin? Burnside? Hadley? MacWatt? Conspiracy to do what? Where? To whom?

No military court of inquiry would consider any of it.

He heard Janet's footsteps. She couldn't sleep either, he supposed, and was coming downstairs to—the kitchen? He wondered if he should join her? He was still pondering the thought when the door to his room opened and she was standing there is a sheer gown, bathed in the soft glow of the vapor light shining through the window. She left the door open and came softly to the side of the bed and hugged her bare shoulders and gave a compulsive shiver.

He rose on one elbow.

She said hoarsely, "I . . . I can't be alone tonight."

He reached out a hand and she took it and got into the bed beside him. He fixed the covers over her and placed his arm beneath her head. She turned toward him and put her head on his shoulder. Her body was like ice but he felt hot tears falling on his arm.

"Oh-h-h, Jonathan," she moaned, "what has happened? Why did Father Dan have to die? What has ... Peter ... done ... ?"

She was crying. Great, racking sobs that shook the bed. He held her closer and stroked her hair and soothed her like a hurt child that needed balm.

After a while she grew quiet and fell into an exhausted sleep. His arm began to cramp. He lifted her head gently with his free hand, flexed his muscles and put her head back on his shoulder.

Sometime during the night she cried out, startling him awake. He was surprised that he had dozed off. He looked at her closely. She hadn't awakened. He adjusted his arm once more and fell asleep again.

During the twilight hours shortly before dawn they made love. Tenderly, without urgency, a simultaneous recognition of mutual needs, a warm and willing giving of one to the other.

Afterward, when she had fallen asleep yet once again, Ward lay engrossed in thought. The gentleness of their lovemaking, his conscious desire to *give* of himself, not simply take, was a new and strange awareness. For the first time after sex he felt ... he didn't know how else to express it ... *manly*. It was as if he had never been with a woman before. He wanted to protect, to comfort, to provide ... to love.

Was this what Susan had meant?

He dismissed thoughts of Susan.

He pulled Janet closer and held her tightly.

He wanted no other woman in his thoughts this night.

20

ELWOOD Hadley pressed the light button on the clock beside his bed. 3:02 AM. Beset by anxieties, he rolled back and stared into the darkness. He was trapped in a no-win situation, a helpless pawn in a power play between two willful generals. How had he stumbled into this abyss? He was not an overly ambitious officer. Nor one of the brightest. He had long ago reconciled himself to his limitations. But he was a competent staff officer who could ramrod a decision through hell or high water once someone else made it. Before the *Cobra One* fiasco he had prided himself on an unerring ability to foresee trouble and sidestep it before it encompassed him. It was a "protect your ass" attitude that all staff officers must adopt or perish.

Now, his career was teetering on the brink.

Dee Hadley emitted the soft snores of deep sleep. Elwood pushed the covers aside gently so not to disturb her and got up. There would be no sleep for him this night.

He grabbed his uniform, shoes and socks and went to the living room to put them on. It was five hours before time to go to work, but he didn't want to stay home. There was always something to do at the office. And it might take his mind off his miseries.

He parked in front of the Quickseal compound in the space

marked EXECUTIVE OFFICER. Two slots away, in the space marked COMMANDER, was General Sabin's five-year-old Chevrolet. The presence of the car wasn't unusual. Quite often Sabin left it at the compound and ran the eight miles to his quarters, then ran back the next morning.

Hadley studied the Chevrolet with amusement. Last summer one of the Quickseal officers, a first lieutenant, arrived at work one morning driving a shiny new Volvo. Sabin summoned the young officer forthwith. The choice of a personal automobile was a matter of individual rights, Sabin assured him. But the lieutenant should know that the general questioned the commitment of any officer who preferred a foreign-made to an American-made car.

Next day the lieutenant traded for a Chevy.

Hadley cleared through the guard gate and walked across the darkened compound to the command building. At his desk he thumbed through several papers in his IN basket, finally selecting the weekly fuel-consumption report to check against allocations. He had just settled into the task when he was surprised by the whine of a generator in the compound yard. It was a familiar sound. The track-mounted gate between the hangars and the outside runway was being opened. But at 3:30 AM? He switched off the lights and went to the window.

A Lear Jet was taxiing from the runway through the gate into the compound. It rolled swiftly past the hangars and braked to a stop at the blockhouse. Hadley recognized the red-and-white jet. It was one of the Consolidated General Aircraft Corporation executive planes. It shuttled between Los Angeles and Kirtland several times a month. But never before at this hour. He pulled down the blind, switched on a desk light and dug through his IN basket until he found the manifest of flights for the day. There was no listing for Consolidated General. The plane couldn't have landed at Kirtland—certainly not on the off-limits Quickseal runway—without clearance from Base Operations. The clearance must have been verbal. Only two officers had that authority—General Burnside and General Sabin.

Hadley returned to the window to see a man in civilian clothes climb down from the plane and enter the blockhouse. The pilot, dimly visible through the cockpit window, remained seated. He didn't shut down the engines.

What the hell was going on?

Hadley left his office and hurried down the hall to the monitor room. He closed the door, switched on the lights and hunted about the huge console for the control to the blockhouse surveillance camera. He found it and switched it on. In a second one of the monitor screens above the console came alive with the image of the blockhouse interior. In the center of the room the man in civilian clothes was talking with—General Bartholomew Sabin.

The man in civvies, a stranger to Hadley, was as tall as Sabin, but huskier, and appeared considerably older. In his sixties, Hadley guessed. He wished he had a clearer view. Instinctively, he reached for the zoom switch. Then, as if he had touched hot metal, he withdrew his hand. What if Sabin noticed the red light on the monitor camera? Hadley's insides shriveled. He was courting disaster. He should switch off the camera. Now. Leave the compound at once.

On the monitor screen Sabin was opening the safe near the XR-2100 trainer. He took out a tiny black box, locked the safe again and went to the trainer. He motioned the stranger to join him.

Hadley couldn't believe it. That box contained a Top Secret *Stargaze* mission package. Ignoring the fear gnawing at his guts, he reached for the zoom switch and calibrated it until the two men on the screen were in close-up focus. Then he pushed a yellow button near the zoom switch. Seconds later a Polaroid photo dropped from a slot into a waiting tray. Hadley grabbed the photo. It was a clear reproduction of the image on the screen.

On the monitor Sabin inserted the *Stargaze* mission package into the trainer.

Hadley pushed the yellow button.

Sabin and the stranger took the computer printout from the trainer to a table to study. The stranger nodded approvingly.

Hadley pushed the yellow button.

Sabin extracted the mission package from the trainer and handed it to the stranger. The stranger put it in his pocket, then picked up the readout and placed it under his arm. He shook hands with Sabin.

Hadley pushed the yellow button.

The stranger left.

Hadley shut down the monitor, grabbed the Polaroid photos and shoved them in his pocket. He rushed back to his office. The Lear Jet was already taxiing through the gate toward the runway. Before the gate was fully closed the plane was on its takeoff roll. Twenty minutes from the time Hadley first spotted it, it was airborne and winging westward in the inky New Mexico sky.

Hadley sat at his desk in the darkness, trembling. The clandestine photos in his pocket felt like live coals searing into his body.

All at once he bolted out of the chair. *My car!* "Oh-h-h-h, Jesus . . ."

He started for the door. He had to move the car before Sabin saw it. He stopped. What if he met Sabin in the hall? Or the general saw him driving away? Or the guards mentioned him?

He returned to his desk. It was four o'clock. Would Sabin leave, or stay in his office for the workday? Either way he might learn of Hadley's presence. Hadley switched on the light and arranged some papers across his desk. If he was going to be discovered it would be best to be found here, working, as if nothing were out of order, as if he had seen nothing unusual.

He would bluff it out.

He sat at the desk and waited.

21

"DO you ever dream?" she asked.

"Sure." Ward was lying on his back, hands folded beneath his head, watching the sunlight play on the pines outside the window. "Do you?"

"Sometimes."

"What about?"

"Peter, mostly. Funny . . . it's always about our good times. Never the bad."

He turned his head on the pillow. "Did you dream of Peter last night?"

She smiled, the first time he'd seen her do that. "No . . . not last night."

She asked, "What do you dream about?"

He was silent.

She pressed. "I told you."

"My father," he said finally.

"Do you have a good relationship?"

"He died when I was a boy."

"Oh . . . I'm sorry."

"It's OK. It was a long time ago. For some reason, though, the older I get the more I think of him. He was . . . a great guy."

"Tell me about him."

He hesitated. Then, suddenly, it poured out. His boyhood. His closeness to his father. Their outings, campouts, overnight hikes, the private pool by the river. She listened intently, knowing intuitively that he had never spoken of these things to anyone before, but had wanted to, needed to, desperately.

She learned that he was ten when his father died. That his mother, never a warm person, turned even more bitter, taking her bitterness out on her son, missing few opportunities to reproach him.

"There was a barn near home. We kids used to play there. One day—it was shortly after my father died—a girl and I slipped into one of the stalls. We were experimenting, kissing, awkward kid stuff . . . I was feeling her up. My mother caught us. I don't know how long she'd been there, watching. She gave us hell—not yelling, or anything like that—just tore us apart with that bitchy voice of hers. She called the girl a little slut. The kid fled in tears. All the way home my mother told me how filthy I was—she used that exact word. Said I was going to burn in hell. I wasn't old enough then to know what a castration complex was. That came later. And I hated her for it, and all the other guilts she laid on me. I left when I was seventeen. Didn't say a word to her. I've never been back."

Janet put her head on his shoulder. "Oh, my darling . . . how could you love any woman after that?" She leaned up and kissed him gently on the lips then smiled wryly. "But we both know you do that very well, don't we?"

It was his turn to smile.

After a moment he said, "She's dying."

Janet drew back with a questioning look.

"She wrote to me . . . had her congressman track me down." He told her about the letter. "She wants to see me. I . . . don't know if I can do that."

They let the silence grow. Then Janet said, "You must, you know. She's reaching out."

He sucked in his breath. "I . . . just don't know."

She decided not to make an issue of it.

"Oh"—she sat up suddenly—"I almost forgot. I've got something for you."

"For me?"

She stood and picked up her silken gown from the floor and slipped it on over her head. "Peter's things. Some books and papers. Probably nothing." She shook the gown down around her body. "There's some of Dad's shaving stuff in the hall bathroom. My toothbrush is the red one. When you're ready, come to the kitchen."

The sheer pink gown clung to her body like a gossamer sheath, caressing every sensuous curve and crevice. He gave her a smoldering look and reached for her again. She stepped back out of his reach. "Later," she said with a saucy smile. "The kitchen . . . OK?"

She blew him a kiss and left.

Twenty minutes later he was seated at the long pine table in the kitchen looking through the stuff Janet had retrieved from the trunk in the barn. It was an assortment of flight logs, temporary duty records, finance records, personnel file entries—basic items any officer might maintain, of no interest to Ward. But one item did interest him. It was a portion of a computer printout, torn in the size of a sheet of tablet paper, folded and creased several times as if it had been carried in a pocket. It was similar to the XR-2100 trainer printouts, with a major difference. It was in binary, thus undecipherable to Ward. In the upper corner of the paper was a penciled annotation:

ARG ALHA $22^h33^m57^s.348$
GAD $-52°40'55".36$
L 30–30 62° + HOR 151° AP AZ
GRID + 40 Km 180/225/270/ INTRA

Ward laid the paper flat on the table and pressed it with his hands. "Janet."

She was measuring grounds into a drip coffee maker. She had showered and dressed in her tan slacks and sweater and had a yellow bath towel wrapped Turkish-style around her still-wet hair. She wore no makeup. But her hazel eyes sparkled, her face bore a radiant glow. "Yes?"

"Is this Peter's handwriting?"

She came to the table. The annotation was printed in block letters and numerals. "Yes." She put a finger on the paper. "He always made twos like that—with that little curly-cue on the tail. Um-m-m . . . you smell good."

He smiled. "Your dad's bay rum."

He indicated the annotation. "Do you have any idea what it is?"

"Me? Heavens no."

"Have you seen it before, or anything like it?"

She shook her head. "No."

Ward suspected as much. If the paper depicted what he thought it did it wasn't the sort of thing Major Peter Crowell should have been working on at home.

Ward looked at the annotation again. Could L 30–30 stand for longitude / latitude? "Do you have an atlas . . . a world map?"

"In the den, on the wall beside the desk."

It was a National Geographic World Map, scale: 395 miles to the inch at the equator. With his finger he plotted 30°N–30°E—a spot approximately eighty miles west of Cairo, Egypt. Sabin had said that *Cobra Two* would operate from a "secret base near Cairo." Sure as hell the computer readout Crowell had filched had something to do with that. But why would he keep something so sensitive in his personal files? Did it have to do with what Moslin revealed last night? *Kronus?* Chemwar in the Middle East, where the Soviets would surely detect it and reveal it to the world within minutes after a drop? The thought was preposterous. Something was badly out of phase.

The smell of frying bacon wafted through the hall into the den. Janet was fixing breakfast. Moslin would be home soon.

There was a phone on the desk. Ward sat down and dialed MacWatt's office at Kirtland. Ann Lucero answered, then, a second later, MacWatt's gruff voice came through the receiver. "Ward . . . where the hell are you?"

"Tres Pinos. I'll be back on base in a couple of hours. I want to talk to a navigator. A good one. You know anybody?"

"The best. Lieutenant Wheeler, General Burnside's pilot. But why?"

"I'll explain later. Next, there's a retired officer—General Henry Rodale . . ."

"Hank Rodale?"

"You know him?"

"We've met. What the hell's he got to do with this?"

"I don't know. Maybe nothing. Can you find out where he is now . . . what he's doing?"

Hesitation. "That might take some doing. I'll try. And I'm awful damned curious."

"I know. One last thing: Try to find out if Rodale and General Sabin ever worked together."

There was no response.

"Colonel?"

"I'm still here," MacWatt replied. "Jonathan"—Ward was surprised. It was the first time MacWatt had ever addressed him by his first name—"sounds to me like you might be flying into stormy skies. Whatever this is about, we can't sit on it much longer."

"I know. I just want to be sure. Two days, remember? I've still got today."

Another pause. "All right. But I want a full report before the day ends."

"You got it." Ward hung up.

Colonel Robert MacWatt stared at the phone on his desk for a full five minutes. Finally he looked at the notes he'd scribbled while Ward talked.

Navigator. No problem.

Sabin/Rodale work together. That would be a matter of personnel records.

Rodale location. MacWatt's brow knitted. He sat back in his chair and laced his fingers across his ample stomach. He hadn't thought of Hank Rodale in years. General Hap Arnold's right-hand man. Brilliant intellect. Father of Air Force Intelligence. A shoo-in in everybody's book to become Chief of Staff. Then, a gross indiscretion, a brazen confrontation with the civilian hierarchy, fired in disgrace by LBJ.

An Air Force legend, and Air Force tragedy.

Why in God's name was Ward interested in Rodale?

And how the hell am I going to find out where he is—if he's still alive?

MacWatt pondered. The World Wide Officer Locator service in Washington was always hit and miss. Personnel Office at the Pentagon? Perhaps, but slow as cold molasses. Then it came to him. There was one office that all retired officers kept informed of their whereabouts—religiously.

MacWatt buzzed Ann Lucero.

"Yes sir?"

"Ann, get me the chief of the Air Force Retiree Pay Section in Denver."

22

ROBERTA Burnside Vancase finished the last of the breakfast dishes and placed them in the drain basket to dry. From time to time she glanced out the kitchen window into the backyard. Pampered by Roberta's green thumb and the beneficent California climate the yard was a veritable Eden. Enclosed by a seven-foot-high redwood fence the lush bluegrass lawn was accented by mature lime and orange trees, a side border of show-quality Peace and American Beauty roses, walls of English ivy, a giant magenta bougainvillaea, flowering bird-of-paradise plants, a miniature jade tree, and a variety of complementing shrubs.

But it wasn't the garden that drew Roberta's attention. In a corner of the yard sheltered by a broad-canopied avocado tree, Roberta's mother lay on a chaise longue with an open book on her lap, gazing blankly into space.

Roberta dried her hands on the dish towel and stepped into the den. Her three-year-old son, still in pajamas, was sprawled on the floor in front of the television, chin resting on his hands, absorbed in an overloud episode of *Mighty Mouse*.

"Louis, I'm going out in the backyard with grandmother for a few minutes."

The boy nodded without comment.

Roberta walked across the yard and sat down in a lawn chair near the lounge. She'd been there a full minute before her mother noticed her.

"Oh . . . Roberta. I was just admiring your yard. It's so . . ."

"Bullshit, Mother."

"Roberta!"

Eileen could not reconcile herself to the younger generation's penchant for accenting their speech with vulgarities. Still, she realized that Roberta meant no disrespect.

"Mother, you're daydreaming again about Father."

"No . . ." Eileen started to protest.

Then, "Oh . . . all right. I guess I was. But I *was* admiring your garden. It reminds me so much of the courtyard outside our room at the Fujia Hotel in Hakone, near Mount Fujiyama, where your father and I spent our honeymoon. It was winter, but the garden was fed by hot springs. Louis and I had breakfast there every morning. It was so . . . lovely."

Roberta moved her chair closer and took her mother's hand in hers. "Mother, I love you dearly . . . we all do. And you're welcome here anytime. But all you've done for over a week now is mope around the house with your mind a million— no, eight hundred—miles away. It's tearing you apart. I understand why you miss Father so. It's your first trip here without him."

Roberta sat back. "Now, I want you to get up, go inside and call Father right now."

"Call him? Oh, Roberta . . . he's at work now. I can't possibly . . ."

"Oh yes you can! Mother, you're fifty-two years old. You've earned the right to do what you want. And it's time you started. Now, go in and call him and tell him that either he catches a plane for L.A. today or you're going to fly to Albuquerque and personally escort him back here. Hell, the Air Force isn't going to fall apart because one of its generals takes a few days off."

Eileen bit her lower lip. "Do you really think I should?"

"Would you like for him to be here with you?"

"Yes . . . I would."

"Then do it."

Eileen's eyes flashed resolve. She threw her feet over the side of the lounge and stood up. "Very well. I will!"

Major General Louis Burnside tore the sheet from the yellow tablet, crumpled it with a curse, then tossed it in the wastebasket where it would be gathered at the end of the workday by the AFRTC security officer and shredded along with the wastebasket contents from the other offices in the command section.

The general had secluded himself at his desk, with orders not to be disturbed. The wastebasket bore ample evidence of the difficulties he was having expressing in writing what was on his mind. Once again he picked up the letter from General McCollum about Sabin, stood and paced the floor while he read: *"It's nothing I can put my finger on, but I know you well enough to suspect that something is bothering you about this officer . . . If there's something I should know about him that isn't in his records please let me know at once . . ."*

"Damn!"

He tossed the letter back on the desk. He despised these "fuck your buddy" reports. Granted, they had kept many misfits from donning stars. But it was the flip side of the coin that bothered Burnside. How many deserving officers had been sacrificed to vindictiveness?

He sat down and picked up his pen. If he finished the letter soon, Lieutenant Wheeler could fly to Washington and deliver it to the Chief of Staff that evening. He pulled the tablet to him and wrote:

2 Oct 80

Dear Gip:

Regarding your letter of 29 Sep 80, please understand that what I am addressing herein is an intuitive uneasiness on my part that can't, to my knowledge, be backed up by any hard evidence. But in the past few months I have become increasingly concerned by what I sense to be a clear and present danger to our . . .

Suddenly, he grimaced and gripped the pen so hard that it broke. An excruciating pain rose in his chest and spread quickly across his shoulder and down his left arm. He pushed the chair back and opened the desk drawer and rummaged for his pills. Then he remembered. They were in the medicine cabinet in the bathroom.

He stood on rubbery legs and started across the room. After a half-dozen faltering steps his knees buckled. He grabbed the nearest chair and lowered himself into it. His breathing came in short rapid gasps. The vise clamped tighter over his sternum and he broke out in a cold sweat. He clutched his tie and tried to loosen it but he didn't have the strength. He knew exactly what was happening to him.

He tried to call out to Ann but his voice wouldn't come.

The intercom.

The button was on his phone. He leaned forward and stretched his arm feebly toward the desk. It was too far, too great an effort. His hand fell to his side, his vision became blurred with tears of agony. Resolutely, he fell back in the chair and turned his head toward the credenza behind his desk. He stared through an opaque film until his eyes found what they were seeking. A silver-framed photograph of his wife, dressed in a colorful kimono, taken in the small courtyard outside their hotel room in Hakone during their honeymoon. With grim determination he kept his eyes focused on that photograph until at last the light failed and he could see no more.

"Eileen," he whispered.

It was the last word he ever said.

Ann Lucero turned off her typewriter and reached for the ringing phone. "General Burnside's office."

"Miss Lucero?"

"Mrs. Burnside . . . how nice to hear your voice," Ann said with sincere warmth.

"Thank you. Is my husband busy?"

Ann hesitated. "He did tell me that he wanted no interruptions. But it's been nearly two hours. I'm sure he'd want to talk to you."

"No . . . no," Eileen said hastily. "Don't disturb him, please. But would you do me a favor?"

"I'd be delighted."

"Tell him I called. Tell him I'll call again this afternoon . . . around one."

"One o'clock. Yes. Are you certain you don't need to talk to him now?"

"No. This afternoon will be fine. Thank you, Ann."

Ann Lucero placed the phone back in the cradle and made a note on her pad. She looked toward the closed door to the commander's office. It was almost noon. General Burnside had been secluded since nine-thirty.

She made a decision. She'd stay at her desk through the lunch hour. If the general hadn't buzzed by then she'd make up some excuse to interrupt him.

23

FIRST Lieutenant William C. "Billy" Wheeler showed his ID card to the security policeman stationed at Ward's quarters. It was mere formality. The SP recognized the handsome young lieutenant readily. As did everyone at Kirtland. For Billy Wheeler was something of an Air Force celebrity.

The fourth son in a large family whose mother encouraged reading from the time her children could hold a book, Billy Wheeler graduated from North Little Rock High School with a perfect four-point grade average. His accomplishment attracted the media. That attracted the politicians who stumbled over themselves to reward the deserving student. Billy Wheeler became the first person from Arkansas to receive simultaneous nominations to the Military Academy at West Point, the Naval Academy at Annapolis, and the Air Force Academy at Colorado Springs.

Billy Wheeler's scholastic abilities would have assured him success in any of the schools. Acceptance as an officer after graduation was another matter.

For Billy Wheeler was black.

After realistic consideration he chose the least tradition-bound, thus the most liberal, of the services—the Air Force. In 1979 he graduated fourth in his class from the USAF Academy, setting a grade record in celestial navigation that was without equal.

On this morning Wheeler wondered what could be so urgent that Colonel MacWatt had ordered him to drop all other duties that day and report to the visiting major.

Ward was seated at his desk, a piece of paper in his hand, when the SP escorted Wheeler inside. The young officer saluted snappily. "Lieutenant Wheeler, sir!"

Ward returned the salute and nodded for the SP to leave. He motioned Wheeler to a chair, then, without preliminaries, shoved the paper across the desk. "What do you make of this, Lieutenant?"

Wheeler picked up the printout with Crowell's annotation and gave it a puzzled look. "What is it, sir?"

Ward's expectations plummeted. "I was hoping you could tell me."

"Oh."

Wheeler studied the paper closer. "Mmm . . . uh huh . . . mmm." He looked up at Ward. "Major, could this have anything to do with star patterns? Celestial navigation maybe?"

That's better, Ward thought. "It very well could have."

"I'll need my books."

"You'll have to do it here."

Wheeler put the paper back on the desk. "I'll be back in twenty minutes."

A half hour later, coat off, sleeves rolled two turns above his umber wrists, Billy Wheeler sat at the limed-oak dining table in Ward's quarters surrounded by books and pamphlets. The digital printout lay flat in front of him. His fingers manipulated the keys of a hand-held calculator. Every few minutes he would write something on a tablet, check it against the reading on the calculator, then refer to one or another of the books.

Ward paced impatiently. From time to time he would stop, bend low and watch the computations. He picked up one of the hefty tomes—*Advanced Celestial Navigation*. He put it down and picked up another—*Plotting the Stars*. When he reached for a third Wheeler shook his head in frustration. "Major . . . please."

Ward straightened up sharply. "Oh. Sorry."

He went to the couch and tried to concern himself with the

air traffic visible from the window. It didn't help. He sat back, fixed his eyes on the activity at the dining table, drummed his fingers on the back of the couch and waited.

Forty-five slow-passing minutes later Billy Wheeler tossed his pencil onto the table and rubbed his eyes with the back of his hands. "Major . . . you don't assign easy chores."

Ward glanced at his watch. Almost noon. He couldn't stall MacWatt much longer. "Keep at it," he said stiffly.

The lieutenant flashed a triumphant smile. "Oh, it's done."

"Done?" Ward bounded to the table. "What? Tell me."

Wheeler pushed the books aside. "Well, what you've got here is a pretty damned weird flight plan. Are you familiar with computerized star-navigation systems . . . like the one in the *Blackbird?*" It was the nickname for the SR-71 spy plane.

"Some," Ward dissembled.

"That system, or something like it, is what this"—Wheeler tapped Crowell's annotation—"is all about. It's an astronomic equation for a flight plan based on the position of a major star. This entry here—ARG—refers to Argus, one of the star's names. Alpha Argus, to be precise, in the constellation Argo Navis. It's the second brightest star in the sky. Sirus outshines it, but Argus is much further away . . . so its probably much larger. Its more common name is Canopus."

"Canopus?"

Wheeler nodded. "King Menelaus's pilot—Greek mythology."

"Oh, sure," Ward quipped. "This, uh, Canopus flight plan—does it pinpoint an exact location?"

"You bet." Wheeler looked around the room. "You got a map of Africa?"

Egypt, Ward thought. His guess in Moslin's den had been right.

He got an atlas from the bookcase and opened it to a map of northern Africa and the Middle East. "Show me."

"Not on this map, I can't."

Ward was puzzled. "But the equation . . . I plotted the co-ordinates. Longitude thirty—latitude thirty." He pointed to the spot west of Cairo, Egypt.

Wheeler laughed. "Major, there're four places on the globe where those parallels and meridians intersect. You picked the wrong latitude. Canopus is a southern hemisphere star." He pulled the atlas to him and flipped through it. "Here . . . this is the location in the equation."

Billy Wheeler's finger was resting at the intersection of grid coordinates 30°E–30°S, on the east coast of the Republic of South Africa.

Ward looked at the map incredulously. "But . . . it . . . are you certain?"

"I'm certain."

Ward expelled a long breath. "What's the target?"

"Target?"

"Uh . . . location." Ward cursed silently at his lapse. "Is there an exact flight path?"

Wheeler picked up a compass and placed the tip at the intersection of the grid lines. He drew an arc from 180° to 270°, forty kilometers from the grid reference. "Right there."

Ward studied the line Wheeler had drawn. *A fan-shaped pattern.*

The arc bisected the bold-printed word TRANSKEI, indicating a small roughly rectangular area color-shaded to distinguish it from the surrounding area. Ward put a finger on the word. "Trans . . ."

"Trans-*kay*," Wheeler said. "Only the northern section, really. It's one of the Bantustans."

Ward made a gesture of incomprehension.

"*Bantustan*," Wheeler repeated. "From the word Bantu— the Afrikaans word for black. The Bantustans are 'designated homelands,' supposedly independent states. In reality they're part of a system of forced segregation, a method of corralling eighty percent of the population onto thirteen percent of the land. You know—apartheid—a way for whitey to keep control."

Wheeler was smiling but there was no humor in his voice.

"You mean"—Ward traced the curved line with his hand— "that everyone in this area is . . . black?"

"You got it."

Suddenly, the diabolical meaning of it struck Ward with magnum force. He sat down in the nearest chair, his face flushed scarlet, his jaw muscles bulged angrily. Then, in a voice that was molten steel, he said, "Those dirty . . . murdering . . . sons-of-bitches!"

"Sir?" Wheeler exclaimed.

Ward didn't respond. For a full five minutes he sat immobile, staring into space, his mind's eye fixed on something Wheeler could neither see nor understand.

Wheeler wondered anew what the major had meant by "target." He debated whether to ask.

Finally, Ward said, "Lieutenant, everything you've learned here . . . everything we've discussed, is Top Secret. Do you understand?"

Wheeler decided not to ask the burning question. "Yes sir."

"One other thing. Is there anything in the equation that reveals a time . . . a date?"

"Not in so many words," Wheeler responded. "But it's there."

Using his pencil for a pointer he pushed the equation across the table to where Ward could see it. "The universe is constantly expanding, but for purposes of a human lifetime the stars can be considered stationary. This entry here—ALHA—stands for 'apparent local hour angle.' GAD means 'geocentric apparent declination.' There's only one time in any year when Canopus is at the precise position above the thirtieth meridian at that exact local hour angle and declination—0200 at the meridian."

"And the date?"

"November fifth."

Ward did a quick mental calculation.

November 5, 1980.

Thirty-four days from now.

24

COLONEL MacWatt stood with his hands clasped behind his back, staring out the window in Ward's quarters, trying to assimilate the major's latest disclosures. Without turning, he said, "This Canopus thing . . . the alleged secret mission . . . what's the purpose? Who's to gain?"

"I don't know," Ward replied.

"Still, you believe that this . . . plot . . . led Major Crowell to crash *Cobra One?*"

"To cause *Cobra One* to crash," Ward corrected. "I believe that his suspicions about his training flights led him to analyze them secretly on the Quickseal flight trainer. He learned that once again he was the dupe in a foul plan. That, along with his long-suppressed guilt over Vo Lanh, and learning that he, too, was a victim of *Kronus*, simply drove him over the edge. He picked Kingman Reef because of its remoteness. He wanted to trigger a vast air-sea search—an international attention getter that couldn't be swept under the rug. He hoped that the resulting investigation would uncover the conspiracy—the 'great evil.' But then *Cobra One* was salvaged almost intact, nothing was found wrong with the plane. Sabin limited the investigation and ordered Hadley to find 'pilot error'—to put the blame on Crowell. That would have been the end of Crowell's scheme except for one thing: General Burnside wasn't buying 'pilot error.' When he shot down Hadley's findings and called me into the act, Sabin tried to scare me off. When that failed he changed tactics and massaged my ego. He confided in me about *Cobra Two*'s Middle East spy flights, using the truth as a smoke-screen to throw me off course. A smokescreen that was blown away by the bullet that blew away Father Dan."

MacWatt crossed the room and sat on the edge of the desk facing Ward. "Are you sure that wasn't a hunting accident? It happens every year."

"No, I'm not sure. But Moslin is, and that's what matters."

MacWatt thought it over. "All right, they—whoever *they* are—have the plane, they have *Kronus*, and, for whatever purpose, they have a target. Why not get on with it? What's so magic about two o'clock in the morning on November fifth?"

"Think about it," Ward said cryptically.

"Jonathan, I'm in no mood for games."

"Yes sir. Sorry. Well, I wondered about that too. First I figured the mission was to counteract something planned to occur in that part of the world at that time. But, considering the nature of *Kronus*—its effect is long range, not immediate—I discounted that. I finally concluded that there's only one explanation for the time."

"Which is?"

"There's a seven-hour time lag between the target area and Washington. When it's 2 AM on the fifth there it will be 7 PM the fourth in D.C. Election day. One of the most critical in history according to the pundits. By that time the networks will be dissecting the votes, the country and most of the world will be distracted by the great ballyhoo about who the next American President will be. If you were an American general and wanted to pull off a bootleg clandestine operation . . . what better time to do it?"

MacWatt chuckled. "You've got an answer for everything, haven't you?"

Ward didn't reply.

MacWatt looked at his watch. He was missing lunch. "Still mostly conjecture, though. No smoking gun."

"No," Ward admitted. "No smoking gun."

MacWatt's gut gave a rumble. "You got anything to eat in that refrige?"

Ward stood. "I'll make sandwiches. Mustard or mayonnaise?"

"Both."

Ward brought the food and two beers. MacWatt had moved to the chair behind the desk. He grabbed a sandwich and took a ravenous bite. After a moment he said, "Jonathan, I'd be inclined to discount your story, except . . ." He hesitated.

"Except what?" Ward prompted.

"How much do you know about Henry Rodale?"

"What Moslin told me. I may have heard the name before . . . not much really."

MacWatt took a drink of beer, frowned and looked at the label. It was low-calorie. He uttered an oath and shoved the bottle aside. "Hank Rodale was a brilliant officer, one of the Air Force's first greats. He was to the sneak game what Rickover was to nuclear subs. He recognized the superiority of the MIG years before Korea proved it. He predicted Sputnik thirteen months before it blasted off. He was the first to weed out the Ivy League types from intelligence billets and replace them with engineers and scientists. The CIA pinstripers wanted his scalp. But he had a friend in court—John Kennedy."

"Good friend to have," Ward commented.

MacWatt said, "On Kennedy's inauguration, Rodale pinned on a second star and became Chief of Air Force Intelligence. After Dallas, Lyndon Johnson kept him on. He was LBJ's kind of guy. It was common knowledge that Johnson was grooming him for Chairman of the Joint Chiefs. Everything looked roses. But Rodale had a fatal flaw in his character."

"A flaw?"

"He was a bigot—a white supremacist. He was democratic about it. Hispanic, Negro, Oriental—made no difference to him. He despised them all. By the mid-sixties he had become obsessed by what he saw as the 'ethnic deterioration' of the armed forces. He tried to convince the Chief of Staff to conduct an official study. Of course, the chief refused. So, Rodale did it on his own. Ironically, there was a ready-made laboratory for him . . . Iceland."

"I don't understand."

"Iceland restricted NATO forces stationed there to Caucasians only. The Pentagon and State Department kept it low-key, denied collusion. Nevertheless, our troops there were as lily-white as the delegates to a Klan convention. Rodale chose Iceland as the 'norm' for his study. He tabulated the operational efficiency of American forces there against that of American forces around the globe. He came up with some pretty farfetched conclusions. He insisted that his study showed that when the complement of any unit reached a ratio of less than eighty percent Caucasian, efficiency began to deteriorate. When the ratio reached less than seventy percent, the unit was dangerously below 'optimal performance standards.' "

"Christ!" Ward exclaimed. "That's straight out of the Third Reich."

"You better believe it," MacWatt agreed. "And that's the reaction it got at the Pentagon. Whatever else it was, it was political dynamite. The Secretary ordered Rodale to destroy all records of his study. Instead, the crusty bastard published it on his own."

Ward emitted a low whistle. "And the press had a field day."

"No. With all his fervor, Rodale was still an intelligence officer. He published only a few copies and classified them 'Secret.' He intended to distribute them to selected members of Congress—he had some powerful friends on the hill. First, he hand-carried a copy to Johnson. He actually believed that the President would fall in step with him."

MacWatt's gravelly voice erupted in a raucous guffaw. "What a scene that must have been! The architect of the Great Society—the grand champion of civil rights, presented with a staff study from one of his most prized officers that read like a release from Herr Goebbels."

He paused to savor the thought. "Anyway, the shit hit the fan. That very morning federal marshals sealed Rodale's office and confiscated every last document related to his maverick research project. Every copy of the 'Rodale Report' was destroyed."

"How do you know so well what it contained?"

"How else?" MacWatt snorted. "LBJ was never one to let a

good story go untold. He confided in cronies, and of course it leaked.

"Johnson asked Rodale to retire. He refused. The President was afraid to make an issue of it. Instead, he relieved Rodale from the Pentagon and—you'll be interested in this—assigned him to Vietnam for the duration of the war, or until he requested retirement."

"Interesting indeed," Ward agreed. "And his whereabouts now . . . were you able to track him down?"

MacWatt pulled a piece of paper from his pocket, forced on his too-small glasses, and read: "Henry R. Rodale, Major General, USAF Retired. Address-of-record for pension: Kruger Enterprises, Limited, New Kingsmeade Park Road . . . Durban, South Africa." He peered over his glasses at Ward. "Within spitting distance of Transkei."

"And . . . Sabin?"

"In 1966, Rodale's last year as Chief of Intelligence, his operations officer for the African desk was Captain Bartholomew Sabin."

A tremor shot through Ward's body. Father Dan's death had been the catalyst to shatter Moslin's obduracy—to bring the professor to reveal a long-suppressed secret that provided the key to understanding the crash of *Cobra One*. Even so, a part of Ward had remained poised on the raw edge of doubt, had kept alive the hope that there was a reasonable explanation for things, a logical purpose that Crowell hadn't known about. Evidence, perhaps, that the major, blinded by anguish and guilt, had misinterpreted his startling findings and died for a false cause. Now, listening to MacWatt, Ward realized that his hopes were futile.

MacWatt folded the paper and shoved it and his glasses into his pocket. He stood. "You know, of course, what I must do."

"Yes," Ward nodded. Irrefutably now, the needs of the investigation were beyond his powers.

"It's still too circumstantial," MacWatt said. "We need hard evidence. I'll arrange for you to brief General Burnside first thing after lunch. Then the OSI will . . ."

The phone on the desk jangled. Ward started to rise, but the colonel picked up the instrument. "MacWatt."

Ward remained on the edge of the couch expectantly. Janet had this number.

All at once, MacWatt's face went ashen. He slumped down in the chair. "Oh my God . . ." he moaned. "When . . . where . . . ?"

A minute later, hand trembling, he placed the phone back in the cradle. "Lou . . . is dead."

"Lou?" Ward didn't comprehend. Then: "General Burnside?!"

"Ann found him"—MacWatt's voice was a hoarse whisper—"heart attack . . . his office. I . . . ." He started to rise, then sat back down as if his strength had failed him and stared into space, his countenance a study in agony.

Suddenly, the aggrieved eyes sparked alive with a new realization. "Jonathan . . . you are without authority."

"What?"

"Don't you understand? Sabin is senior officer now—by default, commander. He can cut you off—end the investigation—with the stroke of a pen."

"No!" Ward protested. "Not after . . ."

MacWatt silenced him with the wave of a hand. "Let me think."

He pushed himself from the chair and began to pace. There would be time for grief later. "He's going to be looking for you. Sure as hell that phone's going to ring any moment . . ."

He stopped and stood silent for a full minute. "Jonathan . . . how far do you think Professor Moslin is prepared to go to avenge his dead friend?"

"As far as necessary," Ward replied.

MacWatt leaned back on the desk. "It's a long shot, and it would mean putting our asses on the line. I owe that much to Lou. You don't. If after hearing me out you don't want to go along you're off the hook . . . and no hard feelings. Agreed?"

"Agreed."

"First, you've got to get off the base . . . stay out of sight. I'll make up some story to stall Sabin, make him think I'm trying to track you down. Around noon tomorrow I'll tell him that I've located you and ordered you to report to him at thirteen-hundred. I'll go to the meeting with you."

"Sure . . . but I don't get it."

MacWatt said, "I've done a few favors here and there over the years, collected some pretty high-level IOUs. It's time I called some of them in. You know where Moslin is now?"

"Yes."

"Good . . . now, here's what you must do . . ."

25

AT first glance the office appeared unchanged. Same leather wing chairs and couch, same cerulean rug and drapes, same overlarge mahogany desk. But it was the absence of things, however small, that aggrieved MacWatt. The silver-framed photograph of Eileen no longer graced the credenza. The blue flag with the two silver stars had been replaced with one bearing a single star. The personal items that had marked this room as Lou's had been packed away. Most incongruous was the man behind the desk—so young, sitting proudly erect, confidently taking possession of a greater domain. Suddenly MacWatt felt terribly old and beyond his time.

MacWatt and Ward sat facing the desk. On the couch, hardly able to contain his elation over this opportune turn of events, Gerald Coffman regarded the colonel and the major with a supercilious smirk.

For several minutes Sabin had been mouthing platitudes—". . . loss of a fine officer . . . ," ". . . work must continue without interruption . . ."

MacWatt was barely listening. In his mind he was in the ADCC in Japan ("Topkick . . . this is Blue Knight Two . . ."); playing liars dice with a laughing friend at the Itazuke Officers Club bar one long-ago Christmas Eve; in the control tower at

Keflavik watching an indignant commander bravely recall an outbound passenger flight . . .

Through the haze he heard reference to *Cobra One*. He forced his attention to the present. Sabin was addressing Ward.

". . . was entirely superfluous, an unnecessary duplication. Have you kept any notes, Major?"

"No sir . . . no notes."

"Very well. Colonel MacWatt, please have orders cut at once relieving Major Ward from duty at Kirtland and returning him to Andrews. The shuttle departs at fourteen-hundred. I expect you to be on it, Major. And I remind you of the Quickseal classification. You will not discuss the program, or any of your work here, with anyone. Is that understood?"

Ward made no reply.

"I asked you, Major . . . Is that understood?"

Ward picked up his attaché case and snapped it open. "General, there's a tape you should hear."

"Major," Sabin said irritably, "I thought I made myself clear. I am approving Colonel Hadley's report. I have no need for an input from you." The general rose stiffly. "You are dismissed, gentlemen."

Undeterred, Ward took a cassette recorder from the attaché case and placed it on the end table. "I really think you should hear this, sir. It's a fascinating commentary . . . about a star. I call it *Canopus Thirty*."

A sharp gasp sounded from the couch area and MacWatt saw Coffman's face pale to a sickly hue. *So you're in on it too, you little prick.*

Sabin's expression was unchanged. For a suspended moment he remained standing. Then, without a word, he sat down.

Ward switched the recorder to PLAY.

The tape was thirty minutes long. The first voice was Ward's. He analyzed his findings, emphasizing the discovery of the cross-wired *Stargaze* unit that led him to conclude that Major Crowell had sabotaged *Cobra One*, forfeiting his life in the act.

The voice on the tape changed. In a solemn recital Professor James Moslin told about Delta Group, General Rodale, *Kronus*, the raid on Vo Lanh, Crowell's inexpiable guilt. He described his and Abernathy's lucrative grants for research never performed. He told of Crowell's suspicions about the aberrant test flights ordered by Sabin, Crowell's surprise encounter with Rodale at Edwards, his suspicion that a third XR-2100, built from plans secreted from the country, was being readied somewhere in the world for chemical warfare. He ended with a description of Father Dan's death and his conviction that the priest died from a bullet meant to silence himself.

In the final segment Ward described the discovery of the Canopus equation, how it was deciphered, the diabolical scheme it revealed. Ward concluded:

> "It is my opinion that the evidence indicates the existence of an international conspiracy involving members of the United States Air Force—particularly members of the Quickseal Test Group—to appropriate classified material for the purpose of committing unlawful acts of war. I further submit that the evidence warrants the immediate initiation of a comprehensive investigation by the Office of Strategic Investigation and other appropriate agencies of the Federal government.
>
> "Major Jonathan Ward, United States Air Force, 2230 hours, 2 October 1980. End of recording."

It was a chilling indictment. Throughout the playback Coffman stared at the recorder like a man witnessing the onrush of doom.

Sabin's stony countenance had not altered an iota. Now, he turned on Ward with a vengeance. "I can hardly believe, Major, that an officer of your reputed intelligence would attempt to validate such an outrageous assortment of innuendos, suspicions, half truths and false assumptions. Do you realize that by this allegation against a senior officer you have destroyed your career?"

Nice try, MacWatt thought, but no cigar.

"General," the colonel said, "I'm sure that you're aware that an officially appointed investigating officer is immune from repercussions for his conclusions, and that threats against him, or command interference in his duties, are offenses under the Uniform Code of Military Justice."

Sabin glared, but before he could respond, Ward reached for his attaché case again. "Perhaps, General, you would prefer evidence a bit less circumstantial."

He withdrew two sheets of paper, handed one across the

desk to Sabin and the other to MacWatt. "They're both the same."

MacWatt put on his glasses. The paper was a Xerox reproduction of a montage of photographs showing Sabin and a man in civilian clothes conducting strange business in what was unmistakably the Quickseal blockhouse.

"Well I'll be damned," MacWatt exclaimed. "Hank Rodale."

"I suspected as much," Ward said.

Sabin's vaunted imperturbability failed him. "Where . . . how did you get this?"

"This morning. How, or from whom, doesn't matter right now. What matters is that Henry Rodale is no longer on active duty. He doesn't possess a Quickseal clearance or have any lawful reason for access to the Quickseal compound. I suggest that these photographs alone are prima-facie evidence of a serious breech of security."

Coffman squirmed on the couch, his left eyelid fluttered like the wing of a frightened bat.

Sabin, vulnerable and knowing it, shot Coffman a scornful glance, then, holding the photocopy, he said to Ward, "You have the originals with you?"

Ward's face twisted into a sardonic grin. "Not hardly . . . sir."

Surprisingly, Sabin acknowledged Ward's wry smile with one of his own—a mutual recognition of the bold intent behind the question. The general put down the photocopy, swiveled back in his chair and gazed toward the ceiling in thought.

Ward waited. The ball was in Sabin's court.

For a long while no one spoke. Then, Sabin said, "Gentlemen, I believe we can reach accommodation." He brought the chair back to normal position. "We wear the same uniform, share a common bond. I ask you to hear me out before deciding what course you will take."

His tone of voice, the very posture of his body underwent transformation. The authoritarian mien dissolved, the iceberg blue eyes fixed the two officers with an expression that radiated sincerity and a suggestion of deference.

Ward put himself on guard. He'd seen it before, the suave

manner, the ingratiating appeal to discretion. He knew from experience that when the occasion demanded, Sabin could mesmerize a statue.

Sabin began: "Historically, America has been blessed with leaders—military and civilian—who were unafraid to make the hard decisions necessary to advance and preserve our great nation. At the end of World War Two we were hailed as the most powerful country on earth. It was the accomplishment of superior men—men of indomitable will who left us a sterling heritage. A heritage, gentlemen, that in three short decades has been gutlessly squandered.

"Just consider the debacles since 1950. Korea—we capitulated in a stalemate; the Cuban missile crisis—we delivered the Monroe Doctrine to Khrushchev on a platter; Vietnam—a humiliation. Today—Iran says it all. In just thirty years a series of head-in-the-sand politicians have brought us to the brink of disaster."

He sat back in the chair. "Some of our colleagues, gentlemen, a few in quite influential positions, patriots all, recognize that a reversal of our power decline is imperative. They have pledged themselves and their fortunes to that end. You'll understand if I'm not more specific. However, one resolute goal is germane to our discussion—the reestablishment of absolute military superiority. A priority in that goal is the development and testing of chemical and biological weapons . . ."

Ward interjected, "In violation of a standing executive order, reaffirmed by three presidents."

Sabin shrugged. "Why quibble? Yes . . . a violation. It was a naive order. The Soviets are neither naive nor squeamish about chemical warfare. They are light-years ahead of us. There's a gulag in Siberia where felons and political prisoners are systematically sacrificed in chemwar testing. Afghanistan has afforded them a real-war proving ground. Thousands have died there from phosgene oxime, mustard gas, mycotoxins, lewisite, toxic smoke—what our media poetically call 'yellow rain.' We can no longer ignore these facts. Chemical warfare is a reality, it exists, it is a weapon of tremendous potential.

"Which brings us, gentlemen, to the greatest scientific breakthrough in chemwar history—*Kronus.*"

There was a sudden grunt of approval from Coffman. The chunky technical advisor was perched on the edge of the couch nodding his head in fervent agreement.

Ward said, "*Kronus* is extremely unpredictable, General. Vo Lanh proved that."

"Vo Lanh was ten years ago, Major. Since then, thanks to General Rodale's farsightedness, the formula has been perfected. Recent tests on higher primates resulted in a ninety-percent permanent male sterility rate without other physical defects. All that was lacking for an actual field test was a sophisticated delivery system. During my work on the XR-Twenty-One-Hundred I recognized that the aircraft was ideal for the purpose. I informed General Rodale and . . . certain interested friends."

"Sir," Ward said, "we know that General Rodale is in South Africa. And that he's working with the retired chief of their Air Force—General Jan Kruger."

"Great man, great country," Sabin said laconically.

"And you arranged for them to obtain plans to the plane."

"No . . . the plane itself."

Ward was taken aback. "But . . . how . . .?"

"Ah, hell," MacWatt said, comprehending. "Spare parts."

Sabin said nothing.

Ward looked at the colonel for an explanation.

"It's an old procurement trick," MacWatt said. "When you want a dozen of something and Congress appropriates money for only ten, you pad your spare parts requirements to make up the difference. That third plane was probably shipped piece by piece from Consolidated General as spare parts, then diverted to South Africa."

Ward looked back at Sabin.

Sabin said, "Like the colonel says, it's an old trick."

"And this so called 'actual field test'—you ordered Major Crowell to fly a prototype pattern, then cross-programmed his flight data into the Canopus mission."

"It was a capability Rodale lacked."

"And he came here—in a Consolidated Aircraft plane—to personally take delivery of the programmed chip."

Sabin indicated the photocopy on his desk. "You seem to have that evidence."

"Yes," Ward agreed.

He paused to think things over. Sabin was appe ..ing to their patriotism to convince them of the righteousn^ s of the cause. Wasn't there a famous quotation, Ward mu ed, about patriotism being the last refuge of the scoundrel?

Now, Ward asked the question that had b en burning in his brain since his meeting with Billy Wheele the day before. "General . . . why Transkei?"

"Topography," Sabin replied. "Are yo familiar with the Bantustans, Major?"

"Some."

"Geographically they are enclaves. Transkei is the designated homeland of the Xosha tribe, a remote, primitive area, entirely surrounded by the Republic of South Africa. Each morning the men of the tribe cross the border to jobs in South Africa, then return home each night. The pattern provides an ideal laboratory. Afrikaner physicians can monitor the Xoshan's medical progress on a day-to-day basis. The birthrate in the homeland is readily available. The effectiveness of *Kronus* can be methodically studied."

He made the sordid revelation without passion, speaking in a coldly efficient, businesslike tone of voice as if he were discussing nothing more consequential than the weather for tomorrow's flight operations.

Ward felt the uneasy stirrings of new emotions. He was a professional engineer, committed to a world of oscilloscopes, sonographs, sines, cosines, tangents—impersonal, bloodless, predictable. Nothing else had ever been important, nothing outside his tight little realm mattered. Until this moment.

Through bloodless lips he said, "General, what you're proposing is utter genocide."

"No," Sabin protested. "No killing, no pain. Male sterility only. Millions of human fetuses are aborted in this country alone every year. Certainly *Kronus* is more humane than that. No potential weapon is more so."

Ward kept his voice under control. "Then it's a mere test— a simple field application of a potential *humane* weapon?"

"Nothing more," Sabin said.

"And the target was selected only because of its topography—its isolation?"

"Precisely."

Ward took a deep breath. "General . . . you're a liar."

Coffman gasped.

MacWatt shifted uneasily in his seat.

Sabin gripped the armrests so hard his knuckles turned white.

His voice on the edge of fury, Ward said, "I suggest, General, that *Kronus* is no longer a *potential* weapon—that the Canopus mission is not a mere field test. I suggest that you and General Rodale and your circle of so-called influential patriots chose the Transkei with grim purpose. I suggest that your *field tests* will not end with the Xoshans. There'll be other such tests— in Bophuthatswana, Venda, in all the Bantustans, where the tribal population is conveniently corralled like cattle. I suggest that your purpose is unmistakable . . . and obscene."

MacWatt cringed inwardly. This time Ward had gone too far.

In deafening silence the general and the major, like gladiators locked in combat, held each other's gaze without flinching. Then, ignoring Ward's insolence, Sabin said without rancor, "And I suggest to you, Major, that what you conceive to be an obscenity is in reality . . . salvation."

An immense feeling of relief shot through MacWatt. The General was still trying to negotiate. Ward had been right! Under no other circumstance would Ward have gotten away with a personal attack on Bartholomew Sabin.

Ward, too, had expected a Sabin onslaught. Taken unawares, he waited for the general to make his point.

"Equalitarian thinking is hogwash, Major," Sabin said. "Political rhetoric notwithstanding, wars are not fought for 'human rights' or to 'make the world safe for democracy' or any such gibberish. Wars are fought to gain or protect material advantage. This country is crucially dependent on foreign sources for a most critical resource—strategic minerals. Bauxite—we import ninety-four percent; platinum—eighty-eight percent; chromium—ninety percent; cobalt—ninety-three percent; tantalum—ninety-eight percent. Critical items all, essential for the manufacture or maintenance of jet engines, synthetic fuels, petrochemicals, nuclear power plants, gas turbines, nuclear-propulsion systems, steel. In short, the lifeblood of our industrial society. Where are these minerals found in greatest abundance? South Africa, Major. A geological fact of life that hasn't escaped our ill-wishing friends in the Kremlin.

"Unfortunately for us, eighty-three percent of the South African ethnology is comprised of subcultures whose primitive tribal instincts are communistic. The Soviets are indefatigably exploiting this fact. We must not allow them to succeed there as they have succeeded in Angola and Rhodesia.

"*Kronus* can stop them!" he said, rising. "How better to counter Marxist proliferation than by denying them the human fodders they gorge upon? *Kronus!* In a single generation."

Uncharacteristically effusive now, the general began to pace, staring into the distance as if in a trance. "And it need not stop there. Think of it. Civilization freed from Third World glut. Unlimited space. Unlimited resources. Superior cultures unburdened to develop to their highest potential . . ."

The words were falling on incredulous ears. Transfixed, MacWatt stared at a Sabin he had never seen before.

Ward shuddered. He had read of such men. Crudely defined fanatics from the crazy-world past. Until now, he realized, he had not given serious thought to the possibility that they might exist in his time.

Suddenly, Sabin's eyes fell upon the faces of the two officers and he stopped in midsentence. Those agonized countenances told him more eloquently than words that he had gone beyond bounds. Slowly, he returned to his desk. After a moment he said, "You know . . . both of you . . . that I am right. I ask you to think over carefully what I've said. We'll meet again this evening. Bring Professor Moslin. He, I'm sure, will understand the realities."

Ward shook his head. "I'm afraid that's impossible."

MacWatt looked at his watch. "At this moment, General, Professor Moslin is meeting at the Pentagon with General McCollum. Lieutenant Wheeler flew him out this morning on General Burn . . . on the commander's plane, on my orders. The Professor has a copy of the Canopus tape."

"And the Rodale photographs," Ward added.

Sabin flushed scarlet. The jagged scar below his left eye stood out in angry alabaster against the reddened cheek. He half-rose. It had all been subterfuge, a trap—and he had walked into it blindly. Shaken, he sank back in the chair and looked at MacWatt with scathing contempt. "I suppose, Colonel, that you arranged this deception with great satisfaction."

At that moment MacWatt's eyes were drawn like a magnet to the sky-blue ribbon with the tiny white stars that adorned Sabin's uniform—the emblem of the Congressional Medal of Honor. Sick at heart, he replied, "No sir . . . with great sorrow."

The tension in the room was unbearable.

Coffman moaned unceasingly into his handkerchief.

For a long deliberate time Sabin's eyes surveyed the imposing room—the lofty seat of power he had coveted. At last, mustering that great strength of character for which he was renowned, he sat up to his full height and eyed the two officers imperiously. "Gentlemen . . . you will leave my office."

MacWatt and Ward stood.

Without saluting they turned and obeyed the order.

26

THE message from the Chief of Staff arrived at 6:03 PM that day:

OPS/IMMEDIATE SECRET
DGT 801003/1031Z
FROM: CHF OF STF, USAF
ACTION TO: AFRTC, KAFB, NM
INFO TO: AFSC, ANDREWS AFB, MD
THIS MESSAGE IS IN SEVEN PARTS.

PART I: EFFECTIVE IMMEDIATELY ALL PROJECT QUICKSEAL OPERATIONS ARE PLACED IN INDEFINITE MORATORIUM.

PART II: BRIGADIER GENERAL BARTHOLOMEW SABIN, USAF, IS RELIEVED AS ACTING COMMANDER, AFRTC. OFFICER WILL REMAIN ASSIGNED IN HOLDING STATUS TO KIRTLAND AFB PENDING FURTHER ORDERS.

PART III: COLONEL ROBERT MACWATT, USAF, IS ASSIGNED ACTING COMMANDER, AFRTC. OFFICER WILL UNDERTAKE IMMEDIATE IMPOUNDMENT OF ALL PROJECT QUICKSEAL RECORDS AND SECURE LOCK-DOWN OF QUICKSEAL COMPOUND.

PART IV: ADDRESSEES AND SUBJECT PERSONNEL ARE ADVISED THAT THE PRESIDENT HAS ORDERED THE ATTORNEY GENERAL AND THE AIR FORCE INSPECTOR GENERAL TO INITIATE AN IMMEDIATE JOINT INVESTIGATION

INTO ALL FACETS OF PROJECT QUICKSEAL. IN CONJUNCTION, A JOINT MILITARY/CIVILIAN INVESTIGATING COMMITTEE WILL CONVENE AT KIRTLAND AFB AT THE SOONEST POSSIBLE DATE. NAMES OF COMMITTEE CHAIRMAN AND MEMBERS WILL BE FORWARDED SOONEST.

PART V: ADDRESSEES AND SUBJECT PERSONNEL ARE ADVISED THAT THE PRESIDENT HAS RECALLED MAJOR GENERAL HENRY RODALE, USAF (RETIRED), TO ACTIVE DUTY EFFECTIVE IMMEDIATELY WITH ASSIGNMENT IN HOLDING STATUS TO KIRTLAND AFB PENDING FURTHER ORDERS.

PART VI: MAJOR JONATHAN WARD, USAF, IS RELIEVED FROM ASSIGNMENT, ANDREWS AFB AND IS ASSIGNED TO KIRTLAND AFB AS SPECIAL USAF LIAISON OFFICER WITH THE QUICKSEAL INVESTIGATION COMMITTEE.

PART VII: FORMAL ORDERS CONFIRMING THIS MESSAGE WILL BE FORTHCOMING.

27

HANGAR Two was dark.

Outside, a squadron of security policemen swarmed through the compound, sealing safes, locking offices, securing buildings, posting guards.

The hangar would be last.

General Bartholomew Sabin closed the heavy door behind him, reached to the wall and pulled one of the switches mounted there. Overhead, a single row of fluorescent lights flickered, caught, came alive. In the center of the immense floor, *Cobra Two*, majestic, darkly awesome, stood bathed in the subdued light.

He went to the plane. Slowly, deliberately, he circled it, portside to tail, starboard to nose, gently touching the low-slung wing, caressing the underbelly, lingeringly, sensually, like a lover caressing the body of his beloved.

At the front he turned and faced the plane again. It was his brainchild. He had willed it into being when others had failed, had fought for it, lived for it, perfected it. And he had delivered it into proper hands—the hands of resolute men, men of iron will, the will to persevere.

He thought of the Chief of Staff's message and gave a derisive laugh. Rodale called to active duty? *Never!* Rodale had it all now. The plane, *Kronus*, the vital Canopus mission package. He would ignore the President. He would seek asylum and his friends would grant it. *The cause survives.*

With deepfelt pride Sabin brought himself to rigid attention. Fixing his eyes on *Cobra Two—the hope of the world*—he raised his hand in a crisp salute. After several seconds he dropped his hand smartly and wheeled about-face.

Triumphant in defeat, he left the hangar to face destiny.

28

MACWATT pulled the bottle of Glenlivet from his desk drawer and looked at it ruefully. He would have to replenish his stock. He poured the remaining Scotch into two glasses, added water from his desk pitcher and handed one of the glasses to Ward.

Ward took the drink. "I'm surprised that General McCollum could bring the President in on it so quickly."

"I was counting on it," MacWatt replied.

There was a command photograph of General Burnside on the wall. MacWatt swiveled his chair toward the photograph and raised his glass in on it so quickly.

"I wonder how much he actually knew?" Ward asked.

"We'll never know. He suspected something—that was enough."

"When will you move into his office?"

"I won't. I'm just an expediency . . . a stopgap until they find a qualified general. I can't fill Lou's shoes anyway. Damn few officers can."

They sipped their drinks in silence. After a while MacWatt turned the chair back to face Ward. "Your days in the Air Force are numbered, Jonathan. You know that don't you?"

Ward took a breath. "I've wondered about it."

"The new regime won't tolerate the likes of us . . . you, me, McCollum. We brought down the Golden Boy. A genuine hero. Their type of guy. We'll have to pay for that."

"You don't think he'll get away with it, for God's sake?"

MacWatt swirled the Scotch in his glass and shrugged. "Who knows? Depends a lot on the President . . . how hard he pushes . . . what he can get done in the short time he has left. The joint investigation is a good start. But Sabin couldn't have accomplished what he did without powerful friends. They'll hunker down for a spell, bide their time. But they'll influence things. Insidiously now. After the election—with a vengeance."

He gulped the remainder of his drink. "Any ideas for your future?"

Ward considered the question. "I've had some good offers from contractors. But lately I've been giving some thought to the resort business."

"Uh huh . . . up around Tres Pinos, I suspect?"

Ward smiled. "Does it show?"

MacWatt said, "You're not the only person who can detect passion in a voice, you know."

They laughed.

"What about immediately?" MacWatt asked. "It'll take some time for the investigating committee to get organized. I can arrange a leave."

"I'd like that. There're a couple of people I'd like to visit. A girl in Maryland, to bid her a more friendly goodbye. And, an old lady in Kentucky . . . my mother."

"Done."

"One other thing—Hadley's got a couple of years to go until retirement. He'll need that pension check."

"I'll see what I can do."

"What about you?" Ward asked. "Any plans?"

MacWatt pulled open the top drawer of his desk and took out a small black box. "First, I'm going to help a lovely lady get through a trying time in her life."

He opened the box and extracted an exquisite jade ring. "Then, after a decent interval, I'm going to offer her a present . . ." He looked at the ring tenderly, ". . . thirty years late."

The night was cloudless, the sky an ebony dome. Driving

westward on Gibson Boulevard, Jonathan Ward looked to the southwest. On the far horizon a fading tiara of stars dipped slowly toward the desert floor. He wondered if one of them was Canopus? Lieutenant Wheeler had said that sometimes, when conditions were just right, the great star of the Southern Hemisphere could be seen from here.

His thoughts turned to Peter Crowell. That anguished man the stars had led to a tragic destiny. Had his sacrifice been in vain? *Not as long as I have breath and voice!*

At the intersection of I-25 he turned north. Ahead, hovering sapphire-bright above Redondo Peak, was Polaris. His mood lightened. The North Star lighted the way to the Jemez, to Tres Pinos . . . to Janet.

My destiny.

Resolutely, he "locked on" to Polaris and pressed the accelerator closer to the floor.

29

PRIORITY/CONFIDENTIAL
DTG 801104/0345Z
FROM: CHF OF STF, USAF
TO: AFRTC, KAFB, NM

PERSONAL FROM MCCOLLUM TO MACWATT. THE PRESIDENT HAS JUST INFORMED ME THAT THE QUICKSEAL JOINT MILITARY/CIVILIAN INVESTIGATING COMMITTEE WILL BE CHAIRED BY THE HONORABLE NATHAN L. BEAUMONT, RANKING MINORITY MEMBER OF THE SENATE ARMED FORCES COMMITTEE. PLEASE PROVIDE SENATOR BEAUMONT WITH FULL COMMAND COURTESIES AND ASSISTANCE. REGARDS. GIP.